Copyright

Cuffing and Tree Trimming

Book Three, Cuffing Season Series

by C.M. Kars

Cover design by Indigo Chick Designs

Editing by Aquila Editing

CUFFING
AND TREE TRIMMING

C.M.KARS

OTHER WORKS BY C.M. KARS

The Never Been Series

Never Been Kissed

Never Been Nerdy

Never Been Loved

Never Been Under the Mistletoe

Never Been Boxed Set

Sera & Hunter: A Never Been Collection

Never Been Happier

·♥·♥·♥·♥·♥·

The Fangirl Chronicles

Fangirling Over You

To All the Footballers I Loved Before

Bias Wrecked

Pucked Romance

Never Say Never

The Fangirl Chronicles Boxed Set

·♥·♥·♥·♥·♥·

The Cuffing Season Series

WANT TO STAY IN THE KNOW?

Sign up for my newsletter here for free stuff, info on my upcoming releases, cover and blurb reveal, and to talk about all the things there are to fangirl over.

FREE BOOKS

PREWITT FAMILY TREE

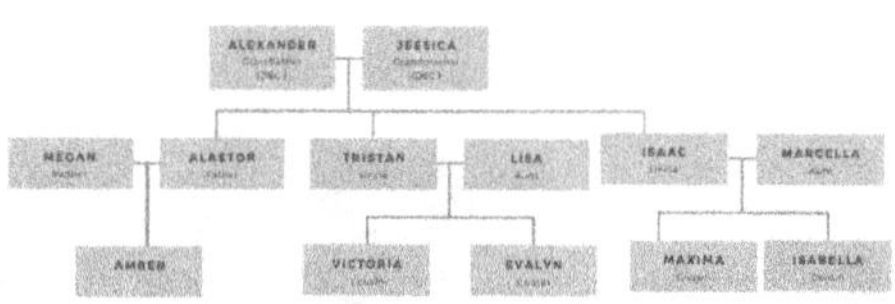

CONTENT WARNINGS

Here are a few content warnings for this book:

- Insidious family toxicity (at least that's what I'm calling it), by which I mean parents who don't validate your worth because you're not following their prescribed script of how they think your future should be
- Sick parent (off the page)
- Death of a parent (off the page)
- Dealing with your family on a holiday when you're the black sheep of the family

If any of these are triggering to you, please proceed with caution. If you have any questions about the above, please DM me on Twitter @cmkars.

I hope you enjoy Max's story.

ONE

Early December, one year later...

The pink staining the back of my eyelids means that I was a dumbass last night and forgot to close my bedroom curtains. It's just my luck that the sun is strong and shining, waking me up before I want to deal with the world.

I huff out an annoyed breath through my nose and attempt to move over onto my side.

Awareness starts coming back in bits and pieces, streaming through my sleepy brain no matter how hard I try to fight it.

My head's pounding, and it's not from spending all day in my editing cave, trying to finish up all my pre-filmed videos ready for Vlogmas, where YouTubers tend to upload a video every single day for December leading up to Christmas.

My body hurts, a rolling wave of nausea hits my stomach, and last night comes back in fits and starts.

My phone chimes, and it takes me an embarrassingly long time to find it in the sea of blankets. I finally manage to squint at the screen to see who's calling.

Shit, it's 12:30 in the afternoon already?

God, I have so much work to do, and half the day is already gone.

"Hello?" I croak into the phone, rolling over onto my other side. My stomach isn't happy with the decision. There's a queasiness that sits on top of my chest like a lead weight. I breathe deeply through my nose and try to convince my stomach that the food should stay on the inside of my body, and not the other way around.

"Holy shit, Max, you sound like garbage," Vick, my cousin, says. "Seriously. It's like you swapped your vocal cords for a toad."

"Thanks for that," I mumble, still refusing to open my eyes. I mean, I'm my boss, and I work from home. I can totally give myself five more minutes in bed, right?

I scratch at my cheek, grunt when I finally open my eyes and find remnants of mascara on my fingers. *Nice. Just what I needed this morning. My skin's going to hate me.*

"I was calling to make sure we're still good for tonight. I've left about a hundred texts on your phone from the morning and since I know you're pretty good about texting back, I was getting worried."

I yawn, blink slowly at one of the walls of my bedroom. One of the strings of the fairy lights has come undone, ruining the whole cozy vibe with that jarring break in the symmetry. I even forgot to plug in the small tree I put up in my bedroom. It sits there, still not trimmed, the naked limbs looking sad and lonely. I *still* have to put up the big tree in the living room. It's been on my to-do list since November.

I take a deep breath in, the smell wafting off my Christmas-scented candle taking the nausea up to a hard eight on ten. And I love gingerbread cookies, but not this morning.

"How did last night go?" Vick asks on a hum. She's probably with her trainer boyfriend, and they've probably already had a protein-dense breakfast and been to the gym already while I'm barely out of bed.

And I used to be the one Prewitt cousin who had all her shit together.

So much can happen in a year, huh?

"I'm in bed alone, if that's what you're getting at," I groan, forcing myself to sit upright. My vanity is just off-center to my bed, and I can see the horror show that is my face in my reflection.

Me? Not double cleanse after a full day of wearing makeup? Who am I?

I must've been really out of it last night. *Really out of it.*

"Now my skin's going to be so angry at me, and I was finally in a good place. Shit," I groan, dragging my fingers across my cheek.

Vick laughs, and I can hear the slide of a balcony door opening on her end of the conversation. I turn to my window and find the bright December sunlight streaming through, trying to fool me into thinking it's warm outside.

I bet it's at least ten below without factoring in the windchill.

"So what happened last night? Tell me. I'm dying to know."

I yawn hard enough to crack something along my jaw. "I don't know, Vick." Jesus, why do I sound so dejected?

"Nothing really. I didn't find anyone special. But I do have a mother of a hangover. Is this what getting older is like? Having too many glasses of wine that didn't *used to be* that many? My head's pounding and my stomach isn't happy."

Vick hums in sympathy, sniffs a little. "Yeah, but I thought you were going to put Operation Get Max a Christmas Date into play. Wasn't that the whole point of going out last night? I mean, you wanted to take advantage of all those corporate Christmas parties that are happening around your neighborhood."

I sigh, roll my aching eyeballs and then wince. I wish I didn't do that.

I slide my body down the bed so I'm almost back to being totally horizontal. Life just seems that much better when you're lying down.

"That was a dumb idea. As if I could convince some rando that we should get together for Christmas. Although crippling family obligations and the fact that I am not yet married bothers my parents more than they should, asking a stranger to help shoulder that is a lot to ask for. And besides, time's running out. There's like, just under two weeks until Christmas."

"Or, you could meet a really cool person since there's still time, and I never knew you to be a quitter. Just saying." I close my eyes, ignore the wave of hurt that rolls over me.

Sometimes, all I want to do is quit.

I shake my head, shut my eyes and try to convince my stomach, that no, we are not moving, and there's no reason to be tossing and turning like that.

"You know me. I'm too bright and loud and wear too much makeup for these random Montreal guys." I clench my blankets into a tight fist, squeezing down hard enough that my knuckles twinge.

Vick grunts. "It's literally your job, and you do things with bright colors on your eyeballs that is pure art, okay?"

I blink at my ceiling, strangely moved. "Vick, that might be the nicest thing you've ever said to me."

Vick scoffs. "I mean, yeah, I get that. Well, I was hoping you'd be able to bring someone to Aunt Ella's house, too. We both know how your parents get. Honestly, I don't really understand it."

I wince. "Yeah, I know, I know."

"Like, it's super weird how different they treat you and Izzy, still."

"Vick, please. I can't do this in the morning."

"It's literally the afternoon. Get your ass out of bed, go take a shower, and make yourself some greasy eggs and toast, or something. Amber and I are coming over later, hangover or not."

I rub at my forehead, at the ache sitting behind my eyes. "I have so much work to do, though..."

"Nope, nope. It's our weekly get-together and we're hanging out. You promised."

"But I have, like, a trillion videos to edit, Vick! I've got work to do!" My voice goes high with panic, and my chest tightens at the prospect of losing out on more time today when I *should* be working.

"There's this thing, called work-life balance? Have you heard of it?"

I snort, covering the smile up with a hand like my cousin can somehow see me over here. I frown when I clonk my head with the sharp edge of a ring I apparently wore last night – another thing I forgot to remove when I got home.

Jesus, that's so out of character for me. How much did I drink last night to forget to do that?

I pull my left hand back, blink my eyes open towards the streaming sunlight and stare at a rock the size of Jupiter that's nestled into a ring that's currently on a *very* important finger.

"What the fuck?"

"What? What is it?" Vick squawks on my phone, while my belly drops towards the basement of my building.

I blink down at the pretty twinkle, swallow the hot bile that burns its way up my throat. I sit up so quickly that I get dizzy. "That better not be what I think it is. Holy fucking shit. *Holy fucking shit!*"

"Max? Maxima!"

"You don't have to pull out the full name, Victoria."

"Well, you don't sound too good right now, so tell me what's wrong."

"My ring," I mumble, trying to find the right words to explain myself. "This isn't my ring."

"What ring? Max, put me on a video call, right now."

"Always so bossy, now that you look like a superhero," I grumble, but I do press the right buttons and see Vick staring back at me. She has the decency to not start screaming her head off at the sight of me.

That is unconditional love.

"You look like shit. What the hell happened last night?"

"This," I say, waving a hand around my face. "This isn't the problem. I can fix this," I say, glancing around my dirty bedroom. "I don't know what the hell this is," I say, flipping the camera around, so Vick can see my left hand.

"What is that?"

I bite my lip. "Jesus, Vick, what does it look like? I stole somebody's ring last night! And right before Christmas, too! I'm going to hell for sure!"

Vick frowns at me and pushes her mermaid-teal hair out of her face. She's wearing her winter coat and clearly standing outside. Her pale cheeks and nose are already turning red, which further cements my decision *not* to go outside today.

"Well, take it off. See if there's an engraving inside of it or something, some kind of identifying mark."

I grunt, because yeah, that's a good idea.

"And you have no memory of this ring?" Vick's voice comes from somewhere in my sheets as I struggle to pull off the ring. It's a perfect fit, and now with my fingers a little swollen in the morning from last night's alcohol, well, it doesn't want to come off.

My stomach twists, and it feels like I've gone and swallowed a lead ball of dread.

"I'm going to have to lather myself in butter to get this thing off," I grunt, ineffectually pulling at it, but the ring still refuses to budge.

"Or maybe we'll cut off your finger," Vick snorts, and I don't appreciate the visual.

My stomach heaves, and I place a hand over my mouth, breathe deeply through my nose. I pull up my phone to stare at my cousin. "Gross. Disgusting. Vick, I'm a criminal," I groan, flopping back down onto the pillows. "I have to find a way to give this back. What if some guy I was talking to at the lounge last night had it in his pocket, showed it to me, and I put it on my finger like an idiot?"

Vick frowns. "That doesn't sound like something you would do."

I shrug, worried. "I don't remember any of that. I don't remember a diamond ring being placed on my finger at all, Vick. Or taking it. Ah, what am I going to do? Go back to the bar?"

"How much did you drink, Max?"

"Honestly, not that much."

Vick glares at me. "Did you sleep more than four hours and eat a lot of healthy meals during the day before pounding back the alcohol?"

I grin sheepishly, caught red-handed. "I guess I should go and report it to the police, huh?"

Vick nods. "Amber and I can take you when we get there. I'll text her and let her know what's up."

I groan. "Fine, fine. I'm going to get up and make myself presentable."

"I'll talk to you later, then."

I give Vick a wave, and end the call, turning onto my side in bed, determined to sleep a little more and forget that all this has happened.

I'll fix it, I know I will, I just need to recharge.

I close my eyes, then jar awake when I hear the toilet flush. The toilet...in the bathroom...that I am *not* in.

I hold my breath, wondering if I should scramble underneath the covers to safety as if an intruder is like a monster and won't be able to find me.

I struggle to get upright, freeing myself from the twisted sheets around my body, and push my hair out of my face. I look over to my en suite bathroom to find it empty and gulp hard.

That means I'm going to have to go out into the living room where the main bathroom is and see who the fuck is in my apartment.

My heart slams hard against my ribs, and settles against my throat, making it a struggle to breathe. I'm barefoot, in a giant shirt that isn't going to provide any kind of defense against someone who wants to hurt me.

Sweat slicks the back of my neck and my palms, and I hastily grab my Christmas Morning scented candle as a weapon to chuck at the guy's head.

Oh god, oh god, oh god.

I lick my dry lips, breath rattling in my lungs. I head outside of my bedroom, peering around for the stranger in my home, and quickly figure out that he's behind the bathroom door.

I frown. I can hear the shower running.

Who tries to rob a place, takes a piss, and then a shower before leaving?

"This isn't some Goldilocks bullshit," I murmur to myself.

I reach out, hand shaking, towards the bathroom doorknob, and finally gather my courage to press down the lever.

I step inside, my bladder embarrassingly full, and my head's still pounding. Holy shit, it's so steamy in here, and I'm already getting lightheaded.

I stop in the middle of the floor, holding my candle over my head, ready for launch.

There's a guy all right, a very *naked* guy in my shower.

And while it's been a *while*, and yeah, a part of me notices that said naked guy is pretty gorgeous standing in there, he is, in fact, in *my* shower.

I pull in a deep breath, ready to start screeching like a banshee –

"Don't just stand there. Are you coming in or what, Max?"

TWO

I screech, nearly dropping the heavy candle on my foot. I squint through the frosted glass, only able to see the silhouette of the said stranger. But honestly, I would recognize that voice anywhere.

It's haunted me for a few nights, more than I ever wanted it to.

"Logan?! What the hell are you doing here?" I growl, clutching the candle to my chest.

The bastard pulls back the glass door, giving me a full-frontal view of what I've been missing from that one night we spent together and I bolted.

I look, for like a *second*. It's, unfortunately, a nice view, better than a memory.

"Why are you in my shower? Using my expensive body wash?!" I yell, my own voice bouncing off the tiles and hitting me from different angles. It's so freaking hot in here that I'm starting to melt.

Logan grins at me and slicks back his dark hair, longer than I remember it being. His dark eyes rove over me, spending way too much time on my exposed thighs. For that alone, I want to launch the candle at his head.

"Give me a second to finish up, yeah?"

My headache blazes hot across my forehead. I don't have time for this. I have a shit ton of work to do, a ring to report lost, and now a…a…what? What the hell is Logan except for a giant pain in my ass?

Did I call him over last night and don't remember?

Shit, Max, how much did you drink?

I replay the facts in my head – I woke up alone, and my bedroom door was closed. I think it was locked, even. My en suite was empty.

I leave the bathroom behind, then step back inside to make sure he's got towels. I've already seen pretty much everything I'm going to see, but I also don't need him traipsing around my home buck naked, leaking water all over the place.

"If you use all of the hot water, you're dead," I mumble, throwing a towel down onto the closed lid of the toilet seat. "Hurry up so you can leave."

Logan laughs, and yeah, it's still a great laugh. The kind of laugh that invites you to join in, always.

I groan in despair, head out of the main bathroom, and take some minor refuge in my bedroom. I lock the door for good measure and scramble to put my room to rights.

I run around to fix everything, and then finally take the time to take ca of my face, and my morning skincare routine. I pull on sweats, a bra, a clean t-shirt before hiking my dark hair up into a giant bun.

I add fuzzy socks for strength and then shove my feet into the reindeer-shaped slippers I use specifically for this time of year.

The water's still running when I exit my bedroom and head to the kitchen.

Logan's coat is draped over my couch, and the pillows are all out of place, so it stands to reason that he slept there last night.

I frown at the bathroom door, the water still running in there.

So he's purposely trying to steal my hot water and ensure that I kick his ass out of here as soon as he comes out. Typical.

I make a giant pot of coffee that should get me through the day and open my fridge to check my energy drink supply. Today's going to be a long day of work, I just know it.

Once I get Logan out of here.

The bathroom door opens behind me, and I'm not stupid enough to turn around. I've watched all the movies, and I have a romance novel collection that if it weren't for my eReader, would have felled an entire forest. I'm not falling for that trap.

"Am I supposed to talk to your back, or do you want to do this like adults?" Logan asks. Even his tone of voice irritates me.

Logan Porter was nothing more than a series of bad dates, and a [illegible]e-night stand that never should have been. I had my fun, and he was [illegible]sed to be someone I forgot.

[illegible]e *[illegible]his number still in your phone, Max? Why did you call him* [illegible]nd *[illegible]can't you stop thinking about him?*

I wish I knew what happened last night. It's all grainy and fuzzy, and nothing wants to come into focus.

I ignore him in favor of grabbing some water and washing down a couple of ibuprofen tablets. That done, I whirl around to look at him.

He's running the towel through his long, dark hair, droplets falling onto the shoulders of what looks like a thermal shirt that's pretty much hanging onto his body for dear life it's so tight.

Ah, one of my weaknesses. Men in thermals.

I don't stand a chance.

I cross my arms over my chest, bite my inner cheek. I sigh. "What are you doing here?"

Logan moves slowly as if he doesn't want to spook me. He moves to one of the stools at my kitchen island and makes himself at home. I grind my back teeth together, praying that the pain meds I just took start to take effect real soon.

"Max, you invited me here," Logan says, his dark eyes wide and maybe something like sincerity, but I'm still hungover and I don't trust my judgment just yet.

I shake my head. "Why would I go do a stupid thing like that?"

Logan frowns, then drops the towel on his lap, one hand splayed on my counter. He looks at me for a few seconds too long, long enough to make something twist in my chest.

"You called me to the bar you were at last night," he says, keeping his voice low, his tone careful. In contrast to his calm demeanor, I'm the on that's starting to freak out. I even take a step backward and hit my frid

"Did we... did we have sex last night?" I stammer, heart, beating triple time.

Logan groans in annoyance and shakes his head. "Of course not. You were drunk. I slept on the couch, Max." He jerks a thumb over his shoulder, pointing in the direction of the couch.

I raise my eyebrows at him, at his reaction. I rub at my forehead, then pull on my earlobes.

"When did I call you last night?"

"Hold on, you're telling me you don't remember anything?"

I nod slowly, squinting at him. If I didn't know any better, I'd say that Logan looked disappointed. I guess he was waiting to score some kind of jackpot this morning, but all I want is my greasy food and to watch *V for Vendetta* until I feel better.

Logan laughs. He *laughs*, and I hold myself tighter. "Well, I can't say you're not at least partially clairvoyant or some shit," he says, leaving the kitchen stool behind and grabbing something off my couch. He resumes his seat and places his phone on the counter between us.

Logan accesses his voicemail and I hear my voice, clear as day, if a little spacey, coming over the speaker.

"Max, Max," I hear my own name, in my own voice. There's no music in the background, so there's no mistaking anything I'm going to say.

> - well, I – called Logan here, and Max, this is the dumbest idea in [illegible], but who cares, who cares?

e

ge.

Mom and Dad are already *pissed* about everything we do – I do – so like, what have we got to lose, huh? Vick and Amber, they're *happy*, and we're...It's our only chance, Max, seriously.

I can't go through another Christmas with Mom and Dad being dicks. I can't do it."

I roll my eyes. Drunk Max is super dramatic.

"So I'm telling you this because we agreed to it, Max. We're not drunk yet, we've had two glasses of wine. We're fine. We did this with sound mind and body, okay? Give Logan a chance. At least until Christmas is over."

The voicemail recording ends, and I'm left looking at Logan with about a million questions, but I don't know where to start.

I breathe in deeply. "What the hell happened last night?"

Logan slides his other hand across the counter, but I keep my arms crossed. I'm in the middle of a fight-or-flight response. I'm stuck between running away or putting my fists up.

"I honestly thought you would remember," he says, keeping his voice calm and soothing, but I don't want to be soothed. I want *answers.*

My stomach hurts, and there's a heavy weight on my chest as I wait for the other shoe to drop. He's going to tell me something horrific, I just know it.

"If I don't get answers soon, I'm going to start chucking all my candles at your head. *Explain.*" I glare at him, grinding my teeth.

"We talked you and I, last night. We talked about everything." Is that hope in his eyes? And why is he looking at *me* like that?

I squint at him. "I haven't seen you in weeks. Why would I call you? Why would even talk? There was nothing left to say. We went on, like, three dates," I sigh at Logan's silence. "Remind me what we said, then." I look around for one of my candles just in case I don't like what I'm about to hear.

Logan drops his eyes to the counter, dances his fingers across the surface.

I rub my forehead again, trying to stop the headache.

"Do you remember when we went on those few dates, earlier in the fall?"

I roll my eyes, and shit, that hurts, too. "Yeah. I remember that. We didn't mesh, but we had our fun."

Logan nods, like he agrees with me, not like he's trying to placate me.

"I like your place," he says, glancing around. "It looks like a Christmas Town threw up all over."

"Stop trying to change the subject, would you? My brain hurts, I'm hungry but also nauseated enough to yak everything up. What has any of this got to do with what happened over the s*hort* period we dated *and* last night?"

Logan blinks at me, looking almost...hurt. "You really don't remember anything about last night?"

I shake my head. "I remember getting to the bar. The music was shit until they started playing that 90s stuff, and the night got better after that."

"What about me? Do you remember me showing up?"

"Are you telling me that I called you and you just appeared?"

Logan coughs into a fist, looking away.

Well, shit, I'll be damned. Logan Porter looks *uncomfortable.*

Huh.

I panic again, stomach rolling. "We didn't have sex, right?" I ask again, needing to make sure.

Logan shakes his head. "No, no. I promise you we didn't. I stayed out here, and you pretty much locked your bedroom door."

I nod, because yeah, that sounds right.

Everything is so fuzzy this morning, and now with Logan here, I don't know what's up or down. Have I skipped timelines or something? Have I slipped into an alternate reality?

Who freaking knows?

"So you showed up for a booty call," I say, waving a hand around. "What happened next?"

"We were talking," he says, eyes tracking over the back of his hands instead of looking at me. I look down at them, too, trying to figure out what's so interesting about his hands, and the rings he's wearing.

I groan. "Seriously, Logan, this is bullshit. Just tell me already."

Logan glances up at me, dark eyes intense. I stay rooted to my spot, unease trickling icy cold in my chest, an invisible fist gripping it tightly. I don't even want to breathe in case I miss what he's going to say next.

Logan licks his lips, lifts his head, and straightens his posture, making himself look bigger. "I'm the reason why that ring is on your finger."

It takes a second to sink in, for me to connect the dots, but when it does, all I can say is one word. "*No.*"

Logan nods. "Yes."

I shake my head, feel the world tilt on its axis until I can catch myself with my hands on the counter. "No. No way. I wouldn't be that stupid."

"I don't think it was stupid," he says, and I glare at him.

"I'm not asking for your opinion." When I can stand up straight on my own, I clap both hands to my face, shame and embarrassment burning hot in my belly. I pace the kitchen, then pivot to pace it again. "There's no way I did this. This is a next-level fuck up, even for me. Oh my god, what will my parents say?!" I groan.

My mind's starting to buzz with thoughts, and questions, and possible solutions on how to fix this problem, how to make it go *away*.

"We can get it annulled, right? Pretty sure that's a thing. Shit, I didn't think I would have to know that, what the reasons are valid for a marriage annulment."

"Max, Max," Logan calls, and I turn to him. He pushes his stool back and stands up, towering over me.

Did he really have to be so big? And would it kill him to crouch so I feel like I have the upper hand?

"We're not married," I tell him, cutting a hand across the air. "We're not."

Logan raises his eyebrows, and there's a tilt to his mouth that could almost be a smile. "I've got court documents that say we are."

Pressure builds in my head. I clap my hands over my ears, trying to stop myself from listening. "We can't be married. We can't. I don't even love you or believe in marriage."

"What?" Logan asks, but I wave off his question.

"I can't deal with this right now, I really can't. You need to go, Logan. Seriously, you need to leave."

"We need to talk about this. We said so much the other night, and you told me things, and I told you things. That's why we did this, Max. We talked about it."

I drop my hands, clench them into fists at my sides. My whole body aches, and I'm not at a hundred percent to fight this fight.

"We talked about it?! For what, like an hour? You don't make this kind of decision in an hour, Logan! I don't even *like* you," I hiss, scowling at him, hoping he can't tell that I'm lying my face off. "And I don't know why you're here."

"You invited me in last night after we got married, and then you might have barricaded your door," he says, crossing his impressive arms across an equally impressive chest.

Now is not the time to notice that shit, Max. Focus. You have to focus.

"I honestly can't do this right now. You need to go." I wave my hands towards the door, shooing Logan in that general direction.

"I think I'd rather stick around with my wife."

I gasp so loudly and quickly that I start choking on air, practically coughing up a lung. "Don't call me that! Don't ever call me that!"

"I've got a fancy government paper that says I can," he grins at me, showing off the single dimple he has.

I wave my hands in front of him, shake my head. "Nope. I'm not your wife. I'm going to fix this. This never happened. I'll get it annulled; you'll see."

Logan grins, and icy fear slithers and slides across my heart. "Yeah, good luck with that." He takes his time glancing down at a simple white gold band on his left ring finger, admiring it.

I bite my inner cheeks, trying to keep myself from screeching.

"I guess I'll see you later, wife," he says, and I do yell this time, pretending to Sparta-kick him from all the way in my kitchen as he makes his way over to my living room.

What's worse? The asshole just laughs at my rage, like I'm being cute.

I'll show him cute when I launch a candle at his head.

But first, I have to figure out how to annul this marriage, preferably before my cousins get here, before they find out about the worst mistake I've ever made in my entire life.

And I've made mistakes — I didn't blend out my loose powder under my eyes once and walked around outside like that. I looked like I had a wad of snow sitting on my face for no good reason, or that I fell face-first into some powdered doughnuts or other illegal substances.

I fume as Logan grabs his coat from the couch, pulling it on glacially slow, smiling at me as I stand there, keeping my hands clenched tightly into fists. Otherwise, I'm pretty sure I'm liable to tackle him to the ground and start throttling him.

Then you'd have a dead husband on your hands and a police investigation. That will ruin Christmas for sure.

Logan checks his pockets slowly, double-checking that his wallet is where it's supposed to be. He picks up his phone with his left hand, the wedding band glinting in the light, a constant reminder of what I've done.

What *we* did.

I want to go hide under the covers and go back to sleep. I want to pretend that none of this has happened. I want to pretend that I have my shit together and that I didn't take a hard right off the path in the direction my life was going.

"I'll call you later," he says, flashing another grin as he pulls on his boots. I stand at a safe distance and watch him open my front door. "Wife."

I start running but end up colliding with the door, practically bouncing off it while I can totally hear Logan laughing on the other side.

Why did I go and marry a guy like him? *Why* did I do that?

I flop down on my couch, then spring back up as if encountering boiling water. The blankets I usually snuggle in *smell* like him, the woodsy cologne that I always loved if it didn't come with Logan's personality.

I work the rest of the afternoon to get rid of all traces that Logan was in my home – I wash my sheets and pillowcases, along with my nesting blankets that sit on the couch. I clean my kitchen counter, making sure that whatever surfaces he touched are clean and proper.

To soothe myself, I light all my candles, and soon my home smells like a peppermint sugar cookie, and my world feels a little bit brighter, happier.

I flop back onto my couch, twisting the ring on my left hand, turning it and turning it, tugging at it gently every time only to find that it's not budging.

I research how to remove a ring that doesn't want to be removed, mounting panic sitting in my chest like an inflating balloon, expanding and expanding until it gets hard to breathe.

I bounce on my toes when my phone rings later that evening, appalled that my cousins are going to find me tonight with this stupid fucking ring on my finger and demand explanations that I don't have.

Explanations that I, too, would like, but Logan's being an obstinate asshole, and I can't deal with any more confrontation today.

Plus, I'm hungry and irritated, and the world feels like it's falling apart.

What in hell would possess me to marry a guy like Logan?

Did Logan offer me money to marry him? I don't need it.

Was I duped by his wonderful companionship? I'd rather run through a wall at full speed and be smushed cartoon-style because I need Logan in my life like I need a hole in the head.

I buzz my cousins in, my left hand wrapped in a tea towel, hiding that it's slicked up with butter.

I grin nervously at the pair of them, wave awkwardly.

Vick points at my left hand, toeing off her sneakers. "What the hell happened to your hand?"

I hide my left hand behind my back, squeeze my eyes shut. I shake off the nerves and embarrassment as much as I can.

"I'm trying to get that ring off," I say, the whole truth wanting to come out. I snap my mouth shut, keeping it locked inside.

Amber and Vick share a look, and I die a little on the inside, knowing I'm already caught. I can't keep a secret to save my life.

"Please. You're lying about something, Max. Spill it," Amber says.

THREE

"We're going to need a lot of wine for this," I say, flopping down onto my couch.

Vick heads to the fridge without further prompting and pulls out the sweetest rosé I've got in there and carts it into the living room.

Amber's the one that orders the food for supper, and then there's nothing else to do but tell them the truth and nothing but the truth.

I squeeze my eyes shut, my entire body burning with shame and embarrassment.

"I did something really stupid. Really fucking stupid." I peek at the two of them, and I don't find murderous rage or condemnation on their faces. So far, so good.

"And it has something to do with that ring?" Vick says, jutting her chin out towards my left hand.

I wipe off the butter with the dish towel and show off said hand.

"Shit, that's pretty swollen. You need ice," Amber says, moving to get off the couch. I grab her arm to keep her in her spot.

"I'll get it in a second. Let me just tell you what I need to." I pull in deep breaths, the invisible weight on my chest not making it easy. Tears of frustration start to well in my eyes. "I kinda...sorta...got married."

"WHAT?" Vick yells, springing to her feet, looking about ready to fight an invisible opponent. She's wearing her usual thermal and joggers, and her shoulders look like boulders. Maybe I should sic her on Logan.

"Vick, sit down," Amber snaps, and my other cousin plops onto the couch, her head in her hands. "You," Amber jabs a finger at me. "What happened? Were you coerced? The last I knew about anything is that you went out last night, trying to find a date for Christmas." Amber's mouth thins, and I roll my eyes.

"I know, I know, you don't approve. But honestly, the two of you are living your best lives with super supportive boyfriends, and I'm stuck here, overworked, overtired, and extremely lonely. I took matters into my own hands. I went trolling for a hot date for Christmas last night, but it didn't go so well."

"I'll say," Vick snickers, reaching for my left hand. "It's a pretty ring, though, Max."

"I'd rather cut my finger off than keep it on another second," I sigh dramatically.

Amber and Vick laugh, which was the whole point.

"So, who's your husband?" Amber asks.

That hot well of shame yawns ever wider in my chest when Amber uses that word.

"Please don't call him that," I whine. "His name's Logan. And I'm getting this shit annulled as soon as possible. It'll all be like a bad dream. Over before you know it." I nod to myself, trying to convince everyone in the room that I have my shit together.

My left hand is throbbing with all the tugging and prying I've done on it, I'm hungry and irritated, and a little heartsick that I stooped so low into getting married to a virtual stranger.

Must have been one hell of a conversation, Max, to consider marrying a guy like Logan.

If only I could remember what I was thinking, what I felt, but last night is basically a blank slate. The last thing I remember is being all morose and shit, sitting at the bar by myself and buying myself drink after drink.

"Logan, *Logan?* That guy you were into, and then you Maxed out?" Vick gapes at me. "Didn't you go out with him a few weeks ago as part of this whole 'get a Christmas date' thing? I thought he was off your contender list."

I shake my head. "I don't understand either, trust me."

Amber doesn't say anything and that makes me nervous.

"He even hates Christmas. I can't be with someone who hates Christmas. I mean, look at this place." My cousins take a glance around my home.

I've got a Christmas tree in almost every single room (even the bathrooms). I have a wreath outside my door *and* on the inside. I have Christmas-themed dinnerware and glassware. I have about four hundred ugly Christmas sweaters, and a mug collection specific for the holiday season that could easily have everyone in the building having a cup of coffee.

I *live* for Christmas every single year. It's the best.

"Don't tell that was the first question you asked him on your date, Max."

I nod. "Obviously not. Or else I would have cut it short and got home and maybe slept the allotted seven hours I'm supposed to. Instead, I listened to him ramble on and on about his life, and why he's so great, ugh. The second and third dates weren't any better. He's the worst. His looks are so misleading. He looks like a quick wham-and-bam and instead I got a cuddly boyfriend ready to sleep in with me on the weekend and bring me breakfast in bed."

Vick gets to her feet again and starts pacing my living room.

"What happened next?"

I shrug, not wanting to get into it. "We came back here last night, uh, this morning. He assures me that I barricaded myself in my bedroom, and yeah, my door was locked from the inside this morning," I sigh, rubbing at my forehead. I frown when I get a whiff of the butter that's made my skin too shiny, and hastily wipe at the grease on my forehead.

"We came back here, and I woke up to find him in that shower this morning." I point, and both Vick and Amber look toward the open bathroom, as if Logan's hiding there, ready to give them the jump-scare of their lives.

"Why did he go along with it, if you guys didn't hit it off a couple of weeks ago?"

"Hell if I know. I remember nothing about last night. But I heard a voicemail of me, speaking to myself." At their blank looks, I continue. "I basically told myself that I chose this being of sound mind and body, and all that. I guess we were drinking after we...we got...I can't even *say* it. Honestly, it's not like I'm already on my parents' shit list. What else is new?"

"You're not on their shit list, Max," Amber says, slapping at my thigh hard enough for it to sting. "And I'm sorry that they compare you to Izzy all of the time."

"She's the baby, I get it, kind of. Maybe. Do you know what she told me the other day? She told me that my father, the man who gave me shit for moving out on my own for choosing a non-conventional job, for not falling in line – he's offered to put the down payment on a condo for her. Can you believe it?"

The sharp pain feels fresh again as if I just heard the news from my little sister.

"I'm sorry," Amber says, Vick tacking on a *'me, too'*.

I shrug again, sniff hard to chase away the unshed tears. "I don't want to talk about it. Not anymore. I'm tired of not living up to expectations that keep moving around, you know? Whatever I do, it's not good enough. And this year, I didn't want to feel like shit at Christmas, I didn't want to field comments or backhanded compliments that sting and pinch instead of enjoying my food and the company about my lack of a love life. Now, I've royally fucked up." I hold my left hand up, glare at the ring that refuses to budge.

Vick heads to the bathroom and returns to the couch with a wad of toilet paper in her hands. She mops up my face when the tears spill over and then gives me some tough love by flicking me on the forehead.

I groan, rub at the throbbing skin.

Amber rolls her eyes at the pair of us and rearranges herself so she can start pouring the wine. Sushi should be coming soon, too. Everyone knows that sushi makes *everything* better, at least for a little while.

"How about you don't tell anyone else that you're married? I mean, you take off that ring, and no one would know," Amber says after handing me a glass.

I drink it down, and hum at the sweetness. Vick hands me the wad of toilet paper and resumes her seat on my other side. I'm stuck in a Prewitt cousin sandwich, and it feels pretty good now that I know they don't hate me for doing what I did.

"You guys are taking all of this much better than I did," I say on a sniff.

Vick rubs my back. "You made a mistake. So you got married, big deal. There's nothing that can't be fixed, right? This isn't life-ending, Max."

I nod slowly, staring down into the depths of my wine glass. I trace over the frosted glass with snowflakes imprinted all over it, knowing that I shouldn't be taking time off from work right now, but needing it all the same.

"You guys ever feel like you're stuck? Like no matter what you do, you can't move forward?" I mumble.

"Oh, *all the time*," Amber laughs. "Always. It never stops."

I stare at her, blink a few times to make sure she's real. "Yeah?"

"Me, too," Vick says. "I think that's supposed to happen every once in a while. You have to stop and figure out where you want to go next. That's all this is. A pit stop."

I glare up at the ceiling, feel the tears fall down my cheeks and temples. "And I had to get married!" I cry, covering my eyes with my hand. "I had to get married to a sweet guy that will have to see all that shit on Christmas." I shudder, trying to control the deluge of tears that clearly doesn't want to be stopped. "And I'm going to look like such an idiot in front of everyone at our dinner."

"Seriously, though, this isn't a problem. We get the ring off you, and no one has to know. I'm not going to tell anybody," Amber says, holding up her right hand. I slide my gaze over to Vick.

"Hey, you know I won't tell anybody, either. Unless it's under duress. The biggest problem we have here is that you can't keep a secret for anything."

"Don't you think I know that? It's like two weeks until Christmas and *everything* is getting ruined because I had to go and get married."

"Max...is there anything else that's bothering you?" Amber asks gently, and more tears fall because she's being so nice to me.

I shake my head, hiccup. "I'm just tired. Really tired. I've been working sixteen-hour days for the past three years, trying to grow my channel. My brain's tired. I hate how I'm always trying to think of the next possibly viral video idea, or how best to showcase the makeup that I already have instead of buying more. I'm always thinking about it, always. I'm tired, guys, just tired."

"Okay, you cry it out," Vick says, rubbing my back in soothing circles. It reminds me of when I was little and used to get the flu practically every six months, and my mom liked me better then. "We're going to be here for you. We're both here."

I sniff, mop up my face with ineffectual sodden toilet paper. "I'm really hungry, too."

Amber laughs and runs a hand down my hair. "So that's the real reason you're so upset, huh?"

I scoff, shaking my head.

"You'll fix this. All you need is a quick annulment, and that's it. Forget about it."

"I don't even know what I was thinking, though. Me? Get married? I don't even really believe in marriage. Have you seen my parents? They're miserable."

"Not everyone married is miserable, though," Vick says, her voice small.

I turn to stare at her. I was too busy throwing my pity party that I didn't notice Vick's ring on her own very important finger. It's not sparkly, but that's not Vick's vibe, either.

"Are you engaged and you didn't tell me!?" I screech, a waterfall of tears falling down my face.

I try to ignore the twist of sharp jealousy that slices through my insides, or the heat of shame and embarrassment that comes as a chaser right after. I try to ignore the way Vick looks so incredibly happy when I'm not.

I force all of it down and think of my cousin.

"You and Michael? Yeah?"

"No, Max, I'm getting married to my *other* next-door neighbor. Obviously, it's Michael. Jesus. I was lucky he made the first move, or I'd still be single."

I laugh because it's true. This time last year, Vick was in bad shape in all areas of her life. Kind of like where I currently find myself.

Who knows who *I'll* be one year from now?

I hug her tight enough around the ribs that she lets out a nervous laugh, and then it's Amber's turn to take my place. We talk about Vick's impending nuptials for the upcoming late summer, but my cousin doesn't want to talk details yet.

The sushi we ordered between the congratulations finally arrives, and we stuff ourselves full of too many of them to count. Amber pulls up *Pacific Rim* so we can all drool over Idris Elba and Charlie Hunnam.

Amid the violence and the chaos, Amber murmurs, "What does Logan think of all of this?"

I shrug. "I don't know. I kind of kicked him out as soon as I could this morning – earlier today after I woke up. I didn't want him here."

"Does he seem open to an annulment?"

"Like I'm going to give him a choice. I don't want to be married. And if I wanted to, it's not going to be without a giant party. No way. And especially not to someone like Logan."

Amber nods like she knows something I don't. Vick shushes us as if she hasn't seen this movie a hundred times and doesn't know what happens next.

I lean further back into the couch, bringing my knees up to my chest, appetite ruined. "You think that'll be a problem, getting an annulment?"

"I don't know. I know not one thing about annulments." She squints into the distance. "I don't know if that's a word. Maybe not. Look, don't beat yourself too much about this, okay? You made a mistake. You didn't ruin someone's life."

"I mean, I ruined my life, but okay, then."

Amber shakes her head, gives me a sharp smile. "We all know that you're even more rigid than me. You have to-do lists and schedules for almost every second of your life. You didn't allow for this kind of detour, but that's all it is. A detour. You'll still get to where you need to go."

"Excuse me, now is not the time to be needling me about my exceptional time management skills."

Amber rolls her eyes, and Vick shushes us again. We both ignore her. "I'm not saying don't do what you want. I'll never do that."

I hold my breath, then exhale in a quick rush. "But what?" My heart hammers against my ribs. I'm waiting for the worst.

"I'm just saying this is a pretty cool story, even if it doesn't work out."

"God, you're such a romantic."

Amber laughs and swats at my shoulder with a sharp slap. "Yeah, whatever, Max. Feeling a bit better?"

I nod, then twist my head from side to side, not too sure. "I feel like I really screwed up. I've been trying to meet Mom and Dad's expectations for so long that I feel all gross inside just thinking about telling them about this."

"And we said you don't have to do that. No one has to know."

I snort. "Yeah, right. I better become really good at lying in the next three weeks before I blurt everything out in the middle of dinner."

Vick pauses the video, the sound cutting off. "All right, since none of you want to enjoy the *excellence* that this movie provides, I'm coming in for a giant hug. Ready or not!"

Vick dives between us, slinging an arm around each of our shoulders.

After nearly swallowing one of her kneecaps or getting a concussion from one of her swaying elbows, we settle on my couch, watching a hilarious still that throws us into peals of laughter.

I'm finally feeling better, and the people I love the most don't think the worst of me for making this kind of mistake.

I mean, I had a *plan*, I had a schedule. I date when I can, and every other waking moment is spent on thinking about my work, how to grow and expand my business.

I'm not ready for marriage, not at all, even if someone stupendous were to come along.

At the end of the night, when I'm left alone in my empty apartment, I pick up my phone.

I pull up my messages, thumbs flying across the screen, trying to type it out instead of *thinking* about what I'm writing.

I grunt when a notification comes in from the person I was already going to text.

I shiver on my couch and open Logan's message.

Logan: *I'm sorry about this morning, and that it was such a shock to you. Can we talk?*

Me: *Not tonight. I'm tired. Are you free tomorrow evening, after work? We can meet up at my place. I don't want to have this conversation out in public.*

Plus, I'll be on home turf, and I know where the weapons are.

Logan: *Yeah, sure. I'll see you then, wife.*

I lock my phone quickly and launch it onto the farthest point on my sectional, bellowing like I'm about to go into battle.

Clearly, I'm married to an *asshole.*

I can't wait to get rid of him.

FOUR

I don't expect Logan to bring me flowers, a huge bouquet that's pretty much covered in snow.

I've been working and haven't broken the surface from my insane seven hours of productivity today to look outside and see what's happening. There could be an explosion out on St.-Jacques Street, and I wouldn't even know. Hell, the fire alarm in the building could go off, and I'd be deep in editing mode and hardly hear it.

Still, though, it's a surprise to see how much snow has come down already.

"Thank you," I grunt, afraid of the part in my chest that seems to warm through at the gesture. I've never received flowers before, not once. And to get them from Logan?

It's a trap, it has to be.

"Don't look so happy about it," Logan says, but he's grinning at me, inviting me in on a joke that I'm not sure I want to hear.

I keep my eye-roll to myself, and head to the kitchen, looking for something to put the flowers in.

“Food should be here soon,” I mumble in my crouch, searching the bottom cabinets for a wayward pitcher that has snowmen around the bottom. I pull out my prize and startle when Logan’s suddenly sitting across from me, the whole expanse of the kitchen island keeping us apart.

I want to keep it that way.

The silence stretches, and as it stretches, my shoulders start to hike up towards my ears. I don’t know what to say, I don’t know what *not to* say. I mean, when we had those three dates, Logan was the one filling in most of the conversation. I was the one listening.

I have two things I love to gush about and that’s makeup and my YouTube channel, and the inner workings of my business. I love to watch movies with my cousins and read romance novels. On the surface, I don’t really have that much going for me.

I’m not that interesting of a person.

And I struggle with finding the right words to say *when* to say those right words.

“What did you get us?” Logan asks, jutting his chin towards me. I fill the pitcher with water and start to take care of the flower stems.

“Pizza. Figured you can’t go wrong with pizza.”

“How did you know that I’m not on a gluten-free diet?” he asks, and I stare at him, panicking for a split second.

“Because I’m assuming since you ate a vat of spaghetti *Bolognese* for supper on our first date that you don’t have a sensitivity. Am I wrong?”

Logan shakes his head, his grin a mile long.

"So why the question?"

"I wanted to know what you do remember about our dates. And my food choice wasn't the one thing I thought you'd remember."

I snort, fluffing the bouquet of flowers, arranging them just so they fit in with the rest of my décor. "What a person eats is important, and how they treat their food is important to me, at least."

I glance over to Logan, waiting for the silent judgment, but all he does is nod at me like he wants me to continue.

"Food is meant to be enjoyed, right? And the more important part to me is how you treat the person you're eating with." Because food and I don't have the best relationship and seeing others enjoy their food makes me happy. I don't tell him that, though.

"Are you ever going to tell me why you didn't call after the third date when you said you would?"

I sigh. "I don't want to talk about that. We have enough to discuss without bringing our very short, shared past into the mix, don't you think?"

Logan's grin disappears, and he shakes his head. Maybe I disappointed him, but honestly, he's going to be here for a couple of hours tops – what do I care what answers he wants from me?

"Do you want anything to drink?" I ask, falling back on the manners of a perfect host, so I can avoid the conversation we're about to have a little while longer.

I was able to drown myself in work today, and I'm still editing the last couple of videos I have going up the 22nd and 23rd. Now that I'm not staring at a computer screen, or pulling links and fixing thumbnails for my videos, there's nothing left to do but think about the situation we find ourselves in.

It's not lost on me that Logan is wearing his wedding ring, and it doesn't look like he's been trying to yank his off. My left ring finger refuses to let go of my ring. It's odd, feeling the weight of it throughout the day.

I get why they call spouses the 'old ball and chain'.

"A glass of water, please."

I raise an eyebrow, then turn around and ask another important question: "Sparkling or regular?"

"Uh, regular, I guess." He grins sheepishly. "I don't even know how to talk to you for a glass of water. What are we going to do when we talk about the marriage ceremony?"

I hiss, practically lunge across the island to slap a hand over his mouth. "Don't talk about it like that."

"Max, we're married. We're going to have to talk about it, exactly like you wanted."

"Then try to talk about it without saying the 'M-word."

Logan works his shoulders free of tension and then crosses his fingers together, holding his hands on top of the table. His wedding band catches the light, and I find myself staring at it, mesmerized.

"How am I supposed to do that? We're married, Max. Married."

Goosebumps erupt all over my body, and a shiver races down my spine. "Well, we're not going to be married that much longer, trust me."

Maybe it's better to clear the air now before the food shows up. That way I won't have to feed him and there'll be more pizza left over for me once he inevitably decides to leave.

"Fine, let's talk. You've made yourself comfortable," I say, grabbing a glass from the cupboards. I fill it with water, and hand it over to him, making sure our hands don't touch. "I want an annulment."

Logan nods slowly, then takes a deep gulp of his water, his throat working. He takes it down in a few swallows. There's a part of me that's wondering if he's nervous if *I* make him nervous.

Which makes no sense at all.

"An annulment," he repeats, trying to catch his breath after drinking down his water. "You want to annul our marriage."

I nod. "Yes. Obviously." The silence stretches out between us, and for some reason, my heart rate goes haywire. "Don't you?"

Logan shakes his head, scoffs like he's heard a terrible joke but is still smiling for my sake. "I keep forgetting that you don't remember the other night."

"Honestly, Logan, it doesn't make sense. We didn't have a good time going on those three dates together. Why in hell would I marry you? Why would you marry *me*? Make it make sense." I wave my hands around for emphasis.

Logan's dark eyes bore into me until I'm pretty sure he's looking through me – making me seem insignificant.

I'm not the kind of person that chases feelings or people that make me feel small. Logan's making me feel small.

"We talked for hours the other night. Hours. We didn't get back here until early in the morning."

"So what? Walk me through the steps. How did we go from talking to getting married?"

Logan rubs a hand over his mouth, deliberating. "You told me about your parents."

I snap my mouth shut, an impatient scream locked in my throat. My cheeks burn with embarrassment and hot shame. We weren't at that stage; we were definitely not at the stage where I would tell him about my unique relationship with my family.

"What...what do you know?"

"That they make you feel small, especially at Christmas." Logan lays it all out there like he's telling me the weather, and not the way my parents make me feel.

I nod along, trying to make him hurry up his story. It's a no-go though because my phone rings for entry to the building. I buzz in the delivery kid.

The conversation has to wait as I maneuver the two boxes of all-dressed pizza and plop them on the island. I get us a couple of plates, and Logan skirts the island and starts asking me where things are, helping to set the table.

Once we both have a slice of pizza in front of us, Logan going at his slices with a fork and a knife while I use my own two hands, I blurt, "So what else happened between the two of us?"

Logan chews slowly, his jaw working. It's unfortunate that it's a nice jaw, so incredibly unfortunate.

He carefully wipes his face with a napkin after setting down his utensils and swallows before the conversation can continue.

"We kissed. That's it, I swear."

I glare at him through a squint. "I let you kiss me?"

"You kissed me, actually."

I shake my head, nearly choking on my bite of pizza. "No way, absolutely not. Why would I do that?"

Logan shrugs, and he looks so relaxed that it's infuriating. "Because you wanted to."

"Why?"

"Max, I don't know what was going on in your head. I didn't push you or anything like that. We kissed for five minutes tops after we were married."

I drop my pizza onto the plate, losing my appetite. It's a sad day all around.

"I still want an annulment," I groan, picking up my slice of pizza again. I'll force myself to eat it, even if I'm in pain later.

"What about Christmas?" he asks, and I raise an eyebrow.

"What *about* Christmas? You made it clear that you hate the holiday through and through that first night we had a date together."

"But you love it," Logan says. "And you asked me to help you."

My heart beats triple time and settles at the base of my throat.

"You asked me to go with you to your Christmas family dinner. I agreed."

I shake my head, unable to, yet again, connect the dots. "And how did we end up married?"

Logan shrugs and focuses on slicing his pizza instead of answering me.

The wind howls beyond the curtain covering my balcony door, and I'm already looking forward to crawling into bed alone, fuzzy socks on, eReader in hand, about to read some smut.

When is it too early to throw out your guest?

"We came to the decision together. I wouldn't force you."

I snort. "Look, you don't know me that well, but I don't do things I don't want to do. No one can make me do something I wouldn't want."

Logan's dark eyes leap with mischief, bright with something like happiness. "So you admit to wanting to be married to me."

Well, I walked into that one.

I roll my eyes, ignore that comment and keep eating instead. Trouble is, my stomach gets full before I want it to, and I'm forced into making conversation again.

"I don't want to be married to anyone," I reply, minutes too late.

Logan raises both eyebrows but keeps chewing, thankfully. He doesn't launch into all the reasons I might change my mind like my mom does, or the way my dad still thinks I need to be taken care of when I make enough money on my own to never need anyone to help me out.

"It's not for me. I know it's not for me. That's why none of this makes any sense, Logan. None of it. Why would I agree to marry you?"

"Because we talked and...there was a connection between us."

"A connection? This isn't a movie or a book," I snort, waving it off. Except Logan looks almost hurt by my blasé attitude and I find myself sitting very still, trying to figure him out.

"People make connections with each other, Max. It happens all of the time."

I don't know what to say. I can't tell him that I've never felt a connection like that with a guy. And to not remember what we talked about, what made me feel like it was possible to marry Logan and think it would work out?

It's torture, plain and simple.

"We talked about every little thing. You weren't drunk. You told me a total of eight times throughout the night. We connected in a way we couldn't on our dates." He sighs. "I know I wasn't at my best those three times we went out. I was word-vomiting all over the place, trying to impress you. The more you stayed quiet, the more I talked, and it all ended up in a vicious cycle that had you walking out of my life. Until the other night, when you called me."

I cross my arms over my chest, think about having a third slice of pizza just to keep my mouth occupied. I think about what he's telling me, but without confirmation from not even a hazy memory of the other night, all I have are his words to go on, and I hate it.

He could be lying right to my face and I won't even know it.

"I wish you could remember what we talked about. I really wish you could. I...I don't want an annulment."

"What?! Are you serious?"

Logan licks his lips and works his shoulders in a row of shrugs. "I think this could work."

"You hate Christmas, Logan, one of my favorite times of the year. That's one mark in the *'con'* column. We're not compatible. Why would you want to stay married to me for?"

He stares at me for a time – it could be an eternity or mere seconds, but I find myself getting lost in his dark eyes, trying to find answers to my unasked questions.

Logan smiles slow and soft, and my chest suddenly feels too tight to house my heart. It's unfortunate that he has a great smile, too. Very unfortunate.

"We could be good together," he says staring at me as if trying to share a vision of a near-future where we're both happy together. I don't believe it, and I want no part of it.

"That doesn't matter. We're not meant to be."

Logan bites at his bottom lip, looking shy. "Did you shut me down, too, all those dates that we had, because you couldn't give me a chance?"

"I give everyone chances," I say, unnerved that he's narrowed down to the truth of it. I'd been looking for Mr. Perfect that I've been blind to Mr. Right.

Not that I think Logan is Mr. Right, especially if he wants to be Mr. One and Only.

Did I do that? Did I shut him down based on a potential only I could see and Logan could never meet? Or did I see him for the guy he was, knew that whatever we could have might leave me broken? Did I run and cut my losses before I could get hurt?

It doesn't matter, none of this matters.

"Dinner's over," I say, closing up the pizza box, and sliding off my stool to start packing the leftovers away. "I'm going to get that annulment tomorrow, with or without you."

"You don't need me there," he says. When I give him a questioning look, he just shrugs. "I looked it up this morning. Only one party needs to attend to have it annulled. I had a feeling your mind was going in that general direction."

I'm thankful that Logan stays seated a few feet away from me while I put the pizza in the fridge. I don't need him looming over me the entire time, and making me nervous because of the height difference between the two of us.

"Thanks for letting me know."

Logan shrugs his eyes on the counter instead of on me. "Could I ask for a favor, then?"

"Let's hear it," I say, waiting to reserve judgment. I don't know why I'm giving him the time of day. I have what I want, and I can get what I need tomorrow.

But there's something about his entire demeanor that has me *listening* with other parts of my body instead of my brain.

Logan glances up with his forehead adorably wrinkled.

Did I just think that about him? About his forehead?!

I wrinkle my nose and watch Logan's eyes fill with bright hope. "Can we stay married until Christmas is over?"

"Why?" I snap, moving to stand in front of him, arms crossed.

"I want to help you with your Christmas dinner. But you have to help me with mine." His dark eyes are bright with a secret, and there's a smile hovering around the edges of his mouth.

I smell a trap. A *big* trap.

But I also know that if I have to spend one more Christmas while my parents dismantle everything I'm wearing, or not wearing, and make raging accusations about my lack of love life, I'm liable to lose it.

Christmas is supposed to be about giving to others, about coming together. As much as I love the holiday for that very reason, it's going to take a lot more than Christmas magic to get me back home without a date this year.

It might take a whole Logan Porter at my side to survive.

"And we have to stay married for this?"

Logan nods. I watch him twist his wedding band around his finger, worrying it until he opens his mouth to speak again. "What's less than two weeks of being married to me? We don't even have to spend that much time together if you don't want to."

I shake my head. "I don't want. I don't want to remember that any of this ever happened."

Logan nods but doesn't look happy about it.

A loud ringing noise blasts from both of our phones, which can only mean one thing.

I'm expecting an Amber alert or something like it, but instead, the Emergency Alert message says that the electrical grid in northern Quebec has shut down, and the island of Montreal should experience a rolling blackout over the next twenty-four hours.

I glance up at Logan, wondering if he read the message. He's still mouthing the words to himself when the power goes out, plunging us both into complete and utter darkness.

FIVE

I hastily turn the flashlight on my phone and peer around, screaming when I find Logan standing too close for comfort.

"How do you move that quietly? Whistle or something next time!"

His face is pinched with annoyance, but I don't care. "Do you have a first aid kit?"

I move my phone's light over him, trying to find a wound. "You're not hurt."

"No, I'm not, but it's going to get cold fast if the power is out for long periods of time. Haven't you seen the storm outside?"

"I don't go outside unless I absolutely have to during December. There are too many people outside. And the wind hurts my face."

Logan groans in despair, and I shush at him to calm down.

"Just head down to your car, and you'll get home. It's not that big of a deal. I'm sure the generators will take over."

"Yeah, to keep the water hot and circulating for as long as possible. At least, that's what happens in my building in case of an emergency."

I blink at him, watch him, peer, into the darkness as if he can memorize the layout of my home from memory.

His anxiety ramps up my own nerves, and I'm wondering now if there really is something to be worried about.

As far as I know, it's still snowing, and this isn't like the ice storm back in 1998 when we were bombarded with 100 millimeters of freezing rain on our infrastructure. This can't be as bad as that, right?

Because if it is, I'm looking at being without power for several days, if not *weeks* at this point, and that would be a catastrophe.

I have work to do, food to cook, laundry to wash. I can't sit here and do *nothing*. Vlogmas waits for no influencer. And I don't want to miss the bump in income I get for the month because I'm posting more frequently.

I do not need a storm affecting the electrical lines, thank you very much.

"Okay, well, thanks for stopping by," I say, ushering in the darkness towards what I hope is where my front door is. It's the general direction anyway.

Logan stays in one spot and turns his own phone's light on.

"I have some bad news."

I wince, knowing without really knowing how this is going to go. "You didn't take your car..." I sigh.

Logan shakes his head, looking down at his phone screen. "Nope. I took the metro in. And as of right now, service has been suspended until tomorrow morning."

We both flinch when another emergency alert comes through on our phones, blaring loud enough to wake the dead.

"'Caution is advised: stay at home, if possible,'" I murmur. "What's that supposed to mean?" I whirl around, bark my toe on the foot of the stool and limp towards my balcony door, pulling the curtains open.

It's funny how now that all the lights are out that I can see through to the cloudy dark gray sky. The snow's still swirling around viciously, and if I were outside, I know it would whip around and sting my face.

"I'll call for a ride," Logan says, somewhere behind me. I just press my forehead against the cool glass and look down towards the street. I hiss when two cars collide right before my very eyes.

"No, no," I say without really thinking. "You can sleep on the couch." I whirl around to point my phone's light at him. Logan winces, and I hurriedly drop my hand. "Help me light some candles," I say, pointing to various corners of the room where I've got them stashed.

I search through my junk drawer and pull out one of the hundred and two matchboxes I have in there, lighting up four candles and placing them strategically around the kitchen and living room.

It starts to smell like a mixture of sugar cookies and hot chocolate, and honestly, that doesn't sound so bad right now...if I had electricity with which to bake and make hot chocolate from scratch.

"Are you sure I can stay, Max? I don't want to make you uncomfortable."

I shake my head, turn off my phone flashlight e to save some of the battery. I still have cell tower service, but who knows with the storm rolling in if that's going to last?

See, that's why it pays to pay attention to the outside world, Max. Shit.

"You can stay." I plop myself on the couch, searching around the living room to find something to do. "I have a deck of cards somewhere if you want to pass the time. Or you can read one of my books by candlelight if you want. I've got my eReader that's at 100%."

"I'll be out of your hair by morning, I promise."

I nod, because yeah, that's the plan. And Logan will still be my husband and I'll finally have that Christmas date I'll be looking for.

But at what cost?

"Show me which one on that bookshelf over there is your favorite," he says, moving to stand against the bright, white shelves. He runs a finger over the spines, tracing each one.

"Romance," he says, and I say nothing. I mean, he can read. "Didn't peg you for a romance girl."

I roll my eyes. "Please, I love that shit."

"Doesn't it get to be too predictable, with the happily ever after?"

I snort. "That's like saying that it's too predictable when the good guys win, or when the detective solves the mystery in a police procedural. The answer is: no, *never*. It's always interesting to see how the author's going to do it. How they'll bring it all together for the grand finale. It's my favorite part of the story, the happily ever after."

Logan turns back to me, half his face hidden in shadow, the candlelight flickering over his features and making him look…otherworldly.

Don't do that, Max. Don't do that.

I squint at him. "How do you know about the guaranteed happily ever after? Don't guys like you scoff at the entire romance genre?"

Logan grins, a quick flash of his teeth in the semi-darkness. He moves slowly, pulls a book seemingly at random, and heads back to the couch, sitting on the other side, keeping space between us.

"My mom gave me romance novels to read as soon as I was old enough to talk and think about sex."

"No fucking way," I blurt, turning on my side. I pull my legs up, knees to my chest, and look at him dead on. "No fucking way. You?"

Logan holds onto the book, tracing a finger over the well-loved spine. "My mom called it my education. She wasn't wrong, even if I still had a lot to learn."

"This is blowing my mind right now. If you led with that on our first date, I would have had a better time."

Logan licks his lips, runs a hand over his mouth, that infernal wedding band glinting hot in the candlelight. Suddenly I feel sick to my stomach. Suddenly I want to crawl under the covers and get lost in my own romance novel. I want to dream about the smuttiest parts that could one day happen with a potential partner that I'm not married to. A partner that I didn't have to blackmail to get him to come to Christmas dinner with me.

None of this would have happened if I never left the house and didn't put ludicrous plans into play and get my ass married before Christmas.

"Your mom sounds really cool," I mumble. Logan nods, clearly agreeing with me.

"Do you mind if I read this?" he asks, voice soft.

I clear my throat. "I said you could."

"It feels like you read this one many, many times. The spine's been broken."

I nod, because yeah, true. "You're not wrong."

Logan smiles, but there are no teeth behind it, and it's quick and gone in a flash. "I would like to read it."

My cheeks start to burn and the rest of my body starts to remember that I'm in my home with a man I barely know. A man that yeah, I find attractive physically, but not emotionally. It's not like I have an itch I can't scratch. I don't need Logan to do that for me, not when I'm still trying to understand how we got here – married to each other.

Ugh, that word.

The candles flicker and everything feels a little bit like a dream, soft around the edges, the shadows keeping everything hidden. I wish it was a clear night so that moonlight could have helped me see him better.

"What was so special about this particular book?" he asks.

My heart stutters in my chest. I lick my lips. This was not a question I thought I was going to be asked. "I saw myself in the heroine," I say. "It resonated with me in the way other books haven't."

Logan nods like he understands. I wonder what game he's playing at.

"Why do you want to honor your decision to come to my family dinner? It's not like you're going to get anything from me in the sex department again."

Logan chokes and starts coughing into his hands.

It would be funny if I wasn't worried until he's able to catch his breath.

"I wasn't...I don't expect that from you, Max. I really don't."

I squint at him, trying to find the lie on his face, but come up empty. I'm blaming the shadows and the romantic lighting. Nobody can see anything clearly with it looking like we're filming an old-school soap opera in here.

"So why would you do this for me? Why do you want to stay married?"

"Why don't you?"

I lick my lips, stuff my toes in between the couch cushions. "I don't think I'm the right kind of person for marriage. I don't believe it's the right decision for me. And I know myself, okay? I know that I don't believe in that kind of thing so the very idea that I signed up to marry you after one night of *talking* doesn't make any kind of sense. Not for me. Look around, Logan. Do I look like the kind of person to take that leap of faith?" I shake my head.

Logan keeps his silence as he stares around my home, and I let him. I don't want to talk about this anymore.

"Marriage isn't for everybody," he says, finally. "But this thing between you and me? If you knew what I knew, Max, you wouldn't question it. Face it, we need each other."

"So tell me then, because I really don't understand. I've got holes in my memory and none of this makes sense to me."

I stare down at my socked feet, probing the gaping hole in my memory, trying to fill it in like you would a puzzle with the last few missing pieces. Except nothing comes to the surface.

I curl my hands into fists, tight enough to threaten to mess up my press-ons, and start pinging them off like bullets. I glance at Logan.

"All you have is what I'm going to tell you," Logan says, gently flipping through the pages of one of my novels, holding it carefully like it's some sort of precious treasure. "You wouldn't believe me, even if I told you."

I frown at that, because that's accurate, too.

"That's why I sent the voicemail to myself," I say nodding. I glance around my cozy apartment. I shiver at the slow change in temperature, the way the heat seems to dissipate with every passing minute.

I really hope the power comes back on soon.

I let Logan read as I try to figure out what kind of questions I want to ask him. I waste another twenty minutes trying to order my thoughts, trying to remember something that isn't there. Maybe the memories will come back to me if I don't try so hard. Maybe I need a good night's sleep and a day's rest.

Right, like that's going to happen.

I have so much work to do for the last few days of Vlogmas, and I need to do them as soon as I wake up tomorrow. Maybe Logan and I can skip the awkward breakfast tomorrow morning and continue with our lives.

He'll go back to his place, and I'll stay here. We'll talk through text and try to figure out how best to approach Christmas with my family.

Logan laughs, the sound jarring me from my thoughts. He's grinning down at the book and judging by the number of pages he's holding in his left hand, I think I know which part he's at.

I end up smiling with him, before erasing it off my face by brushing a hand over my mouth.

The hard day's work starts to drag me down and sitting in the quiet with nothing but candlelight to see by has my eyes going gritty. My head weighs enough that a pillow sounds really nice right about now.

"I'm going to get you some extra blankets," I mumble as I stand up. "And some sheets!" I speed away and avoid his questioning look, grabbing the things that I need from my linen closet.

Logan laughs when I plop the pile of them at his feet. "That's great, thanks." He gives me a sunlight smile. For what? Bringing him blankets?

"You're welcome. I'm going to go to bed now. I'll see you in the morning?" *Jesus, Max, why is that a question? Of course, he'll be here in the morning. There's so much more to talk about and to plan.*

Logan nods, his smile fading. He holds up the book in his hands and nods at me.

"Good night, Max. Sweet dreams."

"Good night, Logan." I squirrel away to my bedroom, lock the door, and freeze when I realize how pitch black it is in here. I fumble my way over to the curtains, too lazy to get my phone out.

I hurry my way through washing up for the night, nearly breaking every finger in my hand by misjudging the distance to the faucet, and punching it for all I'm worth.

Too bad it didn't do anything to the ring on my left finger. Nope, that sucker still has not budged. Tomorrow, though.

I have a good feeling about tomorrow.

I bundle up, pull on fuzzy socks, and a hooded sweatshirt on top, hood pulled low on my face. I crawl into bed like that, searching blindly for my eReader, the only bed companion I've had in a very long time.

I squint at the bright light when I turn it on, snuggle down underneath the forty blankets on my bed, and try very hard not to think about the guy sleeping on my couch. The guy reading one of my favorite romances. Who is my *husband*.

My phone buzzes sporadically over the next hour I read. There are random texts from Vick and Amber, even a couple from Izzy in the group family chat.

I message back, though the messages remain unsent and unread. But it's totally fine. We should totally be back to normal tomorrow morning.

I startle when there's a knock on my door, and sniff against the cold. I've made a warm nest in the cocoon of my blankets, and I don't want to get up.

"Yeah?" I call, hoping Logan doesn't take it as an invitation to come in.

"Oh, uh. Never mind, Max. It's all good. Goodnight again."

"' Night," I call out towards my bedroom door and watch the light seeping through underneath the door retreat deeper into the living room.

I continue reading until my eyes burn no matter how much I turn up the brightness on my reading device.

Even with the device powered down, all I have are my thoughts and unanswered questions buzzing around my brain.

So Logan and I are married. And we're going to be each other's plus-ones for respective Christmas dinners. It's going to be great, hopefully.

And maybe this year I can dodge all the backhanded compliments regarding my lackluster love life from both of my parents, and my mom's side of the family. Maybe I'll be able to forget that I'm the eldest on that side and haven't gotten married yet. Maybe I won't even notice the looks the family gives me like I'm diseased because I'm still single.

God, I'm going to have to coach Logan through so much if we want to make this look legit. *So much.*

I'm not going to tell anybody we're married. Like Logan said, I'll take care of that after Christmas and get it annulled once we both get what we want. We're each other's pretend dates despite being legally wed for Christmas.

Throw in the problem that I'm no good at keeping secrets and Logan's about to get tossed to the wolves.

This might be the worst Christmas ever if the truth comes out. It's fine if I have a date for the holiday dinner. It's not *okay* that I went and got married without inviting the entire family.

I squirm in bed, squeezing my eyes shut, trying to dispel all worst-case scenarios from my mind.

Logan and I are going to survive a Prewitt family Christmas.

I just hope we both come out of it all in one piece.

SIX

I stumble into my bathroom in the morning. The toilet seat is cold enough to wake me up from a dead sleep, slamming me into the realm of consciousness.

After washing up and peering out the window to confirm it's still snowing, I try to get some service and see what the forecast has in store today. The app doesn't want to load, so I'm not sure what's going to happen.

Having more snow isn't the worst. The city's ready for that. It's if the snow turns into freezing rain that it's going to be bad. The entire city could be blanketed in ice, and that includes all the infrastructure. Depending on how much there is of it, structures could collapse, electrical cables could snap under the weight. It'll be a repeat of 1998 all over again. You'd be better off going out with skates than trying to walk anywhere.

I flick the light switches, staring up at the blank light, wishing it would light up.

Great.

Now I'm *really* behind on what I have to do.

I have a thousand power banks – I went through a vlogging phase – and I have extra batteries for my camera. None of which help me. I need my computer to work, and that doesn't look like it's going to happen right this minute.

After pulling on some fresh clothes that'll keep me warm, I stumble out into the living room and *meep* like a scared little animal.

Logan's standing in nothing but his boxers, his nipples pebbled against the cool air in the middle of my living room.

And I can't stop *staring*.

Logan laughs awkwardly when he spots me ogling, and I just blink at him. I mean, he never really looked like he was packing that kind of muscle underneath all those clothes. And the one time we had sex, it was dark and I didn't get to look.

I start counting in my head.

"Do you have an eight pack? Seriously? I bet you're boring and basically renounce sugar, too," I mumble, feeling naked without any makeup on, nor a colorful eyeshadow look. I'm not even wearing lip gloss.

We're not standing *that* close, but I'm sure Logan can count my pores if he wants to, not to mention he can see all the acne scars that pockmark my skin from this distance.

There's a wizardry to editing and lighting. I wash myself out with the bright lighting so it's near impossible to see how bad my skin really is underneath my favorite full coverage foundation.

Now?

Logan's looking at my bare face. I hardly share my bare face with my cousins ever since my adult acne went from bad to worse.

All he has to do is say one mean thing and I'll throw him out. One mean thing.

"Good morning." Shit, does his voice have to sound that deep and raspy so early in the morning?

Honestly, Max, you have to stop.

"Morning," I mumble back and work hard to ignore my reaction to looking at his body like some sort of pervert. It's not my fault that he's standing in the middle of my living room, practically naked.

"I'm going to go wash up, and I'll make us some breakfast," he calls over his shoulder, and I force myself not to stare at his retreating back disappearing inside the main bathroom.

God, get a grip, would you? It's Logan. The guy who made comments about your makeup, and the way you looked. The guy you weren't looking for, and the one-night stand that never should have been.

I shake myself out of it while Logan's in the bathroom. I glance around, trying to figure out what to eat.

I ran out of cereal the other day before the blackout, even though I have two full cartons of almond milk in my fridge. Now that the electricity is out, I'm realizing that a third of my food choices to make a meal have gone out the window.

I open my fridge to find most of the food still cool, but I know if the blackout's going to go throughout the entire day, that I'd better put most of my food outside on the balcony.

The bathroom door opens while I'm contemplating what's my fridge. I turn to look at Logan, now fully dressed, thank the makeup gods.

He smiles at me as if he really is happy to see me, not the forced ones I usually give people I recognize or know.

I don't know why he's so happy to see me.

"Did you sleep well?" I ask, jutting my chin towards the couch.

"Oh, yeah. It was great, thanks. I'd offer to do the laundry, but you know, everything's still out."

I hum, pull my phone out of my pants when the blaring sound of another Emergency Alert comes through. I bite my lip, not wanting to look at it if it's going to be bad news.

"Shit," Logan groans, and I hastily read the message, frowning harder after almost every single word.

"The blackout's going to last for a few days," I mumble, my heart starting to beat hard and fast. "No, no fucking way. I have work to do. I have so much work to do. I need electricity."

"The whole city's out," Logan says in awe. I glance up from my phone to look at him. "Everything. No restaurants, no metro lines. Nothing but the hospitals. This is pretty bad, Max."

I frown at him, my mind already jumping to the conclusion I'm not ready to confront just yet.

Where is Logan going to go? The metro lines are down, and people shouldn't be going out if the roads are that bad. You don't mess with icy streets unless you want to break your body like a watermelon meeting the pavement.

"I don't know how much food I have in here. I don't know if it's enough for the both of us for the week." I wave him over after lighting a candle and swiping it off the kitchen counter. We both enter my walk-in pantry, using the candle for light. I have to keep my phone battery going for as long as I can.

"I have almond milk, but not much cereal. Do you have allergies?" I ask, my mind working overtime on meal planning.

"No."

"Good. Because I'm pretty sure everything I have here is allergen city." I point to the bottom shelf. "I have an induction hot plate. It was for the one and only had time I went on a camping trip, don't ask. I've got one pot that could work with it. I also have jugs of water, also from that same camping trip over the fall. They're sealed so we should be okay," I say.

I look over at Logan. His hands are on his hips, and he looks over each shelf with a methodical precision that makes me squirm and expect a whole lot of judgment.

I have a lot of sugary foods, especially around the time of my period. I've got some candy and all the dry ingredients for edible cookie dough ready to go at a moment's notice. I have the palate of a five-year-old.

I wait for Logan to give me shit about it.

I mean, my body looks nowhere near as strong as his body, even though I know I have muscles underneath all the extra cushion I tend to carry around.

I was supposed to do something about it at the start of this year, but I've been working long days since then, building my channel and community and posting as frequently as I can outside of special events.

Time got away from me, as it always seems to do.

"We can make a few meals with this," he says, his eyes sliding over to me. "If I'm allowed to stay, that is."

I shrug, cross my arms over my chest. I shiver underneath my hoodie, but I don't think it's because of the cold.

"My Christmas would be ruined if I knew you got hurt or something because I kicked you out of here," I bite at my lip, worrying the skin. "I guess you can consider yourself invited into my home."

Logan laughs, then beams at me, delighted. I don't know what to do with this much energy, this early in the morning.

I pull out the hot plate, install the requisite batteries. I only have a single pot that works with it, but Logan's already sworn that he could make us scrambled eggs and bacon inside of it.

While he cooks breakfast, I cart as much produce as I can out onto the balcony, insulating it against the icy wind with blankets and a plastic tarp I usually use when I have the urge to dye my hair.

We sit next to each other this time around, almost hip to hip, our stools too close up against the kitchen island.

"Thanks for making breakfast," I mumble, vowing not to complain about the lack of toast. I know I'm not ready for any kind of apocalypse. I'm pissed that I don't have toast with my eggs. If the world ended and I ran out of toilet paper?

I'm the *first one* tapping out.

"I hope you like it," Logan says, and we sit and eat in awkward silence.

Logan does the dishes while I take stock of what's in my pantry one more time, going through it with a pen and paper.

I don't know how much I eat on a regular basis, and Logan's taller than me, so he's bound to need more calories. I suck at my bottom lip, trying to run calculations on serving sizes and if we're going to need to ration some foods over others.

"You look worried." Logan moves to stand right next to me, his shadow against the wall making him seem like a giant.

"I am worried. I really don't know if I'm going to have enough food."

"I can drink water or almond milk. I'm fine with that, Max. I'm happy to have a place to sleep."

I frown at him. "Why are you being so calm about this? There's a city-wide alert that everything's going to be out for the next week. If this is a repeat of 1998, then this might go on for *several* weeks. I don't know if I have enough food for several weeks, Logan." I bite my lip.

How much rice is in a serving? I don't want to use my phone and drain the precious battery to answer that question.

"There's plenty. We can even make a vat of chili and store it outside to keep. There's enough food, Max."

"Water's the next problem. We have running water for now, so maybe we should stockpile it? I don't know. I'm not meant for this end-of-the-world type stuff. I'd be the idiot that tries to take all of my eyeshadow palettes with me into the wilderness when they'd serve no purpose."

Logan grins, but it doesn't feel like he's making fun of me.

"You know, you never did tell me why that third date was the end of the line."

My eyes bug out. "You want to go over this now? Really? We're facing starvation over here."

Logan shrugs, calm as ever. "Seems a good of a time as any."

I shake my head. "No, it doesn't. We have to live with each other for at least a week. We're married for some odd reason, and you want to get into why I didn't think you were right for my dating life? I don't need you being an asshole to me the rest of the time we're cooped up together. I live here, this is my home."

Logan's jaw locks and I wonder if I've poked the beast into fighting back. I eye the candle sitting on the kitchen counter again, the hot chocolate-scented one. That'll make a good missile if I need it to be.

"Why am I always the asshole?"

I clench my jaw tight enough to make my teeth squeak. I shiver at the impact of tooth grinding tooth. "Do you even remember the dates we went on?"

His jaw flexes and I wonder how hard *he's* clenching his jaw. I'm sure if I were to place a lump of coal between his molars, I'd get a diamond in no time.

"I remember every second of every date we went on."

"Oh, really? Quiz time," I say, exiting the pantry. I turn around and slam my hand on the counter, enjoying the burning sting working its way over my palm and out towards my fingers. "What did we talk about?"

"I was the one doing most of the talking, remember? I was trying to get you to open up."

I shake my head, wave off his words as if I can erase them from existence.

"No, no. You talked, and I listened. I couldn't get a word in edge-wise."

Logan's eyebrows lift, and for the first time since I've met him, he looks almost...annoyed. "You and I are remembering the nights very differently. You didn't want to talk to me. I tried getting you to talk. I really fucking tried. But you were too busy on your phone."

I gasp. "Excuse me, the only reason why I was on my phone the entire time was because of work. I was busy."

"Then why go out on a date with someone if you're going to be working? I wanted to get to know you, Max. All I found out that first night was that you were rude."

I hold my fists up, ready for a fight. "I'm not rude. I'm the nicest person I know."

Logan shakes his head, adamant. "Max, if you didn't want to go out on a date with me, you should have told me."

"I scheduled the date. I wanted to go out." My voice trembles. I was forcing it, I know I was forcing myself to go out on a date with him. He looked like a good time, but I didn't sign up for the rest.

"Did you want to go out with me? Or would you have taken anyone?" he asks gently, seemingly curious.

"I'm dating around, if that's what you're asking," I say, squinting at him. "It's not like we were going to get..."

"*Married*," Logan supplies, and I roll my eyes hard enough to make them hurt.

"Yeah, well I wasn't banking on that. It's not my fault that we didn't have any chemistry those few dates, all right?" *Even I believe my lies. Wow.*

"We might have had if you gave it some effort."

My cheeks burn with embarrassment. Okay, so maybe he caught me out, a little bit. I point a finger at him. "You didn't have to make asshole comments about my appearance, though. Admit it."

"What? What did I say?"

I slap my hand to my forehead. "No way, we're not doing this. I'm not going to give you the replay of events so you can twist them later."

"Max, I'm not twisting anything. Let's get one thing straight, all right? Clear the air once and for all. Did you want to go on a date with me because you found me interesting?"

"I go on dates with a lot of different guys for different reasons." *All of them this past month had to do with needing a date for Christmas. I'm not even sorry. Anything to avoid a confrontation with my parents, anything to avoid feeling like I'm not good enough for them, ever.*

"I talked your ear off. I did. I'm sorry. But I was trying to figure out what you wanted to talk about. I got nervous. I ramble when I get nervous."

"Don't we all," I mutter, but wave it off when Logan looks at me, questions in his eyes.

"What did I say that hurt you?" he asks. "Because from where I'm standing, I said nothing intending to hurt you."

I lick my lips, ignore the spike of pain that lances through my chest. "You mentioned what I was wearing." How do I explain that his words stung because it was after I argued with my mom? That his words just brought up the fact that I don't dress the part to get the kind of man that she can approve of? How do I spell that out?

I'm not even going to bring it up.

Logan nods, waiting for me to continue.

Just say it. Say it out loud. Say one small reason why you ended it after three dates, and ignore the main reason, Max.

"You said that I looked like a Christmas tree," I start, and then hiss. "Look, it doesn't matter what you think of me. It really doesn't. What matters is where we're going, right? You're going to come with me to my parents' place, and we have rules to go over."

"No, wait, Max. Max, please. I'm sorry, I'm sorry I hurt you with what I said."

I scoff. "Please, it's not like I haven't been told by a hundred men before that I look like a clown with what I wear, with what I put on my face."

Logan frowns, the skin between his eyebrows pinched tight. "Max, I didn't mean it that way. Not in a hundred years."

"How else am I supposed to take it, Logan? That I look like a campy Christmas tree?! Hello?"

Logan shakes his head, half-reaching for me before he drops his fisted hand at his side. "I thought you looked beautiful, like a Christmas tree in the middle of the night, all lit up. The way it feels like there's magic in the room with the lights on and the ornaments glinting. That's what I meant, Max."

I blink at him, my heart beating fast and hard in my chest. I pull in a deep breath through my nose, trying to find words to say.

Could I really have been so off base?

I was totally too busy to go on those dates, but I forced myself out into the night and into a stranger's company to share a meal. Maybe I did check my phone too many times, checking uploads and schedules and emails – *God,* so many emails.

Maybe I was rude by not trying to add anything to the conversation.

And it looks like I'm as much at fault for the shitty three dates we shared. While Logan was giving me his time and attention, I couldn't reciprocate enough to learn about him as a person.

I was a little selfish, working on the middle of a date, and trying to figure out if Logan had the *'look'* my parents would appreciate.

He has no tattoos, so that's a win. And I can confirm that he doesn't have a huge back piece or anything like that unless there's something hidden underneath his boxers that I didn't pay attention to.

No odd facial piercings that freak me out, and that would definitely anger my old-school father. Logan's attractive enough that my younger sister won't try to show off and take the spotlight from me. Most of all, he has that clean-cut look that my mom would absolutely love.

Maybe that's why I called him the other night, at the bar. The night we ended up getting married.

Maybe I realized I needed Logan Porter in my life – at least until Christmas.

SEVEN

"I owe you an apology. I'm sorry I was such a shitty date," I tell him, clearing my throat to get the words out. I hold my hand out for a shake, and Logan puts our palms together in a business one-two pump.

I wonder if he can tell that I felt something that one night we were together, that special something that freaked me out enough to take off running.

I focus on my breathing, on keeping still, locking the secret behind a locked, padded door in my mind.

We're still holding hands as we look at each other.

"I never meant to hurt you. Fuck, I thought I was complimenting you, Max. Especially with the way you told me how much you love Christmas."

I shrug. "The holiday season is what I live for every single year. It sucks that you don't like it."

Logan frowns, glances away. He drops his hand from mine as if I burned him. I watch him shake it out as if I totally did scald him with my touch alone.

"Yeah, well," Logan says lamely, and I'm left standing here, basking in the awkward silence.

I force myself to laugh, to ease the tension. I swing my arms around to have something to do with myself, working on chest stretches until something in my shoulders pops. I glance around my apartment, where nothing except the battery-powered hot plate works.

"I don't know what to do. I can't do any work. I'm lost."

Logan nods. "My office is closed, too. It's weird, huh? Not having a job to go to?"

I huff. "I feel lazy. Especially when I know I have a ton of shit to get done. I need to at least send out a mass message telling my subscribers that I'm stuck in a storm and without power." I rub my forehead. "Guess I'll use my phone for that." I frown. *If I can get service...*

"What are you at?" Logan asks, holding up his phone.

"I've got 43%. You?"

"Less than that. I've never felt so nervous about not having my phone fully charged."

I hum. "I have power banks that I use for my camera. We can share it."

Logan grins. "It's almost like what's yours is mine."

I roll my eyes. "Don't push it, or you're going to sleep out on the balcony tonight. God, I seriously have no idea what to do with myself." I lock my phone and shove it back in the pocket of my sweats.

"How about resting?" Logan suggests.

"Rest? Me? During Vlogmas? Are you nuts?"

He takes a seat on my couch, huddles into a ball. "We're lucky you live on the upper floors. I wouldn't want to be the basement unit right now."

"It's still going to get cold though." I turn to Logan. "You think the pipes will burst if it gets cold enough?"

"Why are you thinking about that?"

"Because I've got thousands of dollars of equipment in my office that'll need serious replacing if the pipes burst."

"Max, Max, you're stressing me out. Come and sit down."

"No, I need to move," I grunt, pacing the living room back and forth, thinking about all the worst-case scenarios. "Everything's gone to shit, honestly. I've got this stupid ring on my finger that *refuses* to come off, this storm that's ruined my production schedule, and we don't even know how long this is going to *last.*"

Logan watches me pace around the couch, to the kitchen, and back. I'm not wearing any makeup, and I'm dressed like I've been working non-stop for twelve hours when it's still the morning.

"Can I do anything for you?"

That makes me stop in my tracks. I turn my body around to face him, trying to figure out why he'd ask me that question. "Like what?"

Logan shrugs, his head in his palm. "I don't know, you tell me. I'm happy to sit here and read all day long. I haven't done that in ages. But I can help you if you let me know what you need."

I shake my head and ignore the tightness in my chest "Nah, I'm good, thanks. I'm going to disappear in my office for a bit, actually. I need to write some stuff down. The food's there," I point to the general direction of the kitchen as if Logan doesn't know where it is. "Make yourself at home. I've got extra blankets in that closet over there if you need."

I rush inside my office and close the door behind me, the room strangely quiet. There's no welcoming hum coming from my computer. The floors are cold underneath my socked feet, and the room feels oddly empty without the regular noise that comes with all the machines I have in here, none of them is charging or in sleep mode.

I huddle in my chair and get to work, mapping out scenarios and planning for the rest of the week, and into the next with a plan of action I hope will work.

If I hadn't pre-filmed so many videos before December, I would've been screwed. After some quick calculations, I'm missing two videos for the few days before Christmas, and the day itself.

I'm hoping that the storm doesn't last that long, but it's Montreal, and nobody knows what'll happen in the aftermath, either. It's not like things go back to normal right away after the storm lets up.

While I was stressing over my production and release schedule, my phone's been charging through one of my power banks. Service is still out, but I send out the requisite *'I'm alive and okay'* message to the family group chat anyway.

After only working for an hour and a half, I quickly realize that there's nothing else I can do. It's an itch underneath my skin where I can't scratch, catapulting me to leave my office behind and head to the living room.

Only to be confronted by Logan sitting on my couch, legs spread out, covered in blankets, and reading the same romance novel that he was reading last night.

He turns to look at me over his shoulder and gives me a soft smile that I'm not sure I deserve. Unfortunately, my chest is alight with a warm glow, and it's all Logan's fault.

"I'm almost at the middle," he says, holding the book aloft.

I nod slowly, unsure of what to say.

He sits up, though, eyebrows pinched in a frown. "Is something wrong?"

I shake my head. I nod. I shrug. "I'm restless. I can't do anything to accomplish what I need to do before the day is over, and it's pissing me off. I don't know what to *do* with myself, Logan."

He raises his eyebrows, runs a hand through his dark hair. "Push-ups always help me when I'm feeling like I'm a hamster on a wheel."

I don't comment on him getting right down to the root of what I'm feeling. Guess I look as frazzled as I feel. There's nothing about this entire situation that I can control "Push-ups? Really? I don't even know if I can do one."

"Try it. See how many you can do. You can do standing ones, too."

I amble aimlessly into the kitchen instead, halt in front of my fridge, searching for a snack that'll take away the bite of bitterness at a productive day lost forever.

I twist and grab an apple off my fruit basket instead, wash it quickly in the sink, and start thinking about water again.

"I've filled up some pots with water," Logan calls, jarring me from my thoughts. Can he read minds?

Jesus, Max, you're glaring at the faucet like it went and called you an asshole. It doesn't take much deducing to figure you out.

"So we have some sitting at room temperature first."

I nod. "Thanks. You didn't have to do that. I would have gotten around to it."

"I know," Logan says, moving to stand after carefully inserting a napkin in between the pages as a bookmark. "I wanted to help."

I feel weird about him snooping in my kitchen, even though I expressly told him to make himself at home.

"Well, thanks, but you didn't have to."

Logan's the one this time to roll his eyes. I stop and stare, and point. "Max, let me help. It's the least I could do. I got you into all of this mess."

I raise an eyebrow. "Which mess are we talking about?"

Logan's cheeks turn a little pink with something like a blush. "I'm sorry I got you roped into this. I am, truly. And we stop whenever you want to."

I lick my lips. "I need you to come with me to Christmas dinner. That's a non-negotiable for me. In return, I think me letting you live here is enough of a repayment, right?"

Logan slumps, his shoulders drooping. He sighs and wraps the blanket more tightly around his body. "You're right. I could be walking I don't know how many hours to try and get back to my place. I'm incredibly grateful that you're letting me stay."

Well, shit. Way to make me feel guilty.

"We can't keep talking to each other like this," I say, pointing between the two of us. "Because my parents? They're like sharks. They can smell a wounded fish, or a shitty backstory any day of the week from a mile away."

Logan snorts, smiles. It drops right off his face when I don't return it. "You're being serious?"

I nod. "Deadly. My cousins are going to be at the dinner with their boyfriends, so maybe you guys will end up bros for life. Who knows?" I take a giant bite of my apple. My feet are icy cold in my socks, and I wish I bought those new slippers I promised myself for Christmas earlier than the day of. "I don't want all that attention on me. Not that kind of attention."

Logan tilts his head, bird-like. I stare right back, my heart starting to beat faster in my chest.

What does he see? What *doesn't* he see?

What makes me worthy of being a wife to him? What the fuck did we talk about that made all of this somehow work?

Why did I think I was cut out for marriage if Logan was the guy I was married to?

None of it makes any kind of sense. And the hole in my memory is really starting to drive me up the wall.

"We need to make it look real for the old folks."

Logan stays still, so very still that I wonder for a split second if he's breathing. "You have to be very explicit with me. Spell it out."

"We have to be comfortable with each other. Physically, not *physically*."

Logan shakes his head. "You lost me."

I take another bite of my apple, choke it down. "We have to look at ease in each other's company. Like every romance couple ever do in the history of every romance novel ever written. Not like how we are right now."

"Maybe you need to read some more books, Max."

I jab my finger in the air. "Maybe you do. Because I know what those couples look like, how *together* they seem. We have to do that, the both of us."

"So what do you want to do?"

"Uh, not right now. I think I should go run up and down the hall or something, try to get rid of this feeling first. Then take a scalding hot shower for a short amount of time. Then maybe we'll talk about it."

Logan takes a step forward, looking absolutely ridiculous (and unfortunately adorable) with the blanket about to trip him up.

"That sounds like you're running away, Max."

I nearly choke on my damn snack. "Excuse me? That's a joke, right?"

He shakes his head, and I concentrate on swallowing. "Not at all."

I gulp. "I'm not running away. I need to move around or I'm liable to start throwing things. That's just the way it is."

"Or it could be that I've been encroaching in on your space since last night, and I can't get gone."

I blink at him. "Did I say that? Because I don't remember it leaving my mouth."

Logan stares too long at my lips, and my entire body freezes on the spot. I mean, I don't think Logan would marry me if he didn't think I was a teeny bit attractive. That makes sense.

And of course, *he's* attractive too. But looking good isn't the best criteria in evaluating how to choose a marriage partner.

I still don't know what I was thinking.

"You're unhappy about something," Logan says.

I gulp. My stupid face always gives everything away. "I just told you what I'm pissed off about."

Logan smiles, and my heart's doing weird, acrobatic things in my chest. "Max, that's not what I said."

"Pissed off and unhappy basically mean the same thing."

"No. No, they don't," he says gently, gentle enough that something pinches and twinges inside me.

I glance away, appalled at the tears welling in my eyes. Seriously, Logan decides to make a distinction and I'm the one who's getting emotional? Absolutely not.

"I'm unhappy with a lot of things," I say to the wall, unable to turn and look at him. My place feels too small, too tight, for everything I'm feeling, colliding with the space that Logan currently occupies. "I need to get some air. I'll be back."

He doesn't say anything when I don my boots and heavy winter coat. He doesn't say anything when I leave the apartment, and he doesn't come out into the hall to call me back like you would see some guys do in the movies.

I head down the metal staircase, stomping hard enough against the metal slats that somehow ease my frustration. I fish my phone out of the pocket of my sweats, stuff it in my coat, and try to navigate the zipper while walking down the stairs.

The lobby is empty, quiet. There is no humming of the lights overhead, or the sound of elevators going up and down, up and down. The world outside is blanketed with white swirling snow, sharp and deadly, not soft and pretty like you see inside snow globes.

I hesitate at the lobby doors, belatedly realizing that I didn't take my keys. I completely forgot that the power is out, and whatever is holding the front door locked probably isn't anymore.

I stay inside the lobby, breathing in and out, struggling to come to terms with what I'm feeling, with what I want.

I feel like an epic failure that I'm going to ruin Vlogmas this year for my subscribers. I had fun things planned, and I wanted to interact on the daily with everyone, answering comments, being *present* on the platform, but that's not happening.

I also don't want it to look like I ghosted everyone and dropped videos just like that. It's not me, that's not what I'm about.

I love talking to my subscribers, to the people who comment. And now I can't.

Like a glacier moving along the ocean's surface, it's only the very tip of the iceberg that's bothering me.

This memory loss thing is doing me in. It's frustrating as all hell, and no matter how much I poke and prod, and try to figure out what parts of the night I'm missing, the memories seem that much more elusive.

Plus, there's this whole marriage thing. My husband's upstairs, waiting for me. *My husband* who is reading one of my favorite books and asking me questions I barely ask myself.

Everything's confusing, and I don't know why I truly did this to myself. I mean, did Logan manipulate me into marrying him so I could get him over to my mom's house for Christmas?

I know myself. Plus, there's the voicemail that clearly has me saying what I need to do.

I wasn't coerced. Nope, this is *all* Maxima Prewitt, at her lowest.

Shit.

I stomp back upstairs, legs aching and totally out of breath once I reach my floor. I shove the front door open and stumble inside to a heavenly smell wafting from my kitchen.

Logan's ditched the blankets in favor of wearing one of my Canadiens tuques, keeping his head warm. He's rolling out some dough on the floured surface of my counter, and I swear there's butter and apples and sugar melting in the pot on the induction plate.

My mouth waters, and if I'm not careful, I'll start to drool.

Because Logan's making some kind of dessert, not because Logan is in the kitchen, baking for me.

That would be stupid.

The last thing I need is to start getting a crush on him when this marriage has to be annulled ASAP.

"What are you making?"

Logan smiles over at me, making my heart rattle in my chest. I hastily pull off my boots and coat, tucking them away for future use. I make sure the door is locked and move to the kitchen slowly. I sniff the air like a cartoon character, close my eyes at the way the butter and sugar are mixing together with the apples.

"I'm making apple turnover filling. We can have it with ice cream for dessert. Or as a meal. Whatever you want."

"How do you know how to make apple turnover filling from scratch? Who are you?"

He grins, stoops down to kiss the top of my head in a burst of affection I wasn't ready for. "I bake a lot when I feel helpless. It gives me something to do with my hands." He holds up the dough for emphasis. "I'm going to try to make a few turnovers in your Dutch oven. I'm going to have to rig the pots together so it feels like an oven, but it might work."

I bite at my lip. "Should we be eating this much food so early on?"

"We need to eat, and the apples would eventually spoil."

He looks at home in my kitchen, standing there, baking.

I rarely had any guys over to my apartment. Now Logan looks completely at home and I don't know what to do with the image seared into my brain.

"I'm upset at myself," I say, out loud for all to hear.

Logan glances at me makes the kind of eye contact that tells me he's *seeing* me, in a way I haven't been seen before. "Why, Max?"

I clench my jaw tight, clench my fists at my sides. "You don't have to cook and bake for me, you know, just because I'm letting you stay here."

His eyebrows jump high up his forehead, practically disappearing under the tuque. "I know that. But I want to. Get used to it, Max." He smiles at me like we're sharing a secret, then gets back to work, concentrating on the pots in front of him.

Get used to it? We're going to end this farce of a marriage after Christmas.

Get used to it? Yeah, right.

EIGHT

"I'll get you some more blankets," I say, heading off towards the linen closet. It's empty. I've used every single spare blanket that I have in my apartment to throw over my bed, or Logan's makeshift bed on the couch.

We're in a blanket scarce economy and the temperature's supposed to hit 25 below with the wind chill tonight.

I lean back, and bump into a very solid chest, and well, the rest of his body, too.

"Sorry, Max," Logan says, not sounding sorry at all. I'm about to start throwing elbows, but Logan takes a few steps back, giving me my space. "If I can tape a blanket over the balcony door and the windows here in the living room, I bet it would be a lot warmer in here."

I nod, because yeah, that makes sense.

The living room is blanketed in candlelight again, and my bedroom looks dark and ominous and a whole lot lonely.

"I don't have enough blankets though for that. I've got extra sheets that might work," I say.

Logan hums an affirmative sound, and I help him tape up some sheets over the living room windows, and then pull the curtains over top of them.

"Does that feel better, or am I making it up in my head?" I ask. Logan laughs, running a hand over the curtains, trying to detect any cold air that might be seeping through.

"No, it does feel better, absolutely. Hey, leave the dishes, I'll do them tomorrow morning."

I snort. "You're really on your best behavior, huh?"

Logan stills as he stands next to me, and I tense up, too.

"What? What did I say?"

"Why do you think I'm trying to trick you?"

"I didn't say that, Logan."

"But it's what you meant, though, right?"

I roll my eyes. We've been alone together for one whole night and one whole day and we're about to kill each other. How are we going to survive a stressful Christmas dinner that's bound to end in disaster?

"I'm doing my part. That's what happens between people when they're sharing the same space. You don't take advantage of the other person," Logan says, moving to the couch and plopping himself on it. "I don't know what I can do to make you comfortable around me, Max. I'm trying."

"I'm as comfortable as can be," I say, lying through my teeth. My cheeks are on fire, and my voice wobbles with the lie, effectively convincing no one. "I've got a lot of unanswered questions I'm not sure I *want* answers to. Do you understand?"

Logan stares at me, the candlelight flickering in his dark eyes. Shit, he looks pretty amazing in the soft, warm glow, not that it matters.

We're in this together now, whether we like it or not.

"You nearly chopped off your finger earlier, making supper," he groans, tilting his head back to look at the ceiling. He leans down to glare at me. "And you ran off to the bathroom by yourself without letting me look at it."

"Oh, is that what this is about? Seriously? I'm used to taking care of myself," I scoff. "What were you going to do? Put the giant bandage on my finger? What for? What's the point?"

Logan's eyebrows move thunderously low over his eyes, and I think I'm in for it. My belly does a disconcerting swoop, and I have the oddest urge to start twisting my hair around my fingers.

"A couple that has been going out for some time, to be serious enough to invite each other over for the holiday, is used to doing things for one another. You're the one that said we have to sell it."

I fight not to roll my eyes. "Well, this is who I am. This is who you *married*."

Logan shakes his head. "No, not really," he says and leaves it at that. "But she's under there, somewhere. If you let her out."

There are words left unsaid, some of them boiling up inside of me, too.

I imagine what my parents will look like at the holiday dinner. Mom will be exhausted from cooking all day *and* cleaning every visible inch of the house. My dad will be sitting downstairs, watching whatever dumb sport is playing, instead of helping.

My mom will be snippy with me for not coming over to help prep when my little sister still lives with them. My dad will make a comment about me taking the holiday off, and not working to make sure my nest egg is large enough when I inevitably fail at doing my non-conventional job.

Amber will bring Brody, and Vick will bring Michael. Vick's little sister Evie might have her nose in a book for most of the meal, and my little sister, Izzy, would be the life of the party. My mom's sister will probably show up with *those* set of cousins, making that much more of audience to my demise.

And that's just as soon as we walk into the house. The day's bound to get worse from there on in.

I love Christmas, but I hate Christmas with my parents.

How terrible is that?

Now I imagine how much nicer it'll be to have Logan there, sitting beside me, pretending that he likes me more than my parents currently do. It'd be nice to have someone in my corner besides Vick and Amber. Someone who isn't related to me by blood.

"Seriously, though," I say, holding up the offensive finger. "I'm fine. It bled for like, ten minutes."

"It didn't have to if you let me do the cooking."

I sigh, my shoulders slumping. I feel like a sad, little deflated balloon, discarded on the floor after a righteous birthday party.

"You always do the cooking."

"Max, it's been one day."

"That's exactly it. We've been together one whole freaking day. And you're doing all the cooking. The only thing that I try to do because I can't do anything else." I groan, frustrated. That itch under my skin starts up again. I start rubbing my arms up and down, up and down through my hoodie, trying to chase it away.

"Tell me why you're so frustrated with work," he suggests.

I swallow hard. "You want to hear about my job? Really?"

"I do."

I frown. "Haven't I told you all of this already?"

Logan shakes his head, but I think he's lying.

It's like the dam's been destroyed – I tell him *everything*. I tell him about all of my deadlines that I won't meet, all the cool things I had planned for the week coming up to Christmas that were all time-sensitive.

"I hate letting people down. It makes me feel gross," I say.

Logan rubs his forehead, pushes his hair out of his face. "Because you don't want to disappoint them?"

"Yeah. Look, I know it's dumb, but I don't like doing it."

We're sitting on the couch – his bed – facing each other. His legs are longer than mine, and his feet sit somewhere around my mid-thigh. It all feels very domestic.

If this were real.

I shiver and pull my hood more tightly to my head. Logan adds one more blanket over my shoulders, warm from his body heat.

I don't understand why that makes me blush, but it does.

"So this whole thing with your parents...you don't want to let them down?"

I nod. "When I was younger, everything was easy. I listened, I played the role, I did what they wanted. We started having problems when I barely made it through university. God, I hated every single second of it.

"And then I found makeup, and YouTube, and my entire life changed."

Logan smiles like this story is going to end in a happily ever after.

"I work hard, Logan. Really hard. And my parents...are not supportive. They never will be. We're all very stubborn people."

"What should I do, when I'm there with you?"

"Honestly, act like the ground I walk on was paved in diamonds. Seriously."

Logan laughs, his eyes crinkling closed with it. Unfortunately, he looks really good like that, too.

"Act like everything I say is pure gold. Basically, kiss my ass the entire time, and talk about how wonderful I am. That's it. That's the job description."

"That bad, huh?"

I shrug, wanting to minimize it, make it so small that it barely exists. "It sucks on a gut-deep level to know that your parents aren't proud of you, no matter what you do. I remember," I say, clearing my throat of the tightness. "I remember when I was small, and I brought home an assignment or a test with a sticker. Wham! It would go on the fridge. Some projects would make it on there as the years passed until there was nothing left to be proud of. Not my grades, not what I wore, or what makeup I put on my face, even though it's my job."

I'm embarrassed suddenly, laying it all out there to a veritable stranger.

"Guess you weren't ready for the heavy stuff," I say, laughing it off.

Logan shakes his head. "I'm sorry that your parents aren't supportive in the way that you need."

I mash my lips together, quelling the absurd urge to laugh. "I like talking with you," I blurt. "I should have done more of it when we went on those dates. I'm sorry about that."

"We can talk now," he says. "We have the time."

"So much time," I agree. "Are you sleepy yet? I'm kinda sitting on your bed."

Logan fights back a yawn, and I know it's my cue to leave.

"Hey," I call once I make sure he's comfortable and start heading to my own room. "Thanks for listening."

He smiles at me. "Always. Good night, Max."

"Good night."

It took a long time for me to fall asleep last night, and I have to brave this morning without a fresh pot of coffee. I've got a caffeine withdrawal headache and a sliver of patience left.

My apartment is gloomy with the storm still happening outside. The curtains have been cast wide, and the sheets taped to the walls to cover all the windows and balcony door are helping to keep the cold out.

Logan's already frying up something that smells delicious in that one pot that works with the induction hot plate.

The experiment of the apple turnovers last night is still sitting in the sink, waiting to be washed. Instead, I hunt for tea bags in my pantry, until I grab some Earl Grey and bring my prizes to the kitchen.

"Good morning," Logan says, sounding incredibly too chipper to how miserable I'm feeling. "What's wrong? Do you have a fever?" His hand comes up and reaches for my forehead.

I dodge before he can make any kind of contact. "I'm fine. Need caffeine," I say, lifting the tea for him to look at. "Are you almost done? I need to boil water." Jesus, I never thought I would appreciate my microwave so very much for zapping water to boiling.

"Almost done. Come and eat something. I'll wash the pot and get some water going for you."

I'm too tired to argue, too fragile. Maybe I said too much last night.

"What do you want to do today?" Logan asks once we're finished breakfast and I've had two cups of Earl Grey all to myself.

"I don't know. I guess we should look over how much food we have left. I brought most of the veggies and other produce inside overnight from the balcony. I hope nothing spoiled."

Logan hums. "I'll take care of it."

I'm about to fight him on it, but ultimately decide to let it go.

"What else?" he asks.

"I don't know. There's not much to do. I can clean, I guess. Try to get more water saved in every kind of pot I own. Other than that, it looks like my day is wide open."

"We can play some card games if you want."

"Most of the games I know need at least three people."

"True," Logan acknowledges. "Did you want to get any work done?"

I think about it. There's a niggling feeling in my chest whenever I do think about work, about this imposed vacation time where I've lost all productivity against my will.

My phone chimes in my pocket, and I let out a surprised squeak.

I get my phone out, find no less than twenty notifications piling in, one after the other. The group family chat is full of everyone checking in and saying they're okay and safe. There are invites if people want to go over to Amber's house if the streets are clear and safe to drive.

My family is safe, and everyone's okay. I'm grateful.

"Hey, Logan, did you get a chance to talk with your family? I just got some random bit of service...Nope, there it goes again. Shit." I mumble around the rim of my mug.

I glance up to find Logan staring down at his phone. Whatever's there isn't good news.

"Is everything all right?" I ask in a whisper.

Logan looks at me, the smile not reaching his eyes this time. It's funny how fast I got used to that smile, and now that it's not the one he usually gives me, I'm a little miffed.

That's the lack of caffeine talking. It must be.

"Yes, for the most part. Everyone's safe, and that's all that matters."

I nod, not wanting to pry. "What are you going to do today besides do my dishes because you won't let me do them?"

"I thought we'd properly meal plan together for the rest of the week, and see where we're at."

I mull it over, anxiety sitting like a second heartbeat at the base of my throat.

"That sounds like a good idea, but also not a good idea. I don't want to think about what happens when we run out of food. That's how all those cannibal movies got made, Logan."

Logan chuckles, but it sounds half-hearted at best. What the hell was on his phone?

None of your business. You're just married to the guy. No big deal.

"You sure everything's okay?" I ask, slurping up some more tea. It's hot enough to burn my throat, but it's warming me through from the inside out. Honestly, I don't know how many layers I'm supposed to be wearing to be warm all the time. I've already got two of everything.

Logan nods but doesn't say anything. I take that as my cue not to pry.

Except, it's fine and dandy when he gets me to talk, but when it comes to what's going on with him? I'd be better off trying to scale a wall covered in ice, and all I have are my bare hands and feet to help me get over.

"I was going to read some more, actually," he says finally as if keeping your nose in a book isn't the perfect way to shut me out.

Logan's allowed to have his space, though, and reading was also designed to escape reality.

"Sure, sure. Do you want to do the food inventory now or after?"

We speed through meal planning for the rest of the week. By the end of the eighth day, we'll have rice left over, and maybe some produce. I have some frozen meals that could work as well, as long as the cold outside keeps them from rotting.

"Not bad, not bad," I say, looking down at Logan's pretty handwriting. "Okay, I feel better about this. Doesn't feel so end-of-the-world, you know?"

Logan hums and makes a few notes to himself. He's been suspiciously quiet since getting that message earlier, and my curiosity is dying to know what happened.

But we don't know each other that well yet, even if it always feels like Logan knows everything about me when I barely know anything about him.

Whose fault is it that you weren't listening to him the first time around, Max?

Yeah, yeah. I get it, I get it.

When Logan sits down on the couch to read, it's my cue to hide in my office like I've done for the past day. When I step inside my empty office, the lifeless atmosphere does nothing for my head, so I head back out into the living room instead.

I make a nest on the ground, blankets covering every single cold surface. I've pulled another blanket over me and set up my notes on the coffee table. Logan doesn't say anything as I sit there, writing out my plans for the new year, making the adjustments in my schedule.

When that's done, I cart out a bucket full of makeup and use what little daylight that comes through the taped-up sheets to do my face and eyes.

It calms me, the quick application of eyeshadow – a boring brown smoky eye. The foundation and base routine comes next, then bronzer and blush. The entire process is almost meditative.

For the first time in a while, it feels like I can breathe.

When I'm done, I turn to find Logan looking at me, his stare intense.

"What?" I ask.

Logan shakes his head and goes back to his book. "You look like a Christmas tree," he says, not even paying attention to me.

Now I know what those words mean.

My heart is about ready to explode from my chest.

NINE

Logan slept on the couch again.

I slept in my huge bed but stayed huddled in a small corner to try to keep my warm bubble occupied.

This morning, though, everything feels extra cold. The floors are icy underneath my double socked feet. The surfaces in my kitchen are icy to the touch. My candles have been burning steadily for the past few days now, and even I, a candle fiend, am wondering if we're going to run out of my supply soon.

The morning's still gray like and the from what I can tell when I step outside to the cold and wet to check on the produce, the snow has turned into freezing rain.

It's warmer, which is a good thing, but from experience, if the temperature hovers where it is for the next few days, all we're going to get is freezing rain. We might just get a repeat of the 1998 ice storm.

Shit.

Logan makes us breakfast, again.

We both huddle around the pot of boiling hot water and move our hands close to the pot to try and get some heat waves on our cold fingers. Breakfast is hot, and I know we're luckier than a lot of people who might not have the means to cook.

"What are you going to do today?" I ask, munching around my fried egg sandwich that's as close to toast as I'm going to get. "Because if you wanted, I kind of would like your help with something."

I deliberated all morning if I wanted to let Logan into my office.

It's an organized kind of chaos that drives me insane but also keeps me on my toes. It's high time I organize it once and for all.

Logan finishes up his scrambled eggs and nods. "I thought we could also decorate your tree today."

"It's all the way in my storage unit. I haven't had the time to bring up the main event."

"We can do that together today, if you wanted."

It's a good idea, a really good idea. But I don't know if having Logan trim my Christmas tree with me *is* a good idea. Because whatever happens after Christmas between the two of us...it's going to change how I look at that Christmas tree.

"Or not, Max. No pressure."

"No, no. We could do that. Drag it out so it burns up a couple of hours at least."

Logan laughs, and I find myself smiling at him. "You let me know when you're ready to head downstairs."

It takes a good half hour after we finish breakfast and wash the dishes to bring up all of my special ornaments and the box that holds my giant tree.

Logan keeps the central piece straight for me, and then finally snaps the upper third of the tree in place due to his superior height.

"I would usually have Christmas music blaring in the background. Maybe I'd be drinking an eggnog latte or something," I say to chase away the silence. I carefully lay out all the boxes of ornaments, hardly sparkling under the gray light coming through the windows. "It feels stupid to put up the tree without Christmas music."

Logan hums, but doesn't say anything.

I find myself wanting to fill in the silence. Ever since the power went out, everything is so damn quiet, except for the rain outside I never thought I breathed so loud until there was such an absence of noise around me.

I've become even more aware of my heartbeat, thumping in my chest.

"Max, can I ask you something?"

"It depends if it's going to be a bad question or a good question."

Logan helps me rearrange the branches, laying them down at different angles to cover up some of the spaces. It's looking like half a tree, and we haven't even decorated it yet.

"What's a good question?"

"If it won't make me want to throw you out," I say, fussing with a particular section of the tree that doesn't want to cooperate with the rest of its brethren. "Don't be mean, is all I'm asking."

"I would never intentionally hurt you, Max," Logan says.

I still, hold my breath. "So, what, that means you'll do it unintentionally?"

Logan steps to the side so I can see him perfectly instead of him hiding behind the tree. "Everyone hurts each other unintentionally. It's up to all of us to say something when it happens, so we can keep it from happening again."

I stare at him, watching him stare back. "Okay," I whisper, then get back to paying attention to what's *really important* – my Christmas tree.

When we're done an hour later, Logan was entirely too gracious with my nitpicky ways, the tree still looks sad.

"It's really not that majestic without the lights on." I wave my hand up and down. The ornaments don't sparkle with the gray light seeping through the sheets, and the only music we both hear is the sound of freezing rain coming down, down, down.

"I thought that would take us longer than it actually did," Logan says, looking at me.

"Is it time for lunch yet?"

Logan shakes his head after moving to check where his phone is charging from one of the power banks I have. "Not in real-world terms."

I snort. "What's that supposed to mean?"

"We don't have to have a set time to eat, we can eat whenever we want."

I shake my head. "Not with having to be careful about food. Nah, I'll have a banana. See? It's so cold in here, they're barely ripening. These might last the week without going all brown and gross."

Logan laughs. "When you told me you work a lot, I really had no idea what you meant."

I smirk. "I'm a workaholic. It doesn't leave much time for a lot else."

Logan hums. "But you still found time to go on a date with me."

I wince.

"What? What is it?"

I lick my lips, ignore the jump of my insides. "Look, we are both aware that I fucked up that night, okay. You don't have to stick salt in the wound."

Logan tilts his head. It's like he already knows that he can wait me out, and I'll babble every little thought that comes into my head to fill the silence.

"Your dating profile. It read one way...and I ended up getting something else."

Logan frowns and takes a seat on my couch. I stay standing. "I'm going to ask you that question now," he says.

I nod, crossing my arms over my chest. I'm wearing four hundred layers and my nose is still cold and starting to drip. "If I was such a terrible date, then why did you call me the other night?"

I lick my lips, my heart acting up in my rib cage. "Your dating profile. Like I said, it reads one way."

"Max..."

"Fine, fine, I'll tell you." I rock my weight from foot to foot, but I don't have to go to the bathroom. Although putting my cold feet in a vat of hot water sounds heavily right about now.

"You sell your online self a different way. I thought I was getting a hotshot heartbreaker type that would scratch my itch and do what I asked him to do. When we parted ways, I wouldn't care. I wasn't prepared for what I got. Plus, I know I was incredibly rude, not interacting with you when I should have been. But boy, did I listen to almost everything you had to say."

"That's why you thought I was being awful to you."

I tilt my head to the side in silent question.

Logan sits up straighter on the couch, eager to explain. "Because you were expecting me to be awful. And I wasn't."

"I don't know of any girl who takes the time to dress up and feel really good about herself to waste time in front of a man that compares her to a Christmas tree. You talked my ear off but didn't ask about me. And I know, I know," I say, holding my hand up to cut off any interruptions. "I know that I didn't give you a chance. We had that one night together, and that was all I was looking for. So, I never called you back." *Way to go with the half-truths, Max. Nice.*

"Until the other night," Logan says, and honestly, I don't know what to say to that. "Until the other night when you called me, and I showed up."

"Did I push you into marrying me, or something?" I ask because it needs to be asked. I still don't remember.

Logan smiles at me, all warm and fond and I'm not sure I deserve it. No matter how much I prod at those hazy, empty spaces where the memory's supposed to be, it doesn't help me any in recollecting what actually happened.

"No. I asked you to marry me. You said yes. I didn't know you were that against marriage, actually. It never came up."

I shrug, kick at the floor, not wanting to get into it. So many people like me grew up with parents who were miserable with each other and didn't do anything about it or couldn't do anything about it. I'm not special. "Seems a bit odd to me, is all."

"And now that you're married? Does it feel any different?"

I scoff. "We're not going to stay married, Logan."

"Just until Christmas."

I nod. "Just until then." We stare at each other, until Logan pats at the couch cushion, inviting me to sit down in my own home.

I sit across from him gingerly, as if afraid to startle a wild beast that's about to go for my throat. There's nothing in the way Logan's sitting that indicates any of that, but I'm still nervous for some reason.

"Relax, Max. I don't expect anything of you."

I let out a long breath and stay still. It takes me a while to unwind my legs from being so close to my chest and to stretch out on my own damn couch.

"Are you going to do your makeup today?" he asks.

"I'm too antsy to try and figure out what I want to do for my eyes," I say, waving a hand over my eyelids.

"Can I pick out some colors?" he asks, looking delighted at having the chance to do so.

"Really?" I blink at him.

"Yeah. I want to see what you'll come up with if that's okay."

I nod slowly. "I can do that. You should, uh...You should probably come into my office then and pick out a few things."

I keep my office door closed for a reason. It separates the chaos from the rest of my home. But to have Logan walk in on it?

It feels a lot like letting him paw at my underwear drawer – intimate and a little scary.

I open the door and we both walk inside. To his credit, Logan doesn't say anything, just takes it all in.

"I didn't know what goes into managing your channel, but fuck, Max. This is a lot." He looks at me with wide eyes. "How do you do it all?"

My cheeks burn with a blush. At least there's some warmth in my body, and I'm not entirely made of a Max-sized chunk of ice. "Not very well. As you can see by the state of this place."

"Do you need help organizing?"

The tightness in my chest loosens, little by little, and a trickle of relief comes wafting in. "Yes, yes, I would like that."

We spend a good portion of the afternoon organizing and separating items from PR into baskets. I have a new system of what has to be reviewed and featured on my channel, and the leftovers of what can be donated to family and friends, and to the local women's shelter.

It's only the waning daylight that chases us out of my office and back into the living room.

"I didn't get to see what you'd be wearing on your eyes today," Logan says, sounding almost petulant.

"Tomorrow," I tell him. "Tomorrow you pick the colors."

"Yeah?" Shit, he looks *excited*.

Logan wasn't at all like the guy I was expecting to date. I wanted an asshole-type that didn't have any skin in the game, that could pretend to be enamored with me. Logan's more dangerous though, because I know I wouldn't be able to tell where the line between and reality is.

That's why I ran after our one night together. On some visceral, maybe even magical, level, I knew that Logan could be *it* for me.

"I would like to ask you another question now, if that's all right, Max."

I swallow hard, already nervous at what words he's going to string together for his question. I give him a shallow nod.

"Why did you leave that night, after we slept together?"

I close my eyes, focus on my breathing for a few seconds. I knew that he was going to ask, I knew it like I know I have over a hundred eyeshadow palettes stashed in my office that I love dearly. I lick my dry lips.

"Well," I start, then stop. I try again. "You weren't what I bargained for," I laugh. "Honestly, I just wanted someone to come with me to my family dinner and treat me like they're in love with me."

Logan frowns at me as he moves about my home, lighting all the candles. He brings one to the living room, setting it on the coffee table as the gloom starts to make shadows. "I thought you said my profile was making me sound like a dick."

"Oh, it did. But I wasn't expecting you." *And I didn't want to use you.*

He continues to frown until there are furrows on his forehead that I want to soothe and kiss away.

The problem was never that I wasn't attracted to Logan. The problem is that he seemed like a nice guy, and even though I gave in to the physical chemistry we had, I didn't want to use him like that for a family dinner.

Then again, Drunk Max thought it was a good idea to marry the guy, so here I am with a whole husband instead of a date.

"So if I truly was an asshole, you'd have signed up for this anyway?" Logan asks, pointing between the two of us. "I'm trying to understand."

"There's nothing to understand, Logan. Honestly. I'm the asshole who needs to have someone beside her to avoid confrontation. I love my parents, I do, but they hurt me despite that love. I'm sick of it."

Logan nods. "Then what do you need me to do?"

I stare at him, unblinking. "Should I tell you how it's going to go?" I take his silence as a yes. "When we both walk in, my mom will be suspicious. I haven't talked about you, or anything like that, or told her that I was bringing a guest to dinner. We're lucky that the power's out, so that text message I can say was lost to the aether or whatever."

Logan looks nothing but calm and collected, and there's a part of me that wants to rile him up, to ruffle his feathers.

"They'll look you over, score you from a one-to-ten in their heads, just by looking at you, if you and I fit together as a couple."

"Doesn't every parent do that, even if they don't tell you about it?"

I shrug. "I don't know. There are going to be questions...how we met, how long we've been dating, hell, maybe even where we've gone together. You'll sit next to me at supper, of course."

"Of course."

I pull my mouth into a grin, then get back to the story. "We'll be grilled. Every inch of our body language will be analyzed."

"Holy shit, Max. You're making it sound like our lives depend on it."

"Well, mine does. My mom might give me some backhanded compliment. It could be about my weight, my lack of real-world accomplishments, something. Don't rise to the bait. Pretend like you never even heard it. Okay? Can you do that for me?"

Logan leans forward, his elbows on his knees, frowning hard enough to make his face stuck that way. "What are you saying?"

"My mom will make comments about my weight even as I get myself a second helping. She'll tell me that I have to exercise more in front of the whole table. She'll lament the fact that I'm not married and that I'm not pushing out grandkids. We will *not* tell her that we're already married. That's going to open up a can of worms that I don't need."

Logan licks his lips, ready to say something. I wait him out. "You had told me some of this, the night we met up."

"Okay, then. I don't remember doing that, but it makes sense. You should know what you're getting into with me."

"Max, there's no getting into anything with you. I'm standing with you. I'm not getting stuck."

I blink at him, squinting hard enough to strain my eyes. "I really don't get you. What kind of person just shows up when they're summoned, and then *marries* that person? Make it make sense."

Logan smiles, big and wide, and it makes my heart do pirouettes. "We talked for hours about everything, anything. I learned a lot about you. Enough to make me want you by my side for the rest of my life."

I frown at him. "After one night? And one night of *talking* at that? Did we even kiss?"

"When I was told to kiss the bride, yes. But you beat me to it." He grins at me.

I roll my eyes. "I still don't remember that, either."

Logan leans closer, close enough to gently tap his fingers on the back of my hand, a careful touch. "Max, I really need you to remember. Please."

I swallow hard. I don't know if I want to do that.

I don't know if I want to remember.

TEN

The wedding night...

I check out my reflection in the women's washroom at the lounge bar I'm at. My feet are starting to hurt with the heels I'm wearing, and my tight dress is starting to feel constricting instead of like a second skin. I look good, but I don't feel it.

This is what you get for hanging out in sweats all day while you work. Nothing will ever feel as comfortable.

There's a ticking clock only I can seem to hear, and desperation never looked attractive on anybody.

I double-check my makeup, leaning in close to my reflection, running one of my nails carefully under each eye to clean up the flakes of mascara that have fallen onto my under-eyes.

I admire my eyeshadow look – a cut crease of teal shimmer against a deep plum outer corner. I already posted the look to my Instagram, and the subscribers from my channel that follow me there want the details.

Guess I have another video idea, ready to go.

I hastily take notes down on my phone and then exit the washroom.

The music's loud and thumping, the bass settling right along with my heartbeat, controlling its rhythm.

My hair's straight and silky, hitting my waist, and my plum dress compliments my eyeshadow.

I was supposed to meet a guy here for drinks, but he didn't show. Something about the clown makeup not doing it for him. Which, I guess is fine, because I would have wasted my time on him anyway.

Operation Get a Max a Christmas Date is still fully in effect.

The stool I was sitting in close to the bar had been stolen. I walk around until I find a small table to myself, order a rum and coke from the waiter while scrolling through my phone.

I don't have hundreds of phone numbers stored in my phone, but enough to ask someone to come and meet me.

My thumb hovers over Logan's name in my contact list, my body stilling from bopping along to the music. I can't blame the almost non-existent alcohol that I've had for the decision I'm about to make.

I message Logan before I can think better of it, wondering if he'll show up.

I never get an answer to my message, and I turn down a guy who wants to *talk*. He doesn't look like Christmas date material so I excuse myself to the washroom again.

I'm wondering about my life choices when I come back and find another seat in the lounge to make my own, adjusting my dress so that I don't give everyone a free show.

Time's running out, and I need someone to go home with me on Christmas, or I might die.

Way to be dramatic, Max.

I don't know what makes me look up, only that I do.

In the dimmed lighting, Logan walks through a crowd of people, parting them like he's some kind of miracle worker. He's dressed casually, dark jeans, and a tight thermal top that looks like a second skin. My heart twists in my chest, and my lips part.

Logan looks amazingly delicious. He walks calmly towards me, a genuine smile on his face when he points to the chair across from me, asking for permission before sitting without saying a single word.

I'm not about to say no to that.

He waves at me from across the table, and I don't know what it is, but I find myself smiling back at him. He points to his ear and then holds up his phone.

I glance down at my own in my hands.

Logan: *Hi! You look great! How have you been?*

I smile down at my screen and quickly type a response.

Me: *Do you want to go and get some food with me? This place sells overpriced nachos and calls it something else.*

I glance up to look at his reaction. Logan nods so hard that I'm afraid he's going to hurt his neck.

This is why I tried to keep away from him, why I slept with him that one night and never wanted to see him again. Because Logan is the quintessential heartbreaker, the kind of guy I could lose myself in, and I'm not looking for that.

So why did you get him over here, Max?

I didn't actually think he was going to show up!

Especially looking like my deepest, darkest boyfriend dreams.

Logan gestures towards the exit, and I follow. I take about two steps before he's ushering me ahead of him, not touching me or directing me in any way, but keeping me close, nonetheless.

Once we both get our checked coats, we head out onto the sidewalk, the cold night air slicing against the exposed skin of my legs.

It's a night for love and magic. The sky is inky dark, looking like velvet. Heavenly smells are coming from late-night restaurants that are waiting for the party crowd and the late-callers.

I'm craving hot dogs and the world's greasiest poutine smothered in gravy and squeaky cheese curds.

"Hi," Logan dips down to say close to my ear, now that I can hear him properly. "Hi, Max."

I can't help it. I'm grinning like an idiot. *This* is what I wanted, but I was too stubborn to ask for it.

It's freezing cold outside, but Logan makes me warm.

"I didn't think you would be calling me again," he says, keeping his stare straight ahead. There's no pressure to answer, no harsh tone that needs to be soothed.

I lick my lips at that, tasting my cupcake-flavored lip gloss. "I didn't think I would call you again, either. You look very handsome, by the way, even bundled up."

Logan tugs on the tuque on top of his head shyly. "How are you?"

"Hungry," I say, then let him in on the plan. I nearly sideswipe on a stretch of black ice in my heeled boots, but Logan's there to catch me before I really hurt myself. "Shit."

"You okay?" He asks, coffee-scented breath close to my face, his cologne somehow strong even through his winter coat. Logan's got a hold of both my arms, balancing me practically on my toes. And all the weight gain I've been worrying about the past few months seems to disappear being held in his arms like this.

Whoosh. Abracadabra, gone!

"Yup, I'm good. You can let go of me now, though."

Logan scrambles to make sure that there are no points of contact between the two of us. There's a sureness, a sense of *rightness* that bathes me in a warm glow as Logan sputters and asks me if I'm okay again. We're supposed to be here, him and I.

We're quiet until we find the restaurant I want and are seated. I'm overdressed. I get the side-eye from the cook when I order ten steamies for myself, and a poutine on the side. I pay for Logan's meal, too, because he came out to see me, after all.

"I'm glad you called, whatever the reason," Logan says once we've collected our food and take our seats at a vinyl booth.

I lick my lips again, chapped and dry now that the lip gloss is gone. Logan sits across from me, his jacket in a pool of cloth around him, elbows on the table.

I tilt my head and squint at him, trying to pull him out of this picture and settle him inside a picture at my own family's Christmas dinner.

He would fit, he would *so* fit. Operation Get Max a Christmas Date might just be complete.

If he says yes, of course.

And looking back on my track record with him, I don't see why he would.

"Hey, what's wrong? Do you feel sick?" he asks, eyes wide, hands reaching for me but not coming in close enough to touch. Everything he does is to make sure that I'm comfortable. Have ever been on a single date where I've been asked for permission so many times before?

The answer's no. I find myself *loving* it.

I shake my head, then glance down at my steamed hot dogs. "I...I wanted to ask you something, but I don't think I have the right to."

Logan smiles softly. "You can ask me anything you want. I don't have to answer."

I nod. "Right, right. Well, uh, I went on those dates with you a while ago because I was looking for something specific. *Someone* specific."

Logan nods, waiting for me to continue. I like how he doesn't rush in and ask a hundred questions. I like that he has patience. The makeup gods know that I don't have any to spare.

I dive in, headfirst and everything. "I need someone to go with me to my Christmas family dinner."

It sounds stupid when I say it out like that. Like I'm a little kid afraid of the monster under the bed. Except the monsters are my parents and their lofty expectations I can never ever seem to meet.

"Okay," Logan says, giving me that soft smile of his.

"Okay, what?" I sit up straighter, hold my breath.

"You know I'm not a big fan of the holiday. I don't have any plans. I can go with you."

"You don't have *plans*? How come?"

Logan's eyes lose that sparkle, and his soft smile is gone. "Maybe I'll tell you one of these days, if I can get a second chance."

It needs to be said. "I used you on those three dates, and I'm sorry."

Logan shrugs, like it's not a big deal.

"I wanted something else. You're not what I wanted, what I was looking for."

"I kind of got the message when you fled my apartment in the middle of the night. Maybe I should be the one apologizing."

I start eating my hot dogs. How do I explain that I hadn't had sex in a long time, and felt particularly vulnerable with him? How do I explain that the night I spent with him was the final nail in the coffin?

I can't. Not yet, anyway. Not after he just agreed to help me.

I keep quiet, watch him eat his food. He hums in happiness after every single bite. "I thought you'd be angry with me. Most men would have been."

Logan moves his shoulders in a semblance of a shrug. "I'm just me, Max."

I wasn't expecting that answer, either. "Yeah, you are."

Logan wipes his mouth carefully with his wad of napkins. Finishes chewing, swallows. "Do you want to start again?"

"Start what again? Dating?"

He nods. "Now that you know who I am, and what you're looking for. Why not?"

My heart leaps in my chest, and I struggle to hold down the wave of excitement that makes me smile. There's magic in the air, there *has* to be. I'm getting everything I want, and Logan together. I don't know what I did to deserve this, but maybe it's all going to go right for me. Maybe.

"We can do that, yeah."

I hold my hand out for a shake, and Logan meets me in the middle of the table. We shake hands, his giant paw engulfing mine.

"I'm Maxima, but everyone calls me, Max."

He grins at me, wide and bright like I'm the one that hooked the stars in the sky, just for him. My belly swoops, and I can feel my pulse in my wrists. Oh, he could get me in so much trouble. *So much.*

But what's the point of waiting around never trying?

"Logan. It's nice to meet you, Max."

We sit in the diner for hours, enough for two bathroom breaks each, and then to order another meal when I start to get hungry again before the sun has even had a chance to rise.

Now that I'm paying attention to him, Logan's maybe one of the more interesting people I've ever met.

He works in video game development, which of course Vick is going to love. I keep thinking if I should blurt about knowing NIKTORIOUS *personally*, but that's not my secret to tell. It would probably get me brownie points, though.

We talk about books for at least two hours. His favorite genres are science fiction and fantasy, but he'll read anything. I tell him about the stories of when I was a kid, sneaking in books to class to try and read them instead of doing the assigned work.

Logan told me about a book he read so many times over his life that the copy he had up and practically disintegrated in his hands the last time he opened it.

I'm no good at talking about video games, but it's fun to see it all from Logan's perspective, from developing the game from the ground up.

To break those last final barriers of ice, I ask him about his most embarrassing story, the one time where he wanted the world to open up and swallow him whole.

We talk about our families, siblings (he's an only child). We talk about expectations.

"My parents are...old school," I say, trying to put it nicely. "They're not terrible people, just limited in the way they think about the world around them."

Logan nods like he understands.

"Are you sure you want to come to Christmas with me?"

"Hey, I'm not going to back down now," Logan says, drowning his last bit of soda. He slams the paper cup on the table when he's done. "I'll be there for you."

I stay quiet, thinking.

"What's up?" Logan asks. I have no more alcohol in my system. I've eaten greasy, delicious food, and I'm wide awake from the caffeine in the soda. I have no reason to tell the truth, no dropped barriers to let it slip out so easily.

"I'm wondering what would have happened if I didn't leave that night. If I had slept over instead."

Logan swallows hard. "You missed out on some really great buttermilk pancakes that morning, too."

I burst out into laughter. I'm buoyant like I'm tied to a hot air balloon on its way up, up, up. "I'm sorry I missed them, then."

Logan glances away, suddenly shy. "I don't know what you're expecting of me, Max."

"Would you like me to tell you, or do you want to try and figure me out for a little while?"

Logan's dark eyes rove over my face. He smiles softly, sweet enough to make my heartache. It's been a long time since I've felt a connection like this. "I'll take my chances. Then you let me know if I'm right or not."

I nod, scared and elated at the same time. He wants to figure me out – no one's ever really wanted to try.

"I have another question for you actually. What scares you the most?"

I gulp, press my back against the booth. "Not being able to learn to live with regret."

"But that's part of life, though, Max."

"I know that. But at this point, I'm always going to be a disappointment to my parents. I have to live with that. I have to *learn* to live with that."

Logan places his chin into his palm. He looks at me like I'm a marvel, even after eating ten steamed hot dogs in front of him. "You're fascinating."

I scoff, cheeks burning. "What? No, I'm not. I'm a workaholic that doesn't know when to take a break."

Logan shakes his head, placing his hands on the table. I want to reach out and thread our fingers together. It would feel right. "And I'm a dreamer that spends most of my day thinking about characters and story structure than I ought to."

I glance around. We're the only two people left besides the cook and some staff manning the cash register and cleaning the grills. "Should we go?" I ask.

"My car's not too far from here if you want me to drive you home. Or we can walk around."

"It's fifteen below outside, Logan, and I'm not exactly dressed for a long walk." Although, I could be persuaded. I don't want the night to end, not yet.

Logan grins sheepishly. "I want to spend more time with you if I can."

"It's not like you won't see me after this," I say, nervous, too, about extending the night, about saying something wrong.

"You already have a habit of running away from me. I don't want to take my eyes off of you. Not tonight." His dark eyes rove over my face, waiting for me to answer.

I don't think I've ever been looked at like this, like I'm just Max, and not all the embellishments I put on my face and hair.

That's a *good* answer. "Well, where should we go?"

"I could use a hot coffee," he says, leaning back in the vinyl booth. "We can catch an early breakfast, again, if you wanted."

It's three in the morning, and I'm starting to get tired. I'm equal parts wired from the food, and from Logan's company. I haven't felt this good about a date in a long time.

Unlike the last few dates we had, he's not talking so much because I'm not impersonating a wall.

That would help, Max. That would help a lot.

"I could have breakfast. Maybe pancakes."

Logan nods. “It’s good to have a baseline. That way, you can taste the superiority of my pancakes when I make them for you.”

I raise an eyebrow, pull on my coat as Logan zips his up. I stand up and out of the booth, my purse over my shoulder. “When do you plan on making me these pancakes?” I ask, thinking about them already.

“When the time’s right, obviously,” he laughs. Logan holds out his hand, and I gently place my palm against his.

He wraps my hand in his grip, his skin almost scalding against my cold fingers.

We walk out like that, the Christmas lights strung up all over the light posts and lightening the dark sky. I feel like we’re in a snow globe as we walk down a few blocks to get to the city’s early breakfast joint.

Logan offers to carry me twice because of my shoes, but it’s better for me to be moving, anyway.

I don’t know what I was truly expecting when Logan showed up back at the lounge bar, but it wasn’t this.

I didn’t expect to be holding his hand and letting him open the door for me, ushering me inside the breakfast diner first. I didn’t expect him to make me laugh while we wait for our breakfast order.

I didn’t expect the perfect first date to end with Logan popping a very *important* question.

I sure as shit didn’t expect to say yes.

ELEVEN

I open my eyes, the dark cover of my own personal blanket burrito blocking out whatever little light is in my bedroom. The breathing hole around my mouth is cold, and my lips feel chapped.

I have to get up, I know I do, but that would mean leaving the relatively warm embrace of my blankets and the warm spot I've managed to make on my mattress throughout the night.

I stay lying down.

Honestly, there's no real pressure to get up – I'm not sticking to a schedule or a routine. All my plans are ruined for the rest of this month, and there's no salvaging them right now. When the power comes back – hopefully soon – I'll hopefully be able to spring back.

Right now, though? I need to sit with my thoughts and the remnants of my dream, the memory of my so-called wedding night.

Maybe the wine made me too loose in the emotional department, maybe I was primed for whatever Logan had to say that night.

Shit, I was right about what I told him before. Logan was not the type of person I was looking for to use to bring to my family dinner. It's easier to fake it with a stranger than someone you could potentially see yourself with.

At least, that's what I thought.

Because me being a shitty date on those nights when Logan and I met up? Maybe it was my own sense of self-preservation or self-sabotage, that kept me from wanting to be closer to him.

I mean, the minute the guy sat down I could tell he was nervous. And my parents would have seen through that right away, even though I was endeared by it.

I even made any kind of excuse to run away from him, even after we slept together.

I apparently have a broken throttle on my emotions and feelings that's out of service, and I don't know how to fix it.

Still, though, remembering pieces of our wedding night isn't helping me much. None of it makes all that much sense to me.

Sure, I felt a connection with the guy, was elated when he showed up after I called him, but to get married after that one act of so-called kindness?

What kind of stupid ass leap of faith did I take?

I slap my heels against the mattress, hiss when I let in some of the cold air in my warm little cocoon.

Gathering the strength to deal with the cold, I haul myself up and glance around my empty bedroom. Everything's clean, immaculate, a complete juxtaposition to the shit show that is my office and beauty room. It's definitely not as warm in here as it is in the living room.

I deliberate, yawning hard enough to bring tears to my eyes.

Logan's right, I wouldn't believe a word he told me about our wedding night. And since my memory is starting to come back, maybe I should spend the whole day taking cat naps, forcing my brain to start replaying those memories like pressing a play button on a movie.

I don't think it works like that.

Sick of overthinking, I haul myself out of bed to my en suite. I take the fastest hot shower that I could, opting to dry shampoo my hair. I couldn't stand feeling cold with wet hair, absolutely not.

I venture out into the living room when I'm done, closing my bedroom door behind me, shocked to find some of Logan's clothes strewn across my couch and on the floor.

Man, I wish I had his body temperature. That would be amazing.

I know he's in the main bathroom – I can hear the water running. I try not to think about a very naked Logan showering behind that closed door, but my brain takes me there for a split second before I can corral it back to figure out breakfast.

I check our meal plan, start making us scrambled eggs with egg whites and some spinach that looks about a couple of days out from going bad.

I'm in the perfect vantage point to see Logan come out of the bathroom through a cloud of steam, like he's the *Terminator*. And of course, he's wearing nothing but a towel around his waist.

Of course.

Even with the curtains open and a wan gray light coming through the sheets across my windows, I can still see *everything*.

"Good morning," Logan says, flashing me a wide grin, teeth practically glinting.

I will not react, I will not react.

I react.

"How are you walking around naked when it's freezing in here? How?"

Logan shrugs. "It feels kind of refreshing, actually. Hey, I was going to make breakfast."

"Yeah, well, I'm doing it now. Get dressed, would you? I'm freezing my ass off just looking at you."

Logan smirks, and I wonder how he can turn it off and on like that, how he can switch from being the nervous guy I had a first date with to *this*.

It might help if you stop staring at him like that, Max. Just a thought.

"You're my wife. You're allowed to see me."

I grit my teeth, threaten him with my hot pink spatula. "What did I say about that word? What did I fucking say?"

Logan makes a show of looking up at the ceiling, searching for a memory. The smile he gives me is charisma turned up to a hundred and four degrees, and I might just be melting under it.

Clearly, someone chose violence this morning, and it wasn't me.

"You said nothing about me calling you my wife. Which you are. You're my wife, Max."

I know, *I know*, he keeps repeating that stupid word for my benefit. I know that. It doesn't help the pressure building in my head or the white-hot anger that blisters my skin.

It's honestly too early in the morning for this.

"How would you like if I keep calling you husband, huh?"

The pleased grin has my belly swooping, and I know I walked into a trap. "I'd love it very much. Enough to ask for a kiss."

I snap my mouth shut and concentrate on making the eggs. I plate them quickly when I realize how well cooked they are, and then work on frying up some sandwich bread in butter for our toast.

Anything to keep me occupied from that shit-eating grin on Logan's face.

My mind flashes to that one night we were together, the one night where I've never been asked permission for so many things.

I loved every second of it.

I fell headfirst into *like* with the guy because he dicked me down good, and then I bolted. This was supposed to be a business transaction, and now what?

Do I want another night with Logan?

If only to share his body heat, and nothing else.

Liar, liar!

I nearly burn the toast from being so occupied over my conclusions, and that would have been a tragic waste of food.

I hurry up and plate everything, then pass the plates across the counter to where Logan and I usually sit, right next to each other.

Would it look weird if I were to space them out a stool apart? Just so I can breathe a little?

The decision is made for me when Logan plops down in the middle stool and puts the ball in my court.

"You're still not dressed," I comment, waving a hand over his body, as if I can magic him some clothes to wear.

He forks up some of his eggs, smiles at me through his first bite. "You can look all you want, wife, but you should ask if you want to touch."

"The only touching I'm going to do is sucker punch you when you least expect it."

Logan laughs, not believing a single word I say. Hell, I don't believe me either.

"This is yours," he says, leaning all the way back in his stool so that I know *exactly* what he is referring to. If I were drinking coffee, I'd spit it out all over him. As I'm not, I choke on good ol' oxygen instead.

"What? What?!" I sputter. "Maybe you should leave now. Yeah, maybe you should just go." I point toward the front door.

Logan's grin gets impossibly wider, and I have questions.

Why is he acting like this? Why is he suddenly being so playful, and like, turning on his charm so high that I'm getting hit over the head with it?

I'd rather take a stun gun to the chest than deal with him when he's like *this.*

"I thought we were supposed to be rehearsing for your parents. I can't have you stammering or blushing every time I say something sweet to you."

"I'm not blushing," I say, lying. My cheeks are on fire. I make a mental note to put on a shit ton of blush for Christmas day. Then I can totally blame it on the makeup. "And you haven't said anything sweet to me this morning."

Logan's eyebrows leap up to his forehead, water droplets from his long hair dripping onto his shoulders and they take mesmerizing curves on the way down his defined chest.

It's *distracting*.

He licks his lips. "You look especially gorgeous when you just wake up in the morning, and I'm honored that I get to see that."

I can't help it. I laugh, right in his face. I finally round the island and sit next to him, pulling my plate in front of me. "Way to lay it on thick."

Even now sitting next to him like this, I can feel his body heat through the fourteen layers I'm wearing on top. How is that even possible?

"Max," Logan calls, voice soft. I turn to look at him, stomach already twisting into knots. "I like you a lot, you know," he says, just as gently.

I frown at him. "What's with you this morning?"

Can he read minds? Can he tell that I started remembering or something?

There's really no other explanation as to why he's being *this* flirtatious, and I haven't even had breakfast yet. Logan somehow knows that I've started remembering.

That's gotta be it.

"Max, I like you," he says again with a finality that has me glaring at him.

My cheeks still burn, and I have to glance away. I haven't been told I've been liked in a very long time. Like, it's simple, high school type shit, but it still makes my heart race away in my chest.

I've had guys comment on my body in the way that they've found me attractive, hot, but it's been forever since someone outright and said that they *like* me for my personality.

"Honestly, I don't what happened to you last night, if there were body snatchers in my home or whatever, but you have to knock it off," I say, my voice losing the heat of anger. Now I just sound scared.

"I didn't mean to upset you."

"You didn't," I tell him. "Eat your food before it freezes because it's so cold in here."

We eat in a strained silence, and I'm aware that it's still morning and we both have hours and *hours* to kill in each other's company.

"I'll go get dressed," Logan says when he's done eating, scarfing it down in practically two bites as if he's rushing to get away from me.

I wouldn't mind the reprieve, and to sit with my thoughts.

I hear the bathroom door shut, and I exhale a long breath. I finish up my breakfast as fast as I can and then clean up the dishes and the lone pot we can use to cook things in.

Now there's *really* nothing to do.

Logan steps out of the bathroom, fully dressed in gray sweats that are as much torture to watch him in as him being practically naked in front of me.

It's also weird that those are *my* sweatpants, specifically bought from the men's section, about four sizes too big for me, and extra comfortable. And now Logan's wearing them, and I feel...possessive about it.

"Hi, again," he murmurs, giving me a small, shy smile. Whatever audacity Logan had walked around with practically naked before has left the building, and I'm left behind with the shy version of him that I know how to handle.

I wave at him, not saying a word.

"I'm sorry if I upset you," he says, mopping up the excess moisture in his hair with a towel.

I shake my head. "You didn't upset me."

Logan drops his hand from his hair, and glares at me, his lips parted. "Are you kidding me? What's it going to take for you to let me in?"

I take a step back, my heart beating hard and fast. "What are you talking about?"

"Every single time I talk to you, every single fucking time, Max, all you do is deflect."

I'm about to tell him I *don't* do that, but then I'd be proving his point. "It's who I am as a person, or so my cousins tell me."

Logan's eyes go hot and intense, and I can't seem to move, even if I wanted to. "Why can't you tell me what you want? Why can't you just say it instead of always running away?"

"Hey, I'm standing right here. I haven't gone anywhere."

Logan tilts his head to the side, an almost-cruel twist along his mouth. "Haven't you, though?"

I gulp hard, not expecting to be called out like that. Then I get *mad*. "What makes you think that you have a right to me in any way when I know fuck all about you?" *Liar, liar, Max. You know that he cried when he read Charlotte's Web and admitted it to you. You know that he read romance novels for basically sex education as he was growing up. You know some things about him, Max.*

"You don't even ask anything about me, Max, unless it's to help you with something around here."

"Hey, you offered to do that! I didn't put a gun to your head! No one's stopping you from leaving."

Logan crosses his arms over his chest and looks about two seconds from throttling me. Well, the feeling is mutual.

"I want to be here. I want to help you."

"Why? What for if I'm such a giant pain in the ass?" I growl.

Logan's eyes go soft once more, and I swear to everything that's holy that I'm getting emotional whiplash. I don't know how much more that I can take.

"I never said that, Max. You're just filling in the blank spaces with what you want to hear."

I stop breathing, my heart twisting so tight that it's hard to breathe.

Logan stays on his side of the living room, as do I. We're maybe a whole ten feet apart, but there's not enough air in the room to breathe, and Logan's staring at me like I should know what's going on.

"You told me about this, too," he says gently, and I tear my gaze away, staring instead at the front door like I'm the one who needs to take off running.

But then I'd be proving his point, and I don't want to do that.

"You told me that you hear the worst things about yourself because of how you were raised. You told me that you're working through it. You told me that you'd assume the worst of what I said when I told you that I would never intentionally hurt you. Just like I told you the other day."

"People lie," I whisper. "Even by the ones, we love the most." I stare unblinking at the front door, but the tears well in my eyes and spill over anyway. "I don't want to talk about this anymore."

Logan sighs. "Okay, Max. Whatever you want."

I sniff hard, chasing away the tears to the best of my ability. "Why do you even like me? I'm a mess." Maybe I'm waiting for some good ol' material for self-flagellation that I can use later.

"Because you're kind. Because you love your family despite what they've put you through."

"Most people would call that stupidity. Hell, insanity, even." I turn to look at him. Logan's eyes are soft on me, and his arms flexed tight across his chest like he's trying to restrain himself.

Restrain himself from *what*?

"You make me laugh. You see me."

I force a snort, trying to break the tension. "Pretty sure I saw a lot this morning. Thanks for the free show."

Logan's cheeks turn pink, and the tightness in my chest starts to unfurl, little by little. "Don't make a joke about this, please."

"You're the one that decided to marry me," I say, shrugging. "I'm not the walking joke."

I shouldn't have said anything, I *know* I shouldn't have said anything. The look in Logan's eyes cuts me to the quick, a sharp lance of pain centered in my chest. I feel it every single time I take a deep breath, cutting myself on it.

"Max, let me *in*," he says, braver than I've ever been. "Let me in like you did that night. Please."

I shake my head, the fear clogging my throat, the fear of being so open with him. I can't do that. This is only supposed to last until Christmas. Why does he need to see all those sides to me?

What for?

"I...I don't think I can give you what you want, Logan. I don't think I can."

Logan pulls in a deep breath, his chest expanding with it.

And you noticed. Guess you still think he's pretty beautiful.

That doesn't change anything, though.

"No. You don't want to try."

I wince at his words, the implication that I've quit even before I've begun. I bristle at the tone, at the words, but ultimately decide to flip him off, and hide in my bedroom for the rest of the day.

Logan's right. I don't want to try.

It's safer this way.

TWELVE

The wedding night...

Logan and I sit across from each other, waiting for our breakfast. We've both ordered the same thing: eggs with sausage and a side of pancakes.

I'm ready to drown everything in maple syrup.

"Okay?" Logan asks, smiling wide. I don't think he's stopped smiling since we got here, even when he almost spilled his coffee into his lap.

I'm waiting for my second cup, glancing around for the waiter. "Yeah. I'm okay. You?"

"You're not cold or anything?"

I shake my head. "The coffee's doing its job. Just waiting for a refill."

Logan hums, palms the back of his head before ultimately crossing his arms over his chest. He leans back in the booth, taking me all in.

I've never been looked at like this.

I know when a man's attracted to me. Hell, I've seen pupils dilate and everything. But Logan's...different. He doesn't look at me like he wants to consume me, and he doesn't look at me like I'm a precious treasure that'll be ruined if he touches me.

He's looking at me like he sees me, even under all the glittery eyeshadow and the heavy makeup.

At least, I think so.

"I'm really nervous," he admits, smiling sheepishly. And well, it's unfortunate that I find that pretty adorable. "I bet you hear that all the time."

I shake my head, carefully take a sip of water. "No, actually. Guys don't tend to admit that kind of stuff out loud. Especially to the girl they're dating."

"Well, I'm nervous," he says again, nodding to himself. "You make me nervous."

"I'm sorry?"

Logan shakes his head, panicked. "No, no. That's a me problem."

I tilt my head at him. "Logan, I want to ask you something. If I can."

"Yeah, sure. Go ahead," he says, licking his lips.

"Why did you come tonight, when I called?" My heart drums in my chest, and I hastily slurp more water to hide my blush. "Because I wanted you to show up, I did. I didn't expect you to. Not after how I treated you."

"Maybe I'm a glutton for punishment," he says on a forced laugh. I frown. "Or maybe I'm really glad that you called me again. I thought I did something horribly wrong."

I shake my head. "Uh, no, no. I'm the one that messed it all up. I...I told you I was looking for someone else, *something* else."

"And you got me."

"Yeah," I sigh. "I got you."

"Is that a good thing, or a bad thing?" He looks unsure.

I smile for him. "It's a good thing, even if how it all started was less than ideal. I'm sorry I ran away. I wanted to stay, but I just couldn't."

"Why, Max? Not even for pancakes?" He looks at me, aghast.

I know he's trying to make me laugh, I know that. "I...I'm not good with attachments," I say.

Logan does nothing but waits me out, listening to what I have to say. I don't think he realizes how rare of a skill that is.

"I'm not good at relationships. I always end up fizzling after like, the tenth date. So then I just kept it strictly casual. I didn't want to get my hopes up anymore."

"And now? We're technically on our fifth date," he says with a grin. "Three dates before tonight, then date number four when you called me, and now date number five where we're sharing another meal. That counts."

I gulp and nod. "I guess it does." It also means I'm halfway to ghosting him and retreating into my office before I find the courage to try dating all over again.

"You're doing pretty good so far, speaking as the guy you're dating."

I roll my eyes. "Yeah, yeah."

Logan smiles, making the sides of his eyes crinkle closed. It's unfortunate that it's the best he's ever looked, and that's saying something.

"So what's the worst thing that can happen on Christmas? I want to know."

I glance away, not wanting to tell him how much my parents' words bother me, how much their opinion matters to me. I mean, I'll be in my thirties soon. I can't still be hung up on their approval.

But that's exactly what I'm doing.

Shit.

"They're going to push hard. I've never brought anyone home for Christmas before. It's always been strictly a family thing, but this year's different. My cousins are bringing their boyfriends, too, and I hate being the odd one out." I don't get into it how Evie probably won't have a date, and neither will my little sister. It's Amber and Vick I'm worried about. I've always been compared to them as much as I've been to my little sister in the past.

Amber's wicked school-smart and has about four hundred letters after her name with all the studying she's done. Over the past year, we've had our ups and downs together, but we've made it work.

That's what you do with the people you love, and the ones that love you back.

Vick's completely changed her life around and has achieved that elusive work-life balance that I have yet to conquer this past year.

Both of my cousins are doing great in every aspect of their lives: financially, in their careers, hell, even in the health department. I mean, Vick looks like she could audition for a superhero film and headline it.

And then there's me, constantly drowning in work, barely keeping my head above water.

"Max? You went somewhere else in your head for a second."

"Yeah, sorry. Uh, my parents, right. They're going to be nitpicking everything I wear, what my makeup is like. This, right here?" I point to my teal-and-plum smoky eye. "I'll get shit for it. But it makes me happy, and I need every scrap of happiness I can get when it comes to Christmas."

"Why don't you skip it?"

I squint. "Are you trying to get out of our deal, Logan?"

"No," he says, looking like he's about to roll his eyes at me. "Max, if it makes you so miserable, why don't you stay home?"

"Because then I'd get a million phone calls, and about fifty guilt trips. Not to mention the disappointed silent treatment that I absolutely hate." I shake my head. "I'm already at my limit with work. I can't pile on any more shit that I have to deal with, okay?"

"Okay," Logan says, reaching out a hand across the table. "Okay. I'll be there, right next to you the entire time."

I sneer and stare down at his lonely hand. Mine's pretty lonely too. "It's pretty sad, huh? The lengths I'll go to avoid a fight with my parents?"

"I think you're avoiding feeling like shit, but I'm not in your shoes. Everybody wants to avoid that feeling. Besides, I'm going to do my best to make it a good day. I promise."

I want to tell him that he can't promise anything like that, he just can't.

But I really do want to believe him. I want to believe that he could do that for me.

"Okay, then. All right." I nod to myself, swallow hard. I reach out across the expanse of the table's surface, reaching for Logan. When my fingers make contact with the back of his hand, bumping over his knuckles, I swear I hear him suck in a breath, all from my touch alone.

Logan slowly threads our fingers together and I suddenly don't feel so completely alone in this.

Maybe I had to run away from Logan to come running back. Maybe all of this was timed just right, all of it coming into alignment.

This isn't a sci-fi movie, Max. This is real.

The food is eventually placed in front of us, the pancakes steaming, and a perfect cube of butter sliding along the top of the stack.

I let go of Logan's hand to grab my fork, and we both start eating.

Logan starts with the pancakes first, eating diligently.

"What's the verdict?" I ask.

Logan swallows. "Mine are better."

I laugh, cover my smile with a hand. "Yeah? I think you're just talking shit, Logan."

"I'll have to make them for you one day, Max. Whenever you want. Name the time and place, and I'll be there."

Funny thing is, he sounds deadly serious.

I want to take him up on it.

·♥·♥·♥·♥·♥·

I wake up early the next morning, the sky dark enough that no light is coming through my haphazardly closed curtains.

I spent all day long in my bedroom yesterday, and I'm already sick of it.

But then I'd have to go out to the living room and confront Logan and I don't want to do that. Oh, I have to do it, but I still don't want to.

Shit.

I fish for my phone in the sea of blankets until I nab it. The light blinds me as I check the time. As suspected, it's too early to get up, but I head to my en suite anyway and go through my morning routine. Only then do I head out of my room into the living room, to find Logan sleeping on the couch.

An awful, terrible idea comes to mind that would make me somewhat of a terrible person, but after yesterday's talk, I'm feeling raw and sore in places I didn't know I could be.

Logan's been harping on the truth when he hasn't been the one to let me in either. What about that weird text message he got the other day? And what about his non-Christmas plans that he doesn't like to talk about?

I mean, he could be estranged from his family, for all I know. It's not like I *know* him and we've talked about all of this stuff. And yet, we're married.

Shouldn't I know a whole bunch of stuff about him before having decided to do that?

What kind of high was I on to agree to do this with him?

I tiptoe into the living room, and into my office, grabbing what I need by phone flashlight. When I have the eyeshadow palette and the makeup brushes I need, I head back to the living room and carefully get down to my knees right beside the couch that Logan is sleeping on.

His eyes are roving back and forth under his eyelids, and he's clearly in the middle of some dream. I make sure to keep my phone away from him, lamenting the lack of light. But honestly, this is meant to be a prank, and not anything else.

I keep my phone on the ground, the light pointing up to the ceiling. It'll have to be good enough.

I open my eyeshadow palette, looking busted with pressed pigments flying everywhere before I blow it away.

I start working, using my fluffy brushes and a garish nave blue to start on contour on Logan's face, working in fits and starts until I'm sure he's gone to sleep more deeply.

When Logan murmurs my name, though, I freeze, holding my breath. He sighs one last time before snoring a little, and I know I have some more time to do his makeup before he gets up.

By the time I'm done, it's close to seven in the morning, right about the time that Logan's usually up.

I hurriedly grab my stash and shove it into my office, not even bothering to figure out the right place for every little thing.

When I head back out to the living room, it's to find him stirring awake. I bypass the couch and head to the kitchen, nabbing the induction pot and using the faucet for water. I fuss around with the induction plate and get the water boiling as Logan rustles the blankets and eventually sits up to stare straight at me.

He looks at me blearily, eyes still squinted closed, his face contoured with blue eyeshadow. I even went so far as to use some of my precious multi-chrome eyeshadows on him for kicks, and every time he moves his face, I get to see a different sheen of color.

He looks like a merman with iridescent scales that don't belong on my couch.

I guess I should have taken some eyeliner and drawn a giant dick on his cheek instead. Lost opportunity, Max. What a lost opportunity.

Even with the shitty lighting, I did a good job.

"Good morning," he rasps. I get a flutter of *something* in my belly at the sound of his very early morning voice. "How are you?"

I mean, I did a good job and everything, but he still looks ridiculous. I find myself wanting to talk to him now after my little art session.

"Good. Good. Amazing. Did you, uh, sleep well?" I clench my jaw and mash my lips together.

Logan's pouty in the morning and his eyes have slid shut again so he can't see my expression. It makes the makeup look even dumber all over his unfortunately symmetrical face.

"Nah. Couldn't sleep until four."

I sputter. "What? Why? It's not that cold in here. Do you need more blankets?"

Logan leans back into the couch, the sheet dropping from a very naked chest. His nipples pebble against the change in temperature and a shiver makes him wiggle from head to toe. Logan sighs.

I look and look some more.

How can he be so casual with me, after what we said yesterday?

"Why are you half-naked again?" I ask.

Logan squints at me, licks at his lips. "Because I want you to look at me like you want me to be here."

I can't *believe* he just said that *out loud.*

If I was a cartoon character, my jaw would be hitting the floor, and my tongue would come rolling out. "So what? You thought it was a good idea to flaunt your body like that?"

Logan blinks at me. "I remember you liking my body."

I snort. "I remember you liked mine, too. A hell of a lot."

Logan closes his eyes again, a perfect smile on his face at the mention of that memory.

I gulp, that fluttering *something* in my belly heading down south. Honestly, I don't know how this is happening. He's got makeup all over his face, he's half-naked, and he thinks I'm a runner. Why am I reacting like this?

"It was a good night. Until you left."

"Yeah, and still we ended up here, so stop complaining, would you? You want some tea or not?" I hiss, trying to pour the hot water into my prepped mug. Of course, I get some hot water on me, and the steam doesn't help the exposed skin of my wrist any, but I do it anyway.

"Jesus fuck, Max. Why can't you be more careful with yourself?" he groans, getting up from the couch and stalking over to me. He holds his hand out, but I'm the idiot that extends my arm so he can look down at the reddened skin of my wrist.

I hold my breath, half-afraid of what he's going to do next. Is he going to kiss me there? Do I want him to?

Yes, Max. The answer is yes.

"It's just a burn," I stammer as Logan blows cool air onto my throbbing skin. "I'm okay."

Logan looks at me, and I don't even see the botched makeup I've done on his face. Nope, I'm too busy staring into his eyes, trying to read him like he's reading me.

"What do you want for breakfast?" he asks as if we didn't fight yesterday, as if that's all forgotten. I have a feeling that he didn't mean to ask that question, that he wanted to ask me something else.

Now I feel like a petty bitch. *Good thing I didn't draw a dick on his face, huh?*

"We're running out of eggs," I say, trying to cover up the fact that I have a craving for pancakes. "I've got some bread for French toast, though."

"French toast it is. Let me go wash up. You have any aloe for your wrist?"

"I'm fine, Logan, I promise."

He looks at me. "You know, I don't think you would tell me if you weren't." He drops my hand, gently guiding it down to my side. Logan turns on his heel and heads to the bathroom, shutting the door behind him.

There's a shout, and then scrambling to get the door wrenched open again.

"Maxima! What the fuck is this?!" he bellows, pointing to his face.

I shrug, but I can't stop myself from smiling. I mean, he looks stupid, and it's making me feel better. "It'll wash off."

"No, when did you do this? How? I'm a light sleeper."

I shrug again. "Not in this house you're not. It's some eyeshadow. Use the cleansing balm I have in the medicine cabinet, and it'll come right off."

Logan frowns at me, clearly annoyed. "I guess it could have been worse."

"It's just makeup. It's not going to mess with your sexuality or anything."

Logan snorts. "I know that. I thought I'd wake up if you were so close to me before you ran off again."

"What the hell is that supposed to mean?"

"It means, wife," he says, tacking on that stupid, *stupid* word. "That I wouldn't be opposed to you waking me up in the middle of the night if you wanted to be in my arms."

"Over my dead body."

Logan smiles at me like he knows I'm already close to caving in. It's hard getting warm at night, and it's equally hard getting out of bed in the morning, and Logan's clearly stealing all the body heat.

It's not fair.

"All you have to do is ask, Max. I'm not going to say no."

I clamp my lips shut to keep from doing just that.

Because knowing he'll say yes to whatever I want isn't going to do wonders for my own discipline.

Shit.

THIRTEEN

"Here," Logan says, throwing me a blanket that's been warmed through from his own body heat. It's almost like I put the thing in the dryer, it's so warm.

I frown down at the blanket in my lap, then look at him.

"I didn't ask for this," I say.

Logan groans, staring up at the ceiling, elongating the column of his throat.

Unfortunately, he's *this* good-looking. Incredibly unfortunate.

"Just take it. I can see you're cold. And don't lie about it either."

I snap my mouth closed. "You don't have to be so bossy about it," I hiss, unwinding the blanket and covering my shoulders with it. It's unfortunate, too, that it is warm, and is exactly what I needed.

"You should come and sit over here," Logan says, tilting his head back. He's currently finishing up one of my romance novels, and I wonder how he can read them with a straight face.

I don't possess that kind of skill, so I can never read (or listen to) them in public. I'd be a blushing mess, and people would ask questions. Then I'd have to say that I'm reading smut and there'd be even more questions I wouldn't want to get into.

"Why? Besides, you're taking up the whole couch." I wave at his body, sprawled across that portion of the sectional. There's really no room for me.

Unless, of course, that's the point.

Logan smirks, and I know I'm in trouble. "Because it's warmer over here."

"No, it's not. And I'm perfectly fine where I am, thanks."

Logan shakes his head, his teeth flashing in a pleased smile. He goes back to reading his book, while I re-shuffle the cards and go about playing another game of solitaire.

I shiver underneath the blanket and glance up when Logan makes a noise. He's deeply engrossed in the book, and I know he only has a small section of paper left to go.

"What the fuck, that's the ending?" He says, lifting his eyes to meet mine. "Please tell me you have the fourth book."

"The fourth book doesn't come out until next year."

"No," he practically bellows, dropping the book into his lap. "That's terrible."

I snort. Watching him be so upset over a book release he has to wait over a year for, well – it's cute. *He's* cute.

And that's dangerous.

"What am I supposed to do with my life now?"

"Read another book?" I suggest, even as Logan springs to his feet and starts to peruse my bookshelves, searching for his next read.

He pulls one at random, then half-turns to show me the cover. "This one?"

I shake my head. "After that cliffhanger, that one won't satisfy your itch." I wearily get to my feet, the blanket wrapped around me tight enough that I resemble a mummy.

I waddle over to stand next to him, the both of us staring at the spines.

I finally pull one out from its home and hand it to him. "I think you'll like this one. It's got dragons in it."

Logan's eyebrows pump high on his forehead. "Well, shit, okay. Thanks. Hey, do you want supper soon?"

I ignore the way my stomach *leaps* at the sound of yet another meal. Right now, though, all I want is a hot cup of tea, and to read a book of my own. The only problem is that my eReader's going to die, and I'm nowhere finishing my current read.

Plus, I'd rather stay out here, where it's warmer than go into my bedroom. Maybe Logan's giving off enough body heat that he's actually affected the thermodynamics of my living room. I don't know.

"You don't have to cook. I can eat some cereal."

Logan sighs but doesn't say anything after that. I bristle, that itch under my skin is back again, all because of Logan being annoyed with me.

"You know, if you're annoyed with me, just come out and *say* it. Stop with the long-suffering sighs. I didn't ask you to feed me. You should be happy about that."

Logan stills, and turns those dark, intense eyes on me.

I lick my lips, holding very, very still.

If I don't move, maybe he won't see me.

"You're being obstinate because you can."

I hold my breath as Logan comes to stand right in front of me, putting us toe to toe. He's a lot taller than me, so when he drops his head just enough that I have to tilt my head all the way back until he becomes all I can see.

"You're being obstinate and so fucking stubborn, *wife*, because you won't let anyone help you with any little thing."

I want to call him out on his lie, but I do think he has a point. All I can do is blink at him. Smart Max has taken a vacation; Horny Max is standing right here.

It's a bad idea, I *know* it's a bad idea, but I can't help myself.

I let my eyes drag down Logan's face and stop at his mouth, watching his lips move with every single word.

"Your family will see right through us if you can't take what I can give."

I'm pretty sure Logan's talking about something else other than a blanket, but what do I know?

I look up to meet his eyes, knowing I've been caught staring at his mouth. From what I can remember, Logan's a good kisser, patient and considerate — two things I didn't know I wanted or needed.

And it's what I want now. I want him to shut me up with kisses.

"No, they won't."

"Max, you can't even stand for me to give you a fucking blanket. You can't stand to admit you need help with any fucking thing. How is that going to look?"

It should bother me that he's thinking about *how* it's going to look on Christmas instead of paying attention to me right now when I'm standing right in front of him.

"I'm sure you're a good actor," I say, trying to convince myself of the fact.

"Right," he whispers, his voice dropping a whole octave it seems. "Because I'm supposed to pretend like I'm in love with you. I'm supposed to pretend that the ground you walk on is paved in diamonds, Max."

"Yeah," I whisper back, still mesmerized by his moving lips. They're so close, and yet not close enough. I have a distant memory of telling him those things.

"So, what do you want me to do, Max? How do you want me to do that when you can't even stand accepting what little help I want to give you?"

"Pretend," I blurt, gaze still riveted by his mouth. "Pretend you could love me. Pretend." *Please, pretend. Please.*

When I think Logan is going to lean down and kiss me, *finally*, he's the one pulling back, away. He moves around me and I whirl around to watch him take a seat on the couch.

"What the fuck was that?" I growl, pissed off.

Logan raises an eyebrow in a silent question. "Can you take what I give?"

I narrow my eyes. "We're not talking about what I think we're talking about. Are we?"

Logan smiles, and my belly flops over into a series of somersaults. "We're talking about it all, Max."

"You told me I need to be explicit with you, so here I am, being explicit. What do you want to give me?"

"My time, and my attention. To start."

I gape at him. "To start?"

Logan nods. "I'll give you my affection when you feel you need it, when you ask me for it, wife," he says. My heart beats triple time, and my blood whizzes around my body, pounding in my ears. "When you admit to yourself that you can't do everything alone."

"I've been managing just fine for literal decades," I tell him, sarcasm dripping from every single word. To be honest, I've never been so tired in my entire life. Maybe this storm has been a blessing in disguise – if I believed in those types of things.

"But you have me now, Max. Won't you give me what you can't take?"

I mash my lips together, glance away, or else he'll see the tears welling in my eyes. Maybe he can even hear my heart hammering in my chest. I know he can see the way I almost curl in on myself, trying to hide away the pain centered in my heart, where his verbal blow lands.

"I...I don't know how to do that. I've always done everything on my own," I tell the wall. I hear movement, and I know Logan is coming closer to check on me. I can't look at him, not yet.

"Let's start with something small, something easy. What can you give me, Max?"

I've got emotional whiplash. I'm afraid to look at him, I'm afraid he'll see what a mess I am. It's easy to *tell* someone that you're a mess of a human being, it's quite another for them to see it with their own eyes.

"Can you give me a hug?" he asks, standing close enough that all it'll take is for me to take one more step and I'd be in his arms.

Do I want to do that, though?

What about what happens after the hug? The aftermath is where I start to fall deeper into *like* with a guy like Logan Porter when there's already an expiration date on all of this.

"I might just squeeze you to death," I murmur. Logan laughs, sounding like he's happy with me. I think I would do a lot of stupid shit to get him to laugh like that, to be the cause of that laughter.

Better start looking up terrible puns and dad jokes. I bet Logan likes those.

"I wouldn't mind. I bet we'll both be warmer in a hug, too."

I huff. "I already have a blanket," I say.

Logan hums. "I know. But you could share it, Max. You could give me a part of it, too, you know."

I turn to look at him, once and for all.

"Ah, Max. I've made you sad."

"No, no. Not really. I'm always like this when I'm exhausted and flirting with burnout."

Logan nods like he understands but doesn't say anything. I find myself waiting for him to say something, to soothe me. It dawns on me that I'm going to have to ask for it.

"I would like to give you a hug if that's still allowed."

"Of course, wife," he jokes, opening his arms wide so I can step into them. Before I know it, I'm pressed up against his chest, my ear hovering right over his heartbeat, listening to Logan, hearing the very sound that makes him alive. "Do you need me to stop calling you that?" he asks.

I nod my head. "You'll probably let it slip on Christmas, and I don't want to answer any of those kinds of questions."

"All right, Max. I'll stop saying it."

"Thank you. And thanks for the hug. I needed it more than I can say."

Logan hums places a gentle kiss on the top of my head. He holds me close for a while, the blanket wrapped around both of us until we're both swaying to some music we both can't hear.

I don't know how long we stand like that, in each other's arms, only that after we're done, I feel better, lighter.

It's all Logan's fault.

"Are you going to bed?" Logan asks later that evening. The sky is dark and inky black outside, and all the candles are lit in the living room, giving it a warm glow that I don't exactly feel.

Plus, I have something I want to ask Logan, and I'm not sure how he's going to react.

"What do you think of me sleeping here tonight?"

Logan frowns at me, his face half in shadow. "I can sleep in your bed, sure, if that's what you want."

I shake my head, pull in a deep breath to try again. "No, I mean, uh, what if I pulled my mattress in here and we both sleep on it. Together." I gently clap my hands together for emphasis. "Not for sex. For like, warmth and shit."

Logan *laughs*, surprise leaking out of him in a great boom of a sound that I think will wake the neighbors.

"Warmth and shit," he repeats, his laughter petering out. "Funniest shit I've ever heard."

"Oh, shut up. So? What do you think? Is it a bad idea or a good idea?" I ask, my hands on my hips. I know I look ridiculous still wrapped in my blanket cape, but that's not the point.

Logan looks around the living room. "We have to move the coffee table out of the way and push the couch almost all the way back to the windows there," he says, pointing around the room for visual aid.

"Yes, I know. I want to know if you're going to be comfortable with that."

Logan stares at me. "I already told you, Max. I don't expect anything from you. I only take what you decide to give me. Tonight that'll be sharing your mattress in the living room. I'm okay with that as long as you are."

I nod slowly, trying to figure out if my body wants to run or fight. Maybe a little bit of both. "Yep. I'm good with it."

It takes us a while to spread out the furniture in my living room, and then haul my mattress to the middle. We've pushed the couch all the way up against the living room windows, and I can feel it already providing a slight barrier to the cold air seeping in through the windows, strung-up sheets, and curtains.

I bring my own blankets from my bedroom into the living room once the mattress has been transferred, and Logan grabs his own set and plops them right next to my mountain.

We both glance down at the mattress, then back to each other.

I wonder if he's thinking about it, too, the one night we were in bed together. Maybe it's all me, but I don't think so.

My heart rate goes haywire, and I excuse myself with a barely-there sound to hide in my en suite and get changed and washed up for the night. When I'm back in the living room, it's to find that Logan is in the main bathroom, doing his own routine. I quickly blow out all except one candle, and then hop into bed, arranging the blankets just how I like them.

When Logan opens the door, it's to find me with the blankets all the way up to my throat, my hoodie pulled up over my head, my hair tied up in a bun and hidden underneath it.

I don't look ready for love. I look ready to survive another cold night with the guy who's apparently my husband lying down beside me.

He's wearing his sweats and a giant sweatshirt. He's not going to crawl in naked into bed with me, either, but I can't help the hot little flare of disappointment all the same.

Logan gets into bed, and now we're both staring up at the ceiling as if it's going to give us topics for discussion.

I don't know what to say, what to *do*.

We had a heavy afternoon, and yesterday wasn't fun either.

Now we're both lying down next to each other in the middle of a storm, and I hope to everything that is holy that I don't somehow attach myself like a barnacle to Logan as the night drags on.

"Good night, Max," Logan says, his voice shattering the silence.

"Good night, Logan," I murmur back, turning to my side to blow out the last candle.

The apartment is plunged into darkness. It's a little scary actually, being in this much open space with all the dark and no light to see by.

I'm acutely aware of every single move that Logan makes, the way he rolls more deeply onto his side and sighs like he's had a hell of a day, too.

I keep my eyes on the ceiling, the shadows resolving into shapes and movements as my eyes get adjusted to the lack of light.

The storm still rages on outside, the pitter-patter of freezing rain hitting the windows with enough force to be annoying.

The dark, too, makes it easier to confess to half-truths and lies I've told myself, or let myself believe. "I don't believe in marriage because I don't want to end up like my parents," I whisper.

Logan's breathing is even and measured, but there's a part of me that can tell that he's listening.

"I don't believe in marriage because I'm afraid if I do get married, I'll settle for the way that I've learned, knowing the way my parents treat each other. I don't want that for myself."

Logan doesn't say anything. It makes it easier to speak out into the dark like I'm having a conversation with the shadows instead of another human being.

"I've been alone for a long time, too. I don't navigate relationships well, either, as you've clearly seen."

I turn to look at Logan's broad back, aching to reach out and touch his shoulders, to feel that connection.

"I know I keep saying that you need to do all these things for me for Christmas, Logan, but...but if you think it's going to be impossible, or you change your mind, then we don't have to do this. I can go alone. I won't actually die if I go alone."

Logan turns slowly onto his back, and then onto his other side so that he's facing me. "I made you a promise," he whispers in the dark, and a shiver races its way down my spine. "I plan on keeping that promise."

He stares at me with his dark eyes, willing me to believe him.

If only I knew which promise he was talking about – coming to Christmas dinner with me, or this farce of a marriage?

Which one is he talking about?

FOURTEEN

I wake up, my skin boiling. I cling to sleep as I fight to get my hoodie off, trying to navigate and pull it my body without opening my eyes.

My elbow hits something that isn't a pillow, and a grunt of pain whistles out of teeth.

"Max, fuck," Logan groans, but I refuse to open my eyes to see what's going on. I'm still fighting with my hoodie, too tired to move and drag it off my body. "Do you want some help?"

"Mmmm," I murmur, frowning now since I'm more awake than I was a few seconds ago.

I feel Logan's hands move to the bottom hem of my hoodie, grab onto the material and start yanking it over my head. When I'm clear of it, I sigh, shivering in the cold, my skin pebbling in goosebumps.

The blankets are twisted around my legs. I'm *boiling* like I'm inside the heart of a star. I futilely try to kick off the blankets but only succeed to make them more entangled around my body. Now I'm awake.

I groan as I sit up, pulling the blankets off me and placing them on the side, letting the cold air circulating around my apartment cool me down.

"S'too hot," I groan, rolling onto my side, finding a cold patch of the mattress to gratefully sink into.

"Because you're sleeping next to me," Logan says. I shush him. Logan chuckles. "You're really not a morning person, huh?"

"Still dark outside," I point out.

"The curtains are closed, Max. It's morning, I promise you."

"Liar," I groan, hiding my head underneath my pillow, trying to keep the blissful darkness close. It's no use, though. I'm awake.

Shit.

Logan's humming a song underneath his breath, and by the jostling I'm getting, I can tell that he's moved further away from me, taking his scalding body heat with him.

What an asshole.

I shiver in the cold air, the exposed skin of my arms already feeling cool to the touch.

Seems like everything is conspiring against me to get my ass out of bed. "What if I just spend all day in bed?" I murmur to myself once I get clear of the pillow and can breathe fresh air again.

Logan laughs, turns onto his back so that our arms are brushing against each other. He really is scalding hot, in more than one way.

I lift my head to squint at Logan in the semi-darkness. He's lying there, chest and nipples exposed to the wind. I drop my head to the pillow and groan.

"What? What is it?"

"Why are you naked?" I ask, rubbing a hand over my burning cheeks. I use my foot to get my blankets on top of me again, snuggling close to the soft material. "Honestly, it's like you want me to look."

"That's kind of the point, Max."

I turn my head to look at him. What's worse? He turns on his side to face me, and I'm faced with all of that glorious male beauty that I don't really know what to do with this early in the morning.

I know my hair's a mess – it's always a mess in the morning. This close, Logan can probably count my pores and start tracing constellations over the bridge of my nose and my cheeks.

"You know you're hot," I say, licking at my dry lips. "I'm sure you know that."

Logan grins at me, clearly pleased with the roundabout admission. I roll my eyes, keep them closed and try to force myself back to sleep.

"Are you really going back to sleep, or do you want breakfast?" he whispers. "I can make us pancakes."

Pancakes – the meal I was promised if I had stayed the whole night that time we slept together.

I open my eyes to a squint. "I might want to go back to sleep," I say. "But I won't be able to. I really want to stay in bed all day."

Logan grins at me. "Nobody says we can't. There's nothing else to do anyway."

I frown at him. "You're not supposed to give in to what I want. You're supposed to tell me to get my lazy ass off the bed and do something productive with my time."

Logan frowns, his forehead adorably furrowed. This close, I could reach out and touch the skin there, smooth it out with my fingers. Not that I'm going to, of course, despite us sharing my bed.

Even though we're legally husband and wife.

"Max, who told you that?"

I pull the blankets up over my mouth in case I want to let out any more revelations today. Except Logan looks so earnest, and he's right *here*, in my bed with me, in the middle of this fucking storm, and I want...I want him to know me better, to understand me.

"When I told my parents I wanted to do the whole influencer thing full-time, they didn't speak to me for three months straight. It was the longest silent treatment I ever got, and whenever I was around them, they'd give me the *'disappointment eyebrows'*." I show him what I mean, frowning hard. "I wanted to do something for me, and they couldn't handle it."

"Three months?"

I nod. "The longest three months of my life. My dad went so far as to take his name off my car lease, and I lost his corporate discount when it came to my cell phone plan. It was all shit. But I don't think they expected me to double-down and move out when I did."

Logan's eyes flare wide. "That's something to be proud of."

I nod slowly. "I did a lot of it out of spite. A giant '*screw you*' to both of them. It was pretty lonely for a while, but it's better this way."

"How is it better?"

"I can do what I want when I want. Always. That sense of freedom, I wouldn't give it up for anything," I say, looking him dead in the eye.

"Max," he says, my name coming out on a sigh. "Max, is that what this is all about? Why you ran away from me?"

I want to cover my head with the blankets, pretend we're not having this conversation. My throat tightens, and I know the next words are going to be difficult to say.

"I hate disappointing people, I hate it. I…I don't want to disappoint you, either."

"How are you going to disappoint me?" he asks gently, leaning in just that bit more so that I could reach out, skim a touch over his arm, maybe even his cheek if he'd let me.

"I work a lot, Logan. It's kind of the only thing I'm good at. I mean, look at me. I've been going stir crazy for days because I can't be productive."

"That's just a habit you need to break, not a life-long affliction."

I look at him. "And this whole thing, tempting me with your body or whatever? It's distracting."

He grins. "You're supposed to be distracted. I want you to be distracted. Why can't you rest?"

"I wasn't born with that gene, okay? Stop pushing it."

"Because you feel like a failure if you don't try to prove to everyone around you that because you're working so hard, nobody can touch you? Is that it, Max? Because it sounds lonely to me."

"Loneliness never killed anyone."

Logan smiles sadly. "I'm pretty sure you're wrong about that," he says, gently lifting his hand. I watch it move like it's some foreign object streaking across the sky, scared and elated all rolled into one. "Can I touch you?"

I nod. My eyes close at the feel of him running a hand over my head, then trailing down my hair.

"You can move closer if you want to," he says, giving me permission that I'm too scared to ask for.

I don't let guys get this close. I certainly don't intend to lay in bed with them all day unless we're doing other activities.

I slowly inch forward, until my cold nose is pressed to Logan's warm chest. He hisses at the contact, and I marvel that steam isn't wafting off our skin at the temperature change.

"Is this okay?" he asks, holding me close, but not tight enough that I feel like I can't breathe like I couldn't get away if I wanted to.

"You can hold me tighter," I tell him, grunt when he does so. Logan rolls onto his back so I'm lying down on top of him, a mishmash of blankets and two bodies as close as they're going to get.

And because Logan can't see my face, it's easier to talk, pressed close to him like this. "Thank you for even offering to come with me on Christmas Day. I know it might seem like nothing, but it means a lot to me. *A lot.*"

Logan gives me a squeeze. "Yeah, of course."

"And you don't have to pretend to be head over heels in love with me, or pretend I've got diamonds up my ass."

Logan laughs. "I thought the ground you walk on was supposed to be made of diamonds," he says, pressing his cheek against the side of my head.

This is nice. It's *really* nice. So nice in fact, that I'm scared to ruin it.

Like this whole situation can be summed up like that one time my mom put out the very best tablecloth we owned for Christmas dinner years and years ago. I, of course, dropped some gravy on it and had to get up and clean the stain while everyone else was enjoying their meals.

The embarrassment and shame are still hot embers in my chest, and the memory is enough to spark them into a full burning flame.

"It wouldn't be difficult, treating you like that, like how you want to be treated," he says easily.

I hold very still, afraid to breathe. Logan gives me another affectionate squeeze.

"Don't be scared now, Max. I'm going to give you want."

"But I don't want to take it. This isn't fair to you."

"Don't make assumptions on what I feel. You can't do that, Max, not for anyone." Logan runs a hand through my hair, soothing me. I could fall asleep again, just like this. I really, really could.

"So, what do you want, Logan?" I pull back enough to look at him, my hair blocking out the rest of the world so all we can do is look at each other.

"You know, that first night we met, I thought that you were seriously out of my league."

I smile. "It's the eyeshadow. It scares all the wannabes off."

Logan shakes his head. He slowly lifts his hand, telegraphing the movement. I hold still and shiver when he skims his fingers along the apple of my cheek.

"No, I liked everything about you, immediately. And I couldn't fucking stop talking the whole night. It was like I could hear myself from a distance, but I couldn't get myself to shut up.

"And then you smiled at something I said." He mimes an explosion going off beside his head. "You have a really great smile."

"Thanks," I murmur, my cheeks already starting to burn.

"I knew that night, even after stammering like an idiot, and even after I had to pull teeth to get you to talk to me, but when you did? Shit, Max, I knew that I wanted to marry you."

"What? That's *insane*. That's not true. No way. I wasn't even a good date."

"You treated the wait staff with respect, and you offered to pay for your meal at the end of the night. You were kind, even when I was babbling my head off. I'd get high just watching you give me the smallest of smiles."

I shake my head again, my heart beating erratically as I stare down at him.

"Logan, you couldn't have thought that you wanted to marry me that night. No way."

"Fine, I lied. It was after our third date."

I wince.

"Yeah, exactly. After you ran off, I kind of got the point."

"Sorry," I murmur.

Logan grins at me. "Why? I kind of got what I wanted in the end. I put a ring on your finger," he says. His hand rests over my ring finger, traces the ring that refuses to budge.

It defies the laws of physics, honestly.

If I believed in magic, or destiny, or whatever, I'd say there has to be a reason for a ring that doesn't want to be removed from my body. Like it's supposed to be there, for better or for worse.

Yeah, right.

"A ring which we will never mention again, based on the look on your face." Logan grins, playful and sweet.

My heart drums against my ribs, the blood pounds in my ears. I'm warm, too warm, settled on top of Logan like this.

We're close, but we're not skin to skin, not like a part of me wants to be.

Logan moves some of my hair out of my face, looping it carefully behind an ear.

"You're being very gentle with me."

Logan nods. "You don't go barreling into a Christmas tree. You move around it carefully."

I snort. "That was cheesy."

Logan smiles, his eyes crinkling closed. "Yeah, but you loved it. I can tell."

I roll my eyes. "Yeah, right."

"No, I can tell, Max. You smile at me like this when you like what I say to you." He demonstrates a lopsided grin that's been hanging around my mouth too often these past few days. I didn't know I was being that transparent.

"Well, don't let it go to your head."

"Never," he whispers. "Can I kiss you here?" He taps the middle of my forehead.

My skin's on fire, and my arms are starting to shake from holding myself up so I don't crush him to death. "This just sounds like it's me taking from you, again, Logan."

He leans back, giving me time to think. One hand is still absently petting my hair, and it's going to seriously put me to sleep.

My heart beats hard in my chest like I've gone and sprinted up fourteen flights of stairs.

"You've done a lot around here," I say. "It hasn't been terrible living with you these past few days. You're also exceptionally good at making breakfast in a pot."

Logan smiles, his hands trailing down onto my shoulders, down my arms. "Tell me more."

I lick my lips. "You...you take care of me, in the smallest ways. I didn't realize what you were doing, actually, but you have been. Ever since you got here."

Logan nods but keeps his silence.

"And despite the fact that you like walking around my apartment half-naked, you're shy."

Logan groans. "I thought I was hiding it so well."

"And you like fighting with me, even if we're fighting over dumb shit."

Logan pulls his hands back, palms out, caught red-handed.

"You think I'm beautiful, even without all of my makeup on." Logan smiles, nods for me to keep going. "You like that I work hard, and you like that I was able to rest and do things that contribute nothing to the growth of my business."

"Not in so many words," he says, "but yes." He traces the skin along my jaw, the feeling almost ticklish.

"And even though we're married, we're still kind of dating, we're still kind of trying to figure each other out." I lean down, lay my lips against my forehead in a ghost of a kiss.

Logan gasps underneath me, tensing like he's ready to spring.

I lean back. "Was that okay? I guess I should have asked first."

"Fine, it's fine," he rasps, voice cracking. "Do it again."

I snort but oblige him. "Better?"

Logan nods enthusiastically, and my heart flips in my chest. I think I could get used to this, even if I think I'm going to ruin it.

"On Christmas," Logan starts. "How affectionate should I be?"

It jolts me back to the feeling that I'm using him for what I want. I lean up a little more, my arms shaking with the effort.

"Oh, yeah, we need to discuss that. I don't want you to be uncomfortable. Honestly, though, if you have the urge to push me up against the wall and kiss me breathless, I don't think you should fight the feeling."

Logan chokes on air. He coughs hard enough that I'm jostled. I sit fully upright, over his abs as I watch him catch his breath.

"*Max,*" he groans, clenching his jaw tight. "You can't say things like that to me."

"Look, if we're both going to be miserable on that day, we might as well have some fun with it. That's all I'm saying."

I glance down at his exposed skin, my fingers sitting on top of his eight pack. I fight not to move, not to touch without permission.

Logan stares at me, breathless. "Can I kiss you, Max? Please?"

This might be the point in time when I look back and realize that I should've kept my silence. This might be the moment that I'll maybe say where it all went wrong.

But I'm tired of thinking ahead, of trying to be what everybody wants me to be no matter how I fall short of their expectations.

I just want to be Max.

Pretend I'm Logan's wife, for like, *a second*.

Would that be so bad?

"Yes. You can kiss me. *Please.*"

FIFTEEN

Logan stares at me as if he misheard me. He shakes himself, then leans up on his elbows. The movement makes his abs contract, which I *very* much appreciate.

"Are you sure?"

I nod quickly. "I am. Please?" I tilt my head at him, trying to look inviting.

Logan sits up by doing an ab crunch, and I get plunked directly into his lap.

His eyes rove over my face, searching. He gently palms my face, my burning cheeks up against his burning palms. He moves forward inexorably slow to the point where I'm holding my breath, waiting.

My skin tingles all over as Logan moves steadily closer. The hands on my face are infinitely gentle, careful. I still feel like I might just fall apart, that Logan holding me like this is the only thing that's keeping me together.

"Max," he whispers before I get him where I want him.

"Mmm?"

"Don't run away from me this time, okay?"

I close my eyes, waiting for him to kiss me. "Okay."

I've kissed Logan before, those few perfunctory, hungry kisses that were a prelude to sex. The kind of kisses that are rushed, a throwaway of contact, and definitely not the main event.

This kiss is different.

My heart leaps, and my blood sizzles in my veins. I shiver as Logan's lips finally meet mine, nothing but a steadily increasing pressure, at first.

He murmurs my name against my mouth, his lips drinking me in. Logan gently kisses my bottom lip, licking at the swell of it, then pays attention to my top lip.

The way he's being almost methodical in kissing every part of my mouth has me wanting more.

"Okay?" he asks, pulling back for a second.

"Kiss me harder, Logan, *please*," I say, my voice notching high in an almost-whine. I'm acutely aware of every point of contact where our bodies meet, and it's not enough, but it's also too much.

"Logan, come on. Kiss me like you mean it." His hands are still on my face, keeping me in my spot. His dark eyes stay focused on my mouth, but I don't know if he's heard me.

He gives me a wicked grin. My belly swoops, the kind that feels like I've taken my first step out into the dark.

"Only if you do the same. No holding back. No running away."

Honestly, right now, I'll beg if I have to. I'll beg him to kiss me, I'll tell him anything he wants. Anything.

"Kiss me, Logan. *Kiss me.*"

Logan presses his smile right up against my mouth, but I don't get a second to enjoy the moment. His tongue sweeps across the seam of my mouth, delving in deeper until he's tasting me.

Our tongues carefully tangle together, our mouths the hottest point in my entire apartment. My body throbs with the need to touch, to be touched.

We kiss like we fight, a careful parry of back and forth until my emotions get out of control.

I push Logan back down onto the mattress, straddling him.

I kiss him with everything I have, determined to make him as breathless as I feel. It's hot between our mouths and cold everywhere else.

Logan rolls us so that I'm on my back, caged between his arms. He kisses me deep, my hands stroking along the skin of his back, clutching at his defined muscles.

I want so much more, but that would be a terrible idea.

Terrible.

"Logan, Logan," I pant, pushing at his shoulders. He immediately rolls off me, flopping onto his back to stare at the ceiling. We're both panting like we've sprinted a mile.

I turn to look at him, find him already looking at me.

"Are you okay?" he asks.

"Yeah. You?"

Logan nods. "I didn't hurt you?"

"No, no. We just...we need to stop right now. I need to cool down."

"Yeah, of course, Max," he says.

I stare at him, suspicious. I half-expect him to make me feel like shit for putting on the brakes, but he just doesn't.

"Are you hungry yet? I can get started on breakfast," he asks instead.

I could be offended that I'm the one more affected than him, but Logan's very careful about putting the wad of blankets in front of his lap for one sole reason.

I can't stop smiling. "Pancakes?"

"I can make pancakes, sure."

"And then we spend all day long in bed, reading? Or, I might have some battery pack juice left maybe for my tablet. We could watch some of my movie downloads."

"What kind of movies does Maxima really enjoy?" Logan muses to himself, getting to his feet, still holding onto the blanket in front of his crotch.

"I'm sorry about that," I say, jutting my chin in the direction of the wadded-up blankets.

"You have nothing to apologize for. This is a me problem, not yours."

I glance away, strangely moved at how easy Logan just seems to defuse the situation.

"Okay, then. I'll help you with breakfast as soon as I can," I say. I move off the mattress, and head into my freezing cold bedroom and into my bathroom.

I boil myself under the hot water, and quickly wash my hair, racing against an imaginary timer in case all the hot water runs out in the building.

I grab my charging cord and the power bank I've been using for my phone. I doubt I'll get one more full charge, but it's still worth a shot.

I grab my tablet and my second-best power bank and charging cord and bring it into the living room, plopping my treasure on the mattress.

Logan comes out of the bathroom, fully dressed, down to the orange fuzzy socks of mine that he's stretched out with his huge feet.

He smiles at me, a dusting of pink on his cheeks like I've applied the faintest hint of blush there.

Breakfast is awkward, or maybe *I'm* awkward. I steal glances of Logan out of the corner of my eye.

"These pancakes are really good," I say. "Really good. And to think I would have missed out..." I trail off, realizing how that sounds.

Logan freezes mid-chew, turns to look at me.

Panicking, I point to the corner of my mouth, then decide to go for it. I lean forward, licking at the bit of maple syrup that's tucked into the corner of his lips. Logan kisses me back like he's helpless to stop himself.

"There," I whisper as I pull back. "Kind of weird that I get to do that now."

Logan's eyes flutter open like he's waking up from the best kind of dream. I watch him lick his lips and gulp hard.

"Yeah, you get to do that whenever you want."

I laugh. "Finish your breakfast. We can watch a movie after you're done."

I do the dishes because Logan made us pancakes. Out of the corner of my eye, I see Logan arranging and then rearranging the blankets on my mattress. He even looks around the living room, his hands on his hips.

"Can I get some more pillows?" he asks.

Once the dishes are done, and the pillows have been arranged into a tower that we can both comfortably sit on, Logan opens the blankets, inviting me in.

I snuggle down into the covers, Logan close enough to me that I know I'm going to tear off my hoodie sooner than later.

We spend the next couple of hours in bed, watching *Die Hard* on my tablet, my favorite Christmas movie. The hours go by reading books until it gets too dark, always close to one another on my bed.

When I light the candles around the living room as the light of the day starts to fade away, Logan's already napping, the book splayed on his chest, his hands still clutching it.

I get back into bed after a quick bathroom break. It doesn't take long for me to start nodding off.

The Wedding night...

"I don't think I've ever talked with someone so much," I say, voice going hoarse.

Logan laughs, running his thumb over the back of my knuckles. "I don't know if that's a good thing or a bad thing."

I tilt my head. "I'm thinking it's a pretty good thing, right now." I smile.

Logan ducks his head, rubs the back of his neck with his free hand. "Uh, shit, I'm glad to hear it."

"I bet. So what do you want to do now? The sun will be up soon. I can't believe I stayed up all night."

Logan fights back a yawn, hides his face in the crook of his elbow until it disappears. He lifts his head. "Is it just me or does everything feel like it's right?"

My heart's being squeezed by an invisible fist. "I don't know," I say. "This has never happened to me before."

"Me, neither," Logan murmurs.

He strokes his thumb over the back of my hand, hot like a brand. Our plates are eventually picked up by the wait staff, but all I can do is stare at Logan.

"What?"

"I shouldn't have left that night. I should have stayed, and you should have made me pancakes. We would have talked that morning if I did."

Logan grins. "I still got to be here, though, so I'm not too upset." He brings my hand up to place a kiss on my knuckles.

I'm about to melt through the vinyl booth.

"I'm happy you came out tonight," I tell him, watching Logan duck his head again, suddenly too shy in front of me. It makes my heart sing, makes the world seem all the brighter because I made him bashful.

He coughs, clears his throat, but the blush is still there. My heart's suddenly two sizes too big for my rib cage. "It would have been nice. I'm a cuddler."

"Yeah? Then I'm really sorry I missed out on that. I would like to be cuddled."

Loga excuses himself and lets go of my hand. He twists his body until he's holding his phone, his eyes going flat and cold when he looks at the screen. "Sorry, Max, give me a second."

I nod, but he's already turning away.

I finish up my coffee, take a quick bathroom break. By the time I come back to the booth, Logan still hasn't shown up.

I play with my own phone, wondering if I should message Vick and Amber and let them know what's happened, let them know what I'm feeling, maybe for the first time in my life.

I mean, I told them he was a jerk during those first few dates, only because I was the one being a rude date. Can't really blame the guy for trying to talk to a brick wall, and the brick wall doesn't answer back. I get it.

"Sorry," Logan apologizes again, bringing a waft of cold air with him as he takes his seat again opposite me.

"Everything all right?"

Logan shakes his head. "It will be, eventually. But we were discussing further plans for tonight."

I glance out the large window, trying to see through the glare of my reflection. "We could go back to my place to sleep. I could attempt to make you pancakes when I wake back up."

"Or we could climb up the mountain to watch the sunrise," Logan suggests.

It sounds pretty romantic. I don't think I've ever shared a sunset or a sunrise with someone. It's that type of scene in a movie that I always wanted to be a part of.

Now I can be.

This shit never happens to me in real life and it's happening in the space of one night alone.

That's because you were always looking for something different, Max. You were always looking for someone different.

You weren't looking for a guy like Logan, couldn't see yourself with a guy like Logan.

And there he is, sitting right across from you, asking to share a sunrise with you.

"Yeah, that sounds lovely," I say, throat tight. "That sounds great."

·♥·♥·♥·♥·♥·

"Max? Max? I'm sorry, but I have to go use the bathroom," Logan whispers in my ear, pressing kisses to the top of my head.

I'm far too comfortable to move, but the kisses feel nice, and Logan's so warm and perfectly wrapped around me.

"Sweetheart, please?" Logan begs, and I grunt in annoyance before rolling off him.

"I was having a good dream," I mumble as I move to my side of the bed like I have a side like we're an *actual* married couple.

"Then go back to dreaming, okay? I'll be right back."

It's no use, though, I'm awake, left to stare at the ceiling and replay what memories I have of my so-called wedding night.

I glance over to the closed bathroom door, wondering how what I've remembered led me to the conclusion to say *yes* to a very important question.

What is it about Logan that made me want to do this?

I hold up my left hand, twisting it around until it catches the candlelight, throwing sparks of glittery fire. It's beautiful, simple, and understated as I don't tend to dress or be on a regular basis. I love it because it doesn't really fit in with my aesthetic; I love the contrast, the highs, and lows.

That's what life – and marriage, I'm guessing – is all about anyway.

The ups and downs and in between, the contrasts between every single one of those stages.

I pull and tug on the ring, hiss when I tug on a particularly sensitive piece of skin on my ring finger. It throbs gently, a constant reminder that the ring is still there, practically fused to my skin.

Logan plops back down on the mattress after he's done his business, smelling like apple orchard soap. I hold back one more yawn, my stomach growling.

How long did we sleep? I've lost all sense of time, I swear.

Logan pulls me close, making me squeak in alarm, but when he moves to put me at arm's length, I'm not having it.

"Oh, no. Absolutely not. You're the one with all the body heat in this house. Come closer or perish."

Logan snickers, and holds me tight against his chest, our legs tangled together.

"Tell me something that no one else knows," Logan prompts, and I lean back to stare at his face.

"Shouldn't you be the one answering that question? I feel like all I've done is talk and talk and talk."

Logan kisses my forehead again with a happy sigh. I sort of want to drown him in kisses for doing that, but I restrain myself. Barely.

"I like listening to everything you have to say."

I snort. "I guess because I hardly talked on our dates, you're taking full advantage now, huh?"

"You got me. But, that doesn't give you a free pass. Tell me something that no one else knows."

I deliberate, then laugh to myself. "So, uh, I used to write a lot of self-insert fanfic for my favorite romance novels."

"No," Logan breathes, pushing on my shoulders so he can get a good look at me. "Is it published anywhere? Can I read it?"

"Absolutely not. No one knows. Not even my cousins. And it's not published anywhere no. I've got hidden on an external hard drive somewhere under a very innocuous folder name. You'll never find it."

Mischief glints in Logan's eyes. "Is that a challenge?" I shake my head, and Logan snuggles me close again. A girl could get used to this. *I'm the girl, it's me.*

"Can I get to read some of this fanfic one day?" Logan asks.

"I don't know. If you decide to stick around, maybe. We might even try some of those scenes out together," I say with a grin.

"Max," Logan groans, and I laugh. I don't want to name this bubbly feeling inside of me, I don't want to call it something it's not.

"I'm going to have to take a cold fucking shower. Shit."

"What about you?"

Logan frowns at me as I sit up, planting my elbow on the bed, head in my palm. I watch him deliberate, my heart going haywire against my ribs. He's doing nothing but lying next to me and I'm having heart palpitations.

What is this?

Logan shakes his head, runs a hand over his eyes, hiding from view.

"I secretly stole an axolotl from a pet shop once and sold it to a friend back in university. Nobody knows I did that."

"What's an axolotl?" I butcher the word through and through.

"'What's an axolotl?' Max, they're only tiny little cute sea dragons that don't have eyelids. Come on." Logan fishes for his phone in his sweatpants, tugs it out.

I can see from my close vantage point that he has a text notification. I close my eyes to give him some privacy.

"Shit," he hisses, and I quickly scramble away from him, giving him the space to move.

"What's wrong?"

"This not having service really fucking sucks," he growls, glaring down at his phone. He shoves it back into his pocket and looks at me.

"Do you want to be alone right now?"

Logan shakes his head, carefully lies back down on his side.

"You want to go to bed?" I ask to confirm. When Logan nods, I get to my feet to head to my en suite and take care of my night routine. That done, I come back out to the living room and blow out all the candles.

In the darkest dark, I try to find my way back to my mattress. I scream when hands grab me by the waist, my galloping heart not knowing the difference between Logan and some kind of otherworldly creature that lives in the shadows alone.

"Jesus Christ, *don't do that*," I hiss, squirming to get away.

"Max," Logan calls, nuzzling against my cheek. "Haven't you started to remember yet? Please?" He checks in, and then rolls on top of me, practically pinning me in place.

"I'm trying," I whisper. "I really am."

"Please, sweetheart," he says against my mouth. "Please try harder. For me. For the both of us."

It takes a long time for me to fall asleep.

SIXTEEN

The wedding night...

"I've never actually stopped to watch a sunrise before," I say. Logan has his arm slung over my chest, my back up against his front.

"If you get too cold, let me know."

"Ah, we can stay here a little longer. It's a beautiful view."

Logan hums and then starts rocking us from side to side. Our breaths plume pale violet in the morning air, and the cold nips at my legs until I start to lose feeling in them.

I don't want to move yet. I'm practically in a movie scene, and I don't want the director to call out '*cut*!'.

"Max," Logan calls, and I pat his arm to let him know I'm listening. "This has been one of the greatest nights of my life."

I snort, turn my head to look at him. "Yeah, right. All we did was talk, though."

Logan gently turns me so that we're facing each other. Now with the sun coming up, I wonder if the spell we've been under all night long is going to be lifted if I'm going to have to go back to reality.

If I ever needed some Christmas magic, *now* is the time.

Because I may not love Logan, but I could see myself falling in love with him, little by little until I was head over heels and wondering how it all happened.

"Like you said, I haven't spoken so much to one person in a long time."

I nod, throat tightening up for some reason. I talk to my cousins all the time, but they know me, or they know a version of me that I let them see. He may not know *all* of me, but he knows more than any guy I've ever met, and that's something.

This? This is different.

"I know this is crazy. I know, but I'm going to give it a shot anyway," he says, licking his lips nervously.

My stomach pitches left then right.

"Maxima, will you marry me?"

I sputter, choke on my own damn saliva. I whirl around to look at him. "What? What?! Logan, you can't just ask that question after four dates."

He tilts his head with a smile that *does* things to my weak heart. "I thought we said it was five dates."

"Whatever. You don't just ask me that when we barely know each other." I stay still, enjoying the way he holds me way too much. "Logan, can't you see how crazy this is?"

"Why? My dad asked my mom to marry him after one date."

I raise an eyebrow, totally not buying it. "And? Did she say yes?"

"Nope. She strung him along for a year before she finally said yes. He asked her after every single date, up until the last one."

I smile. "That's sweet. But that's not going to work on me."

"Why not?"

"Because...because I'm not the marrying type." I wave a hand in front of my face to indicate *all of me*.

"Jesus, Max, what does that even mean?"

How do I begin to tell him? "I work a lot, all the time. I'm hardly good at taking care of myself without a huge to-do list where I put too many things on it, and inevitably never get to it all. I avoid my family like the plague when I need to, but my cousins are my best friends. I like going out to have fun, pick up a guy, and then go back to my place. I don't want to deal with Christmas alone. Am I painting you a picture?"

Logan shakes his head. I clench my jaw. "You're trying to make me run away this time. I'm not going to do it."

"Marriage is supposed to be for life. I don't know if I'm going to be *this* person for the rest of my life. We don't know that, Logan."

Logan smirks, dips down to kiss my forehead. "Then I'll be married to all the different versions of you that I happen to meet over time."

"You can't be serious," I gape at him. "Why do you want to marry me? And why all of a sudden? This doesn't make any sense."

"People have gotten married for less. People settle for one another all the time, even when they're unhappy."

"Well, what if I make you unhappy?"

"We'll work on it, together."

"This feels a little like signing a contract in blood."

Logan laughs, kisses my forehead again. I bet he knows how much I like it since he keeps doing it. I'm weak in the face of forehead kisses. "I'm only asking the question. You have to decide whether you say yes or not."

"Right. Was this some elaborate ruse from the beginning? Is that why you showed up tonight?"

Logan shakes his head, squeezes my shoulders affectionately. "When life presents you with a second chance, you have to take it, whatever the outcome, right?"

I shrug. "I don't know. I haven't gotten a lot of second chances in my life. Look, I don't know what you want me to say. We're out here, on the mountain. I've just had the best date of my life, and now you want to marry me? Based on what? On this version of me?" I point down to my clothes hidden underneath my coat. "Logan, you're not going to get this shiny version of me all the time. Honestly, I practically live in sweatpants when I'm working."

Logan smiles, but it makes me all that much more stubborn.

"What about you? I don't know much of anything about you. Honestly, who asks someone to marry them after such a short amount of time?"

"I just did," Logan says, his smile warming me right through. Unfortunately, he has such a nice smile. It's unfortunate that I'm already finding myself wanting to make him smile at me like that *always*.

"Yeah, but Logan, this is real life. We can't get married just like that."

"Why not?"

"I just told you why. But most of all, I'm not the marrying type. I don't know if I can make you happy."

Logan pulls me close into a loose hug that I find myself returning, squeezing along his ribs. "You're not supposed to *make* me happy, Max. It's supposed to happen whenever I'm with you. You're supposed to make the day better simply by being who you are."

"Yeah, well, you haven't seen me at my worst," I mumble against his chest and sniff against the cold.

"You forget that you can be very intimidating, sitting across from me and not saying a word at all. As for me, what else do you need to know?"

"Logan, you can't force a marriage together. I mean, shit, we just decided to really start dating. Isn't the usual timeline for this kind of thing at least a year? Aren't we supposed to try living together first? Who knows? Maybe you leave your dirty laundry everywhere, and I'll end up throttling you in your sleep."

Logan laughs, his chest rumbling with it. I feel it through our hug.

"I don't, for the record."

I lean back to look at him. "You're really serious, aren't you?"

"Yeah. I am."

"You've officially lost the plot."

He grins at me, and ducks down to kiss my cheek. It shouldn't affect me as much as it does, but apparently, I'm that person now, flustered by getting kisses from the guy I'm dating.

Who even am I?

I don't even know anymore.

"What's really stopping you from saying yes?"

"Other than knowing not that much about you?"

Logan tilts his head to the side in a nod. "Other than that."

"How about we don't know so many things about each other that this is bound to end in disaster?"

"No one knows anyone a hundred percent. Do you agree?"

I roll my eyes. "I'm not talking about philosophically, Logan. I'm talking about real-life stuff. I've seen you for three nights and then this practically never-ending one. I've never even seen you angry. Or sad. Knowing how you'll react is important."

Logan snuggles me closer, fighting the cold with our combined body heat – well, whatever is left of it through our winter coats. "My mom, she's very sick," he says, the words come out barely on a whisper, barely existing by themselves.

I hold my breath and keep myself very still.

"I'm sad every single day, Max. You've seen me sad."

"I'm sorry that she's sick, Logan. Fuck, I'm really sorry." Jesus, and he's listened to me complain about my parents when his mom's ill. I'm an asshole.

"There's nothing to apologize for. It just is. The point I'm trying to make is that you've seen all these sides to me, even if you didn't know they were there."

"Don't expect me to reciprocate. I'm a raging asshole when I'm angry or upset. Just giving you a head's up."

Logan holds me closer and whispers in my ear, "So what's the real reason you don't want to marry me? Is it because of what you think, or what others might think?"

Well, shit. I didn't expect him to pick that up this quickly.

"I can't believe you want to marry me. This is crazy."

Logan rocks us from side to side again, until we move in a full circle, dancing.

"Crazy enough not to go through with it?"

I've never made rash decisions in my life. I've carefully contemplated and made projections on which direction my life is supposed to head in. I may not have followed conventional wisdom or the safest of choices. I've struck out on my own because of sheer stubbornness, but that doesn't mean the decision was rash.

I knew I could support myself with my channel.

This though?

If this doesn't work out, it's not like I can deal with just calling it quits. I don't do well with failure.

"If I say no, will you never ask me the question again? If we're still together a year from now?"

"I'll keep asking you until you say yes, Max."

I frown at him. "That's going to get really annoying for you, Logan."

"I don't mind. I know you're worth it."

I want to ask a ton of questions – *how* does he know I'm worth it, and how can I see it, too? Do we both have to stare at my reflection together and make myself listen to what he has to say until I believe it?

God, none of this makes any kind of sense.

My heart shrivels in my chest. "I don't think this is a good idea," I say, needing him to know the truth. "We could end up divorced before this year is over."

"That doesn't scare me. I still want to marry you."

"You really see yourself spending the rest of your life with me?"

Logan ducks down enough so that we're both eye to eye, his forehead pressed to mine. "I've been looking for you for a long time, Max. Now that I've found you, I'm not letting you run away again."

"Jesus, you're never going to let me live that down, huh?"

Logan smiles. This close, it's utterly dazzling, more beautiful than the sunrise we're supposed to be watching.

"Maxima, will you marry me?"

Ah, shit. I pull in a deep breath of cold air, searing my lungs. I question again why I live in a place where the air hurts my face and can freeze my lungs with a single breath.

Logan Porter, my husband? Shit, it doesn't even *sound* bad. My blood has fireworks in it, and my head is buzzing. I pull in a deep breath, and then another. Logan waits for me, breathes with me.

And that's ultimately what decides me.

He'll wait as long as I need him to. So why not now if it's going to be *yes* later?

"Yeah, okay. I'll marry you, Logan."

I jolt awake, a heavy weight settled on my back so that I have become one with my mattress. I don't mind it. It's warm and cozy if a little heavy. Okay, scratch that, it's pretty difficult to breathe.

Logan rolls away though before I can start throwing elbows, and I'm able to flop onto my back and stare at the dark ceiling.

It's still dark outside, and I can still hear the freezing rain making contact with the living room windows. I can't tell if it's morning, mid-afternoon, or if I slept the whole day away and we've come back around to evening.

My phone tells me that it's morning, on day 5 (or is it 6) of being snowed in with Logan.

I finally remembered what I was supposed to remember, and I'm...*underwhelmed*. I thought there was going to be a sweeping moment somewhere during that long night that turned into morning where I would be a thousand percent certain about my decision. Like there was going to be butterflies coming out in the middle of winter to fly all around us in some sort of mystical sign that would let me know I'd chosen right.

Where I would feel a hundred percent about marrying Logan, just like that.

I've seen too many movies.

I still don't know what I was thinking, even if I knew what I was feeling.

On some perverse level in my brain, I was thinking that maybe if I were married, my parents would deign to treat me like a whole person, instead of someone walking around with half of themselves missing.

Guilt burns hot in my chest, making me rub at the ache. It doesn't go away. It stays there, heavy like a lead weight, making it hard to breathe.

So I've been using Logan since the very beginning.

I turn to look at Logan, watch his back, the way it moves with every single breath he takes.

His mom is ill. Maybe you both are using each other, huh?

I head to my en suite for a bathroom break and some much-needed alone time. I can't lie and say that I haven't slept better with Logan at my side. I have.

I don't know what I would have done without him these past few days. I think I would have gone stir crazy living by myself, with nothing but these four walls to talk to.

I probably wouldn't have eaten as much as I have, and I probably wouldn't have been thinking in survivalist mode if Logan wasn't here.

I head back to the living room, after my shower and change into a fresh pair of sweats for the top and the bottom. My hair's still wet, the towel not doing much to pull out any more of the moisture.

When I lie back down beside Logan and close my eyes, I get odd flashes of memory, quick glimpses of my wedding night.

Of getting drunk enough to drown the guilt of marrying Logan, of kissing him once the Justice of the Peace proclaimed us husband and wife. I see myself as a character in a play, looking happy, but knowing that my feelings weren't where I needed them to be to feel good about the decision I made. I see myself looking down at my ring, marveling at how it perfectly fits there like it was always supposed to.

And Logan.

Logan looked so happy that the hot guilt caught fire in my chest, burning up my throat, making me want to cry.

Now that I remember everything, I wish I didn't.

Logan turns onto his back, stretches his arms above his head. He *groans*, deep and guttural, reminding me of that one night we shared.

I hold still, slam my eyes shut. If he looks at me, he'll *know* that I remember, he just *will*.

"Max?" he calls, but I don't answer. "Oh," he whispers to himself. "Still sleeping."

The mattress moves as he leaves it, then moves again when he snuggles underneath the blankets. Judging by the page-flipping sounds, he's gotten himself another book from my shelves.

I want to tell him it's probably bad for his eyes since the lighting is so shit in here, but that would require me talking, and I don't want to do that.

Maybe ever again. Then Logan will never be able to tell that I remember our wedding night very differently than the picture he painted for me.

Shit, shit, *shit*.

I keep my eyes closed, fighting for sleep to come back and render me unconscious.

Of course, that's not how it works, not when I need it the most.

I turn my head to find Logan reading, his nose buried in the book that I can't even see his face. I gently place a finger on the novel and push it down, slowly revealing Logan's face.

"Good morning," I murmur, his dark eyes filled with warmth when we make eye contact. "What do you want for breakfast?" I ask, determined to even out the scales. He's been doing so much for me because he's *sure* of me. How could I have gone and married a guy I wasn't sure of?

Which demon fucking possessed me and made me do it?

Maybe it was old Saint Nick, huh?

I deserve a thousand pounds of coal for Christmas.

SEVENTEEN

On the seventh day with no power, the water stops working. The only good news is that the freezing rain has stopped, but the temperature has cooled and the world is covered in a sheet of ice.

I look around worriedly, my stomach twisting into knots. “Logan, we’re in trouble. Water, there’s no more water.”

Logan waves a hand towards the pots where I’ve been keeping some water, the stuff we’ve stockpiled for a few days now.

“We’ll be okay. And if not, we’ll find a shelter to go to.”

I glance around my apartment, feeling a pang of loss even if I’m still right here. “This is my home,” I croak, crossing my arms over my chest.

Logan opens his arms slowly, a silent invitation to move towards him and accept what he’s offering. I take one hesitant step forward and then another and another, until I’m in his arms, letting him hold me up.

It’s nice, *really* nice.

I like how he has answers, I like that I don't have to think it through myself, that I can give him a part of the puzzle to figure it out instead of me going all *lone wolf.*

It could be like this for as long as you want it, Max. As long as you can stand it.

Guilt floods my throat, and I want to tell him, I want to tell him what I have remembered. I want to tell him that I'm terribly sorry for using him the way I am, the way I've been because I basically said yes so I could feel comfortable on Christmas Day.

I didn't think I was that desperate, but apparently, I am.

"We'll be all right, Max. We will be."

"I don't really want to leave here," I say. "I feel safe here." *I feel safe here with you, Logan.*

"I know, I know you do. But if we have to leave, then we have to leave. The forecast says it should be warming up tomorrow, so hopefully we'll get power back soon."

"You're just saying that to make me feel better. You don't know, either."

"No, I don't know," he says, pressing his cheek to the top of my head. "But I know that we're luckier than most. We have a roof over our heads, and enough food to last a few more days before we really start skimping. We have water, too. We're lucky, Max. Besides, you're in really good company."

I snort. "I think I want to go back to bed."

"Then we can go back to bed. What do you want to read?" he asks, holding onto my hand and tugging me to my mattress. I snuggle underneath the covers, and Logan pulls me close until we're facing each other, a book between us.

I can't see Logan's face, but it doesn't matter. As he starts to read to me, his voice soothing and the perfect pitch that I find myself relaxing. I let my brain fill in the picture of what he's describing to me.

It doesn't take long for me to go back to sleep from being warm and snuggled close to Logan.

"Are you paying attention?" Logan asks, his voice floating to me as if from a great distance, even though I know he's right next to me.

I don't open my eyes – when did they close? – but Logan's chuckle is just as nice listening to it without seeing it.

"I'm not here," I mumble, seeking out more sleep so I don't have to deal with the fact that we could run out of water, that we would both have to leave the relative safety of my apartment for a shelter.

"Do you want me to keep going?" he asks, absentmindedly stroking my arm up and down. He's always soothing me when it should be the other way around.

You have to fix this, Max. You have to so it's fair.

I hum. "Yeah, you have a nice voice."

"Uh, well, we're coming up to the first...uh...intimate scene."

I open my eyes and force Logan to lower the book so I can see his face. "Intimate scene?" I squint at him. "Logan, are you blushing? Really?"

"I'm not blushing," he murmurs but hides behind the book anyway.

My muscles tense up, and the question comes out of me like I've been sucker-punched. "Logan, *Logan*, can I kiss you?"

Logan lowers the book again so I can see his pink face. "Right now?"

I scoff. "Of course right now. You're being cute."

Logan laughs and licks his lips. "How the hell am I doing that? I didn't mean to."

I snuggle closer and run my hand along the collar of his shirt. "You know, one second you look about ready to seduce me with a whole bunch of skin on display, and then other times you're so shy."

Logan's cheeks go even pinker. I move my hand to touch the warmth there, smile when Logan turns his head to kiss my palm.

I about melt right through the mattress.

"I'm sorry."

I shake my head. "There's nothing to apologize for. I kind of like it, you being all shy. I like it when you feel confident. I like it all. I like *you*, Logan."

Logan closes his eyes, tries curling in on himself, but he forgets that I'm right there. He somehow rolls the two of us until I'm on my back with Logan lying down on top of me. He groans in the crook of my neck, his cheeks burning against my face.

I've never been this close with someone before other than the times I was having sex. I've never really had this closeness, and it's really...nice.

"Do you remember, Max? Do you remember it all?"

My heart drums faster and I hold Logan more tightly, keeping him close like he's about to slip away through my fingers.

Guilt burns hot in the pit of my stomach and tries to flood up my throat. I swallow it down. "Not all of it yet," I say. Logan leans out of my neck to look down at me, his eyes roving over my face. "I remember some of the night when I met up with you at the bar. And when we went to go get hot dogs, but that's it so far."

I'm not lying, not completely.

Logan's mouth is thin, and he clenches his jaw hard enough that I swear I can hear his teeth grind. "Yeah?"

I nod, squirming underneath his stare. "I'm trying hard to remember what happened, Logan. I am."

Look at me, lying my ass off. It's a Christmas miracle!

He nods, and rolls off me, giving me my space. "Should I continue reading or do want to get up and have something to eat?"

I shake my head, suddenly feeling cold. "No, no. I'll read something on my own." I frown at the book obscuring his face again and wonder what the hell just happened.

What did I say? Was it something I *didn't* say?

I hide under the covers, shivering a little at the temperature change. Now that I've known what it's like to share Logan's body heat with him, going back to having to fend for myself sucks.

When we do talk it's stilted and forced, like we've run out of topics to discuss like after a whole six days, we've forgotten how to speak to each other about anything.

"You're supposed to be my husband," I say, practically jabbing my fork at him.

We're both huddled at the kitchen island, trying to scarf down our rice for supper that's flavored with soy sauce and rice vinegar. It's tasty, but it's just rice.

I mean, I think I would commit a crime for a hamburger with a side of sweet potato fries right now.

I'm definitely not cut out for this end of the world shit. Definitely not.

Logan glances over, his eyebrows practically high fiving his hairline.

I keep jabbing the air with my fork. "You're supposed to be my husband."

"Max, you don't even know what that means," he says, turning his attention back to his rice. Just like that, I've been dismissed.

"What is up your ass today? Has this shitty survivalist lifestyle finally gotten to you?"

Logan sighs, deflating. "Nothing, Max. Nothing's wrong."

I keep pushing. "What is it that you want me to remember so badly, huh? What?" I snap. My heart beats triple time, and my dinner is sitting in my stomach like I've swallowed a block of lead.

"We both...went into this with our eyes wide open."

I nod, because yeah, from what I remember, that's the truth. Except it feels like Logan's keeping something from me, still. I don't know if I want to know what it is.

"And it's really not fair to talk about any of this until you get all of your memory back of that night."

I squint at him. Go back to my rice. We're both avoiding talking about this, and honestly, we might have more important things to discuss.

"We have food for two more days, tops," I say, eating up the last of my supper. It's not enough, not nearly enough, but enough to sate my hunger for now. I should be grateful that I have food at all, but all I'm focusing on lately is what I can't have, what I *don't* have, and that's not right either.

"I know, Max."

"And we only have enough water for two more days after that, according to my calculator," I say to my empty bowl.

"I know, Max."

"So we should stop being jerks to each other and figure this out."

He turns to look at me, ignoring his food. He's eating more slowly than I ate mine, he's showing the kind of restraint that I usually have.

I think and think and calculate the odds until I'm ready to take that step forward on a single journey. I plan accordingly for disaster, but this? I never saw Logan Porter coming in the middle of a storm where we'd have to live together for days.

I didn't see *any* of this coming.

"I'll wash up," he offers, scraping back the stool and rounding the island to head to the sink. "Go ahead and get ready for bed."

It's such a freaking boyfriend, or hell, a *husband* thing to say.

I do my nighttime routine and then stand around the living room, waiting for Logan to finish up, but he's still in the bathroom.

I dive under the covers when the door opens, and I quickly try to hide my face.

I watch Logan walk around the living room, blowing out the candles until the room smells like wax and smoke, and the dying scent of hot chocolate and peppermint sugar cookies.

When Logan crawls into bed, it's to sleep with a space between the two of us, and boy, do I feel every lonely inch.

"What happened today?" I ask, staring at the ceiling.

It's dark enough that I have to strain my eyes to make out where everything is, and I feel safer talking like this. My heart drums in my chest, and my palms clutch the covers tightly.

Logan doesn't answer for a time, but I'm prepared to wait him out.

"I have something to tell you, but I'm afraid you're going to hate me."

I keep still and keep staring up at the ceiling. "Did you hurt me the night that I can't remember?"

Logan hisses, like the thought alone makes him sick. "No, Max. Of course not. I would never do that."

"So what's so terrible that you can't say it out loud? Do you have a criminal record I don't know about?" I ask, delighted to hear his surprised laugh.

"No. I led a pretty boring life until you came into it."

I slap a hand over one cheek, determined to hide my blush even in the dark.

The rustle of sheets and blankets is the only thing that alerts me to the fact that Logan has turned towards me. I look over, trying to discern where his eyes are, the shape of his silhouette.

"I doubt that."

"I'm being serious. Ever since meeting you, my life's been turned upside down, Max."

"Yeah, well...I'm sorry."

Logan snorts. "I'm not. That's why it's so hard to tell you what I need to."

I gulp. "Okay, then tell me. I'm listening."

"When I proposed, a part of me meant it through and through," he says in a whisper.

"That means that there was a part of you that didn't mean it, Logan." My heart beats erratically, and a flash of heat sizzles my skin from head to toe. I kick off the covers to get some respite in the cool air.

"I know. And I'm sorry."

"Okay, that doesn't change anything, though. Not really."

"Of course it does. I'm a piece of shit for even asking when I didn't mean it a hundred percent."

I laugh a little, but it sounds brittle, even to me. I shouldn't be upset, I really shouldn't be. But there's a part of me that wants the magic, that wants the whimsy. I never believed in love at first sight. Logan's the one that made me believe in it because he seemed so *sure* about it, about me.

It made it seem like this was all meant to be, and I kind of fell under the spell of the fairy tale ending when real life doesn't work that way.

I mean, I'm me. I'm pretty terrible at long-term relationships judging by my record, and usually at the first display of intimacy (like what happened the night Logan and I were together), I bolt like a rabbit that got a whiff of a wolf.

"People get married to each other all the time even though they aren't sure about it or each other. So what? You're one of many. It's not that big of a deal," I tell him.

Relief floods through my body. I let myself go completely boneless on the mattress, relaxing.

I'm off the hook, I'm off the hook for saying yes because I wanted him to come over to my parents' for Christmas! Another Christmas miracle!

"I wanted to be sure, Max. I wanted you to deserve that, at least."

I shrug, ignoring the stinging in my eyes. It would have been nice, sure, but it's not like I need it. I *wanted* it, and Logan made me believe.

I'm such an idiot.

My phone pings underneath the covers, and I fumble until I have it in my hand. I squint at the brightness before adjusting the settings. The group family chat comes in with about three hundred texts, everyone talking to each other.

"I've got some service," I say. "Do you need to call someone?" I ask, moving to hand my phone over. Except Logan already has his phone in his hand, squinting at his screen.

I glance over my own messages and look over the family chat, quickly reading everyone's checking-in texts. I send my own '*I'm alive*' message, and get some thumb's up emojis in response.

I'm glad that my family is safe and healthy despite the major inconvenience of the power being out so long. That worm of worry wriggles in my belly at the thought of not having enough food for the day after tomorrow, but I swallow it down, determined not to worry about it for now.

"Fuck," Logan whispers. From the light of his screen, I can see him frowning at his phone. When I look back at my phone, it's to find that the service has gone out again, and I'm left with no bars.

"Were you able to get a message out?"

Logan shakes his head, then slams his phone into the covers. I bite my lip and try to keep quiet. "Shit," he grunts.

"Maybe we'll get service back tomorrow," I say, not really believing it. Tomorrow's going to come soon enough and we're going to have to decide whether to stay here and wait out the power outage or leave my apartment behind.

"Maybe," he sighs, and I know there's more that he wants to say, but just won't.

After living with him around the clock for seven whole days, I'd like to think I know him by now.

Logan picks up after himself and doesn't expect anyone to come cleaning up after him. He doesn't sleep on his side of the bed and likes moving around during the night. While that usually ends up with me snuggled up close and personal, I don't mind.

He cooks good food, especially under the circumstances. He's calm where I'm the one that freaks out at every minor inconvenience. He lends out a helping hand that I've always been too afraid to take, to grab a hold of just in case he decides I'm not worth it and decides to let me go.

"Logan? Can you tell me what's wrong?"

Logan grunts. "I can't, Max. I can't. Not right now." He turns on his side away from me, giving me his broad back. I barnacle myself around his body and hold him tightly until he relaxes. "Please, let me keep this to myself for now."

I could yell at him for doing that, for wanting to keep secrets while he's taken *everything* from me. Except I hear the deep pain in his voice, and I want to do anything to soothe it.

I might not have said yes with the *best* intentions but that doesn't mean I can't try to make things right. It doesn't mean I can't give him back the care he's given me.

It's all about that game of giving and taking, and I have to give more now than I've taken.

Logan could be the one I fall in love with if I let myself, if I let him off the hook and forget about Christmas dinner, forget about trying to please my parents. I can forget about getting their approval – I can do this just for me, and for Logan.

I've basically survived a frozen rain apocalypse. I can face down my parents alone.

Maybe.

It sure would be nice if Logan came with me, though.

It would be really nice.

EIGHTEEN

I wake up to incredible brightness.

The sun has got to be filtering through the curtains, and it's somehow getting directly into my eyeballs.

When the back of my eyelids goes pink, I groan and move over onto my side, trying to hide away from the glow.

Except I'm sleeping in the living room, and the curtains are definitely drawn because of the cold. There should be no light coming through, and there shouldn't be any kind of light in the living room *unless*...

I hike myself up onto my hands and glance around.

All the lights are on in my living room which means I *have power!*

I have power!

I sit upright, smiling so hard my cheeks start to hurt. I lean over and push at Logan's shoulder, shaking him from side to side. When he rolls over onto his back, he blinks up at me, squinting at the brightness.

I point at the overhead lights with the biggest grin on my face. "We have power! Logan, we have power!" I yell, getting up on my knees and moving in to tickle him. When that doesn't work, I flop on top of him and stuff my face in his neck. "Holy shit, we have power. This is *amazing*," I sigh into the skin of his throat, and shove my cold nose there.

Logan hisses but holds me close while my nose warms up.

I lean back and look at him. "This means we have to make an epic breakfast. Shit, if only we had *food*."

Logan smiles. "We could try going out for breakfast if you wanted. There's a diner a block from your building."

I practically leap to my feet, prancing around the mattress to pull the curtains open. I tear off the sheets we'd taped around the windows and throw open the balcony door.

It's pretty warm outside, the kind of warm that means whatever ice we've accumulated might start melting. If the temperature doesn't drop and everything freezes over again, the city might go back to normal.

I rush back inside, hit my thermostat to adjust the temperature, and get it working again. The lights flicker for a split second and then stay on. I sag against the wall in relief and start laughing like a maniac.

I choke on a cough when Logan gets up from bed, his sweatpants hanging low on his hips, his naked chest grabbing *all* of my attention.

I forgot what he looks like under all these bright lights.

He sees me looking and stops his full-blown stretch to let his arms dangle limply at his sides, letting me look my fill.

"We survived!" I squeak, about ready to jump out of my skin. "I want a giant breakfast, Logan. I'm talking eggs and sausage, and a side of waffles. All of it, and I'm going to eat food that *someone else* made."

Logan grins, and, unfortunately, he looks so incredibly delectable just standing there like that, doing nothing but converting oxygen to carbon dioxide.

My belly swoops for a quick second and then stays there as realization slowly starts to dawn on me.

Now that the power is back, there's no reason at all *why* Logan should stay with me. I mean, sleeping in the middle of my living room was out of necessity; living together was nothing but us being in survival mode.

What if now that the power is on we won't be able to accomplish a repeat performance?

My phone chirps somewhere in the blankets, and I grab it and rush inside my freezing cold bedroom to hook it up to my charger. I've never been so happy to charge my phone in my entire life.

I grab an extra charger and bring it to the living room, hand it over. Logan mutters '*thanks*' and plugs his phone in.

I smack my forehead, wince at the sting. "Holy shit, I can do *laundry*. Yes!" I punch the air, and Logan laughs at me, his smile bright.

Whatever broke his heart last night has less of a hold on him right now.

I wish he would tell me, though, but I don't want to push and prod.

I rush around and turn off all the lights, and make sure the thermostat is adjusted in every single room, including my office. The steady hum of my computer makes my heart rate go haywire with happiness. I glance around the office, my desk and chair looking like some sort of alien landscape than a place I usually occupy for more than eight hours a day.

I quickly close the door behind me, not wanting to think about work right now, about how behind I am.

There's nothing like being stuck without any electricity for a whole week to really put shit into perspective.

So I failed Vlogmas. What's the big deal? My subscribers will understand once I sit down and explain it to them.

I zoom around my apartment while Logan watches. I practically kiss all of my appliances, vowing to never take them for granted again.

At the end of my gratitude tour, I plop Logan's old clothes into the washer machine and set it for a cycle with some of my clothes.

Now that the storm is done, there's nothing left to deal with but the aftermath.

Logan helps me get my mattress back onto my bed and helps me clean up around the place now that I can plug my vacuum in and actually clean the floors. He mops right after while I take a shower and get ready for the day.

We swap places so that by the time Logan's done his shower, his clothes are freshly dried and super warm.

I'm able to put on a full face of makeup in my office and wear something that isn't a pair of sweats and a hoodie. I even blow-dried my hair and styled it because I can.

The breakfast diner is packed, and it looks like it's most of the people from my building that have ventured out for someone else to make them food, too.

Logan and I are squeezed into a microscopic booth where the table is narrow enough that with one good swipe of my elbow, plates are going to go everywhere. It doesn't matter. I'm so happy to be here, out of my apartment.

"Look at you, smiling so much," Logan says, one hand holding onto mine. He plays with my left ring finger, the one that's holding the wedding ring hostage, and refuses to let go.

"I'm happy to be out of there. Aren't you?"

"Yes and no." He smirks at me when I keep staring at him. "I liked living with you these past few days. I did." There's something *fragile* in his eyes, and I have a thousand questions, but now's not the time.

Now should be a happy moment. We're free, and we have power.

"Even if I was a general pain in the ass?"

Logan shakes his head. "Max, I've lived with pains in the ass roommates. You're not one of them. I enjoyed my time with you. What? I did."

I lick my lips, butterflies erupting in my stomach. "What are we going to do now? Because the power's back, and..."

He nods. "And Christmas is three days from now, I know."

I gulp.

"I'm going to keep my promise to you like I said. I need to go home first, though, to take care of some things. Pray that the pipes haven't burst and I need to find somewhere else to live."

I cough into my fist. "Well, I mean, if that happens...you know who to call." I wave around my apartment. He has a place here, *with me*.

Logan smiles, slow and sweet. "I thought you were supposed to be a pain in my ass?"

I roll my eyes. "Maybe you're a glutton for punishment. And why are you staring at me like that?"

"Because I like looking at you. It makes me happy."

I pull in a deep breath and hold it, hold it until I have to breathe again. The blush burns from across my cheeks all the way to the tips of my ears. Well, *shit*.

"I like it when I can make you flustered," he says, running his thumbs over the length of my fingers. "I like it all."

It sounds like he's saying one thing but meaning another. And there I go again, jumping to conclusions.

The waiter comes over with our giant breakfasts, placing our individual plates in front of us, forcing Logan to let go of my hand. It sucks, but I'm trading it in for waffles, so it's not all bad.

The conversation in the restaurant is loud and boisterous. Clearly, everybody's happy to have gotten out of their homes, and everyone's enjoying a good, hot meal. But Logan and I share glances while we eat and don't talk much. That familiar anxiety comes roaring back, tightening up my stomach so that I'm slowly losing my appetite.

This is bullshit, seriously.

"What did you want to talk to me about last night?" I ask, pitching my voice high enough so Logan can hear me.

He fastidiously unwinds his napkin and wipes his face only after carefully placing his utensils on the edge of his plate. Now that we're both back out in the wild, it's all about manners and decorum.

I've seen Logan in ratty sweats and no shirt on, scarfing down rice with his fingers like it was going to be his last meal. I've seen what he looks like with dirty hair, and after being lazy and laying in bed all day long.

But I still haven't seen him at his absolute worst. After living a week with me, I haven't even seen him angry or pissed off or upset with me, which is new.

I don't know if I want to see those sides to him.

I mean we've had *arguments*, but he's never been angry enough to call me names or break my heart with the kind of backhanded compliments I'm used to.

He's not like Mom and Dad, Max.

My phone chirps in my coat pocket, and I fish it out to make sure there aren't any emergencies. I've already alerted the family chat that I have my power back, and am ready to start seeing people again if they want to come over. When I open my messages, it's to find everyone looking forward to Christmas.

There are three days left to the big day and my mom must be losing her mind trying to get everything prepared. She usually preps a whole week out but this year that didn't happen.

Maybe she'll be so off her game, that when I bring Logan over for Christmas dinner she won't say anything to embarrass me. *Maybe.*

I put my phone away and glance over at Logan. He's holding his phone in his hands, glaring down at the screen like it's threatened everyone he knows and loves.

"Logan? Everything okay?"

Logan shakes his head and stuffs his phone back in his pocket. "I'm sorry, Max, but I have to cut this short. Text me the details for the Christmas dinner and I'll be there, I promise."

I panic, the hot feeling clawing its way up my throat, permeating my lungs. "What? I thought we'd go together, not that you'd meet me there."

I can't do this alone. Please, I need you there. Please, Logan, please.

Logan's eyes spark with annoyance, and he twists around and pulls out his wallet, dropping a couple of twenties onto the table. "Change of plans," he says, words clipped and short.

He's never been short with me.

You've known the guy a week, Max. One whole week, that's it.

I've lived with him for a week, too. That means something. It has to.

Logan scoots over to leave the booth, leaving me behind with nothing but money lying on the table.

My stomach twists and I don't think I'll be able to finish my breakfast that I was so excited to eat, to share with Logan.

"I'll call you, Max. I'll be there. I promise I'll be there."

"Okay," I mumble, hunching my shoulders in. God, when did it become so hard to look at him? When did it get so hard to talk to him? "Okay." I nod, clearing my throat of the tightness that's already settling in.

"I keep my promises, Max," Logan says. He leans down and leaves a kiss on the top of my head, and then he's gone.

I rub at the spot over my hair where it feels like he's left an imprint. I try to finish my breakfast, even though it's making me sick.

I carefully walk home after I've paid, and hide in my apartment again, glancing at the closed door to my office like it has some sort of siren's call that I'm not hearing just yet.

I want to work, I do, I just don't have the energy.

I don't have the energy because Logan freaking rabbited and left me here, by myself, with nothing but a promise that he'll show up on Christmas.

"But that's all you wanted, right? That's what you wanted, Max. Jesus, just because you've fallen into *like* with the guy doesn't mean it's a lifelong commitment," I growl to myself. I glance down at my left hand, at the way the wedding ring seems to sparkle with the gray light streaming in through the living room windows.

It looks pretty there like it belongs.

My stomach twists again, and even though my apartment has been set to rights, everything feels out of place, like something's missing.

Well, *someone*.

After living with Logan for the week it feels almost wrong not to have him here, talking with me, *existing* with me in the same space, making it appear less empty, less lonely.

I grab my phone and send an SOS message to my cousins, letting them know that I'm home and need help to navigate my feelings, to process what just happened.

Why couldn't Logan tell me what happened when he looked at his phone? Why couldn't he tell me the real reason why he married me? Why was it so important that I remember that I was using him and got a wedding ceremony out of it?

I've got questions and no answers.

I kick at my couch, squawk when I hit my toe just right that I crumple down onto the floor, my ego shot to hell, and perhaps a broken toe to add to the mix.

I can't be here, I can't be here alone just yet.

With my cousins coming over I have to do the one thing I hate the most – go buy groceries.

I lose myself to the simple task, buying all the food I want. I buy boxes of Oreos and tubs of ice cream to soothe my poor little ego.

I buy some vegetables so I don't feel like a total ass. I run the errands I was supposed to run last week before the world seemed to end. And after avoiding it just enough, I return to my empty apartment with the silence pressing down on my ears and taking up too much space without Logan there to make it go away.

I even sent him a quick message: 'I hope everything is okay. Call me if you need me', but I've been left on *read*.

With Christmas three days away I'm feeling pretty fucking nervous that he isn't going to show up when I need him to.

Maybe this whole week together was some kind of fantasy we both found roles to play in. Maybe we were in a snow globe separate from the world. Now that reality has come crashing back into my life, maybe I'm not allowed to have a guy like Logan in my life.

Maybe I'm supposed to go through Christmas all alone, like always.

I stash away my groceries when I get home, a bag of lettuce somehow getting stuck on my wedding ring. With a quick yank, I free the produce and move it to my fridge, but the metal clang on the floor has me freezing on the spot.

I stare down at my left ring finger, finally free of the wedding ring that I've been trying to take off for literal days.

My finger's not even swollen, and there's hardly an indent, or a sign that I was ever really wearing a ring at all. Like Logan and I were never married, and this past week never happened.

My stomach pitches and I get down on my hands and knees, frantic until I'm able to find the ring. I place it on my kitchen counter and watch it like it's a bomb about to go off.

My bottom lip wobbles and the only thing that makes me shore up my feelings is my phone buzzing with an ID for the front door. I let my cousins in, and stand at my front door.

I pull it open before Vick has a chance to knock.

"I fucked up, I think," I tell them.

Amber frowns. "Again?"

NINETEEN

I'm bundled up in a Vick and Amber hug, squeezed tight on all sides, keeping me from falling apart.

"What happened, Max? Wow, you look amazing. Did you go somewhere today?"

I smirk, but it doesn't feel right on my face like it doesn't fit. "Yeah, I did. I don't want to talk about it just yet. I bought groceries. What do you guys want to eat?"

I turn from their hold and head into the kitchen, but I'm practically thrown to the ground when Vick (I think) wraps all her limbs around me in a piggyback from hell.

"Jesus, what the hell?"

"I don't know," Vick practically yells in my ear. "I've missed your face. I'm happy to see you. It feels like it's been *years.*"

"I thought you were having a little honeymoon with Michael the whole time," I murmur. When I'm finally set free, I open the fridge, check what's inside. I start pulling out ingredients to make chicken brochettes.

"Oh, I was. That still doesn't mean I didn't miss the shit out of you, Max. Although, judging by your attitude right now, I might just take it right back."

I glance over my shoulder. Vick's got her arms crossed across her chest, looking like a superhero about to fuck some shit up. Her mermaid-colored hair is piled high on top of her head, and she looks...happy.

Amber on the other hand looks tired. She plops herself on the stool at the kitchen island and pulls out a bottle of wine from her purse. "I figured we would need this," she says, hefting the bottle high. "What's for supper?"

Throughout the entire cooking process, my cousins leave me be. We only talk about food and getting the ingredients ready promptly.

Once the food has been plated, we all move to sit on my couch (Logan's bed) with *Home Alone* on TV, the volume low enough to be decent background noise.

"So? What's up? Why the SOS?" Amber asks after eating a bit of her salad, crunching away. "Because the last time we saw each other you were *married*."

"Oh, yeah, you guys don't know." I clear my throat, my stomach flipping over. "Uh, well...I spoke with Logan the night that everything went out."

"No, Max. Tell me you didn't," Amber groans, dropping her fork on her plate with a clatter.

"What did you want me to do? Kick his ass out of the place when everything had gone dark? He took the metro in, and the emergency alert said for everyone to stay inside. So I let him stay."

"You let him stay?" Vick asks. She swears when a few grains of rice escape her mouth. "Okay, so what happened next?"

"We basically lived together until he left, earlier today, when the lights came back on." I shrug like it's not a big deal. I don't know how to sit with this uncertainty, with this missing part of me. I move my shoulders, trying to ease the pressure along my rib cage, but it doesn't help any.

"Oooooh," Amber says, and I turn to look at her.

"Oh, what? What?" I snap.

Vick pulls in a deep breath, finishes chewing and swallowing. "So you got attached."

"I did *not* get attached," I fire back, knowing that I'm lying through my teeth. These are my cousins; they know when I'm lying.

"Max, you got attached. You've never spent that much time with one guy since the day you were born. Of course, you got attached," Amber says, doling out the facts.

"Don't say it like that," I groan, leaning my head back to stare at the ceiling. "It makes me sound like an idiot."

"Hey, there's nothing wrong with getting attached. As long as it's good for you, you know?" Vick says, running her hand over my arm in a soothing motion. I don't want to be soothed. I want directions on what to do next.

"I don't know if it's good for me. See? This is what happens when you're a late bloomer, and only had romantic validation in your twenties. It skews *everything*, I'm sure of it."

Amber snorts. "Someone's been doing some of their ownsome loose chocolate chips have research." I watch her starting to attack her chicken brochette. "What did you guys do the whole time you were cooped up in here? How cold did it get? Did you keep each other *warm*?"

I snort, even as my cheeks start to burn. "He made all the meals after we meal planned together. We stockpiled water while the pipes were still moving it around. We talked. A lot. I don't think I've ever talked so much to another human being in my entire life."

"Hey," Vick says, affronted.

I snort. This is why I needed them here, to make me feel better. I shrug. "I don't know. He seems like he's a great guy. And I told him why I ran out on him those few dates we had."

"Not because he was an asshole..." Amber says, nodding. She knows too much and it's a problem.

"This whole Operation Get Max a Christmas Date blew up in my face. I didn't ask for a husband. I *didn't*."

"We know, Max. We know. But?" Amber prompts.

"But what?"

"But you look sad that Logan isn't here anymore. Is that true? Is that how you feel?"

"You know this feeling your feelings is absolute bullshit. It's *bullshit*."

"I know, but no less healthy for you. Come on, tell us what happened. We love you and we're here for you. Let it all out." Amber nods.

I start from the beginning, from what I remember of my wedding night.

I run them through all of it – the way I called Logan up to meet me at the bar, the way I was stone-cold sober when I said yes in front of the chalet on the mountain. I tell them about the way he always cooked and cleaned, and how he tried his hardest to help me around the apartment when I didn't even want it. I tell them about the way he made me feel – like I was more than just my workaholic tendencies, that I was someone to be proud of.

I tell them about saying yes to getting married because I planned on using Logan to get what I wanted, I tell them about my selfishness. I also tell them about Logan's unknown reasons for wanting to marry me.

I tell them how he checked his phone at the breakfast diner this morning and then popped out of my life like we didn't just survive a storm with each other, sharing the same space for the past week.

Maybe the experience only changed me and didn't affect Logan at all.

"But he's coming to Christmas dinner, right?" Vick asks, finishing up her meal. She grabs onto our plates when she's done eating and heads to the kitchen. After opening up *all* of my cupboards, she finds the wine glasses and pours out three glasses, then carts them back to the couch.

"He said he was, but I don't know if he will."

"All you can do is take his words at face value. I swear, if Aunt Ella acts like an ass, we're letting her have it this year, Max. I promise you. We are."

"It just sucks that I've already told the family chat today that I'm bringing someone home for Christmas. I shouldn't have started this whole thing, right? How stupid was I?"

Amber shrugs. "It's not wrong to want to avoid feeling shit about yourself. It's wrong when that behavior becomes destructive. And this is not it, Max. You found a guy you like enough to want to spend the day with."

"But I ended up *marrying* him because of it. If this is not the dumbest shit I've ever heard..."

Vick snorts. "Oh, please. We've all done dumb shit. And we'll continue to do dumb shit in the future. That's the way it goes. You don't have to be perfect."

I don't know why those words hit me as hard as they do.

I could blame the fact that we're three days away from Christmas and I won't have Logan to pseudo-shield me from my family.

I could blame it all on finally seeing my cousins after a week-long hiatus that neither of us wanted but were forced to endure. I could also blame it on the fact that I've developed feelings for Logan Porter, and who the fuck knows if he's going to show up when I need him to?

I could blame it on the fact that I haven't spoken to him at all today, and I'm not used to that yet.

But they hurt, those words. They lance right through me and ache and burn in my chest, right over my heart.

"Oh, Max. Oh, shit. Amber fix this, fix it!"

"What do you want me to do? You're the one that made her cry," Amber hisses, but I'm being jostled until both of my cousins are holding me tightly.

"You don't have to be perfect to be my best friend in the world. You don't have to be perfect for the both of us to love you, Max," Vick murmurs, squeezing me tight enough that it gets difficult to breathe. The pressure is exactly what I need.

"Shit, how long have you been feeling like this?" Amber asks, letting me go in increments until she's leaned back enough that I can see her face without going cross-eyed.

I shrug. "Forever?" I chuckle wetly. I brush away the tears from my cheeks, for once not caring about ruining my base. "And this whole storm blowing in when I had so much work to do is absolutely shit."

"Plus Logan staying with you for a whole week."

I nod. "I did get attached. And we're already married, and he thinks that I'm this great person when I said yes but I did it because I'm scared shitless of my parents finding me lacking in any aspect of my life. Isn't that terrible?"

Amber shakes her head. "It's not. Parents, man. They're the worst."

It shouldn't make me laugh, but it does. I rub over my heart where the ache hurts the worst. "I just wish…I wish I could have met Logan at a different time in my life, you know?"

Vick opens her mouth to speak, then shuts it again. "Nope, I'm not going to talk about Michael and his 'timing' philosophy. It all got thrown out the window anyway, and we're still together."

"The wedding ring finally came off my finger today," I murmur, voice small. "I don't want it to mean anything, but I think it kind of does."

"All it means is that your finger wasn't swollen enough to keep the ring there. That's it, Max. Don't go looking for things to hurt yourself with."

I scoff. That's exactly what I'm doing. I knew I needed the two of them here.

"What do you want to do now? Watch the movie or make some brownies?" Vick asks, rubbing her hands together.

"Like that's even a question."

Amber laughs. She runs a hand over my hair, smoothing it down. "I love you, Max. Even if you ruin the brownies."

Vick slaps at my knee, hard enough to sting. "And I love you, even if you're a giant pain in my ass and out doing random shit like bringing a husband to Christmas dinner. Jesus Christ, this is going to be a *story* we're going to laugh about like crazy when we're old ladies."

I snort. Vick helps me off the couch by tugging at my hand. The movie plays on in the background while we go about making a pan of brownies from scratch. The cocoa powder gets everywhere, and there are some loose chocolate chips that have probably found their way under my fridge but I don't care.

My apartment isn't empty, and it's filled with people I love, and who love me back.

Which is more than I can say for when Logan was over.

"What's the face for?" Vick asks, waving a finger in front of my eyes and nose and mouth. "The brownies didn't do anything to you," she says, grabbing onto the pan and shoving it into the oven. Amber sets the timer, and all there is left to do now is stare at each other.

"He hasn't called or messaged me all day long," I say, getting nervous. "I shouldn't care, I know I shouldn't care, but I do."

Amber unwinds her arms and beckons me closer. I get hugged from the front and from the back because Vick doesn't want to be left out.

"We're going to be there for you when dinner rolls around. Besides, there are still like two and a half days left until then. He'll message you then. And if he doesn't, he doesn't. You'll know where he stands."

"How can I get feelings like this?"

Amber snorts, arms banding around my ribs that much more tightly. "Feelings aren't rational, Max. They don't go away because we tell them to."

"Well, they should. I don't have time for this."

Vick laughs. "Come on, let's go relax while we wait for the brownies."

"I don't want to. I think I'm gonna cry."

"Then cry. We're not going to judge. Hell, I bet Amber's going to cry with you."

Amber sighs. "Stop trying to be an asshole, Vick, and let her cry if she needs to. And I bet you fifty bucks that you're going to cry first."

"You're *on*."

My cousins are chaotic, Jesus Christ. We head over to the couch, and I'm practically swaddled in blankets.

"Can you guys sleep over tonight? I have extra sets of pajamas and everything. Please?"

"Yeah, sure. We can do that," Amber says. "Will that make you happy?"

I shrug. "I don't really want to be alone right now."

"Sure, Max. Sure." Vick says.

When they're both distracted by the movie, I ask the question that's been heavy on my mind since the storm came through and messed everything up for me.

"Do you think there's something wrong with me that I don't believe in marriage?"

Amber snorts. "Hell, no. All you have to do is look at the statistics and you're opinion is totally valid. But really, though, Max it depends on the people who are getting married to each other. It's like everything else, it requires a lot of work."

"And I'm so tired of working."

Vick slaps my knee again, and I'd wrestle her to the ground if I had the energy. "This is a different kind of work. Is Logan supportive of what you do?"

"Well, he says he is, but I don't know."

"Listen to Amber, since she's right."

"Thanks," Amber smirks.

Vick rolls her eyes, the signature Prewitt family trait. "You can only take people at their face value. You have to wait and see what happens on Christmas."

"I'm so impatient, though."

"Well, maybe eat some brownies and get some fortitude. It's Christmas. It's your favorite holiday despite all the bullshit that goes down. Enjoy it while you can."

"Even if it all blows up in my face?"

"I mean, what's to blow up?" Amber asks. "So your parents get pissed at you and make some comments. Does that stop the food from being delicious, or the three of us being together after this horror show of a storm?"

"You're right, I know you're right. I'm sick to my stomach with it, though."

"You can always not show up," Vick says.

"And let my parents *win*? Hell, no. They're going to see my beautiful made-up face with my weird eyeshadow colors. And they're going to look me in the eye when they inevitably say something about me. And if Logan's there, great. If not, he's not there."

"Exactly the right attitude. But sweetie, you're crying," Amber says, grabbing some tissues from a nearby box. She hands them over to me.

"I know. You're the one that said I have to feel my feelings, Amber. So really, this is all your fault."

Amber grins. "I know. But cheer up, we're going to have some brownies soon, and then we're all going to bed early. I'll make us a huge breakfast tomorrow morning. And you know, after you feel your feelings, and you survive them, you know what happens after that?"

"What?"

"You know that you can do it all again. And the people who love you are still going to be here."

I sigh. "I wish Logan loved me, too."

"I know, Max, I know. But look. Vick cried first and she owes me fifty bucks."

Vick's totally dabbing at her eyes, looking like she's fighting the urge to sniffle. "There's something in my *eye*, Amber. Seriously, look, there's something in there— "

I love my cousins to the moon and back.

Really.

TWENTY

Christmas dinner...

I've redone my eyeshadow three times. In the end, I go for more 'wearable' colors — deep and rich chocolate browns with a gold shimmer in a halo eye look. I have fun making shapes with my black eyeliner, even if I made it too dramatic for the occasion.

I wear my stockings and layer on my best eating dress, the one that's cinched right underneath my boobs and flows freely around the rest of my body. The only thing stopping me from eating my weight in dinner is the elastic waistband of my stockings.

I'm as ready as I'm going to be.

I have my best playlist queued up for the drive over to my parents' house. I chase the high while I listen to K-pop as I head to the West Island. I've already stopped off for some of my dad's favorite wine and my mom's favorite cognac as last-minute gifts.

I've also got a huge bag of presents in the back of my car for my cousins and little sister. No one can tell me I'm not being generous.

It just means Mom and Dad will comment on something else.

I'm feeling queasy. There's a heavy weight sitting at the base of my throat, my breakfast lodged there, ready for an emergency evacuation at the slightest inconvenience. I practically strangle my steering wheel on the entire drive over.

It doesn't help matters that Logan hasn't contacted me at all today. My heart has sunk somewhere down near my ankles, and there's a lead weight in my stomach. Just when I needed him the most, and he's been ghosting me ever since we had breakfast the other day.

I'm not holding onto any hope that he's going to show up this evening. I'm *not*.

Even if I did wish Logan were going with me. I wish he was sitting next to me in my car, I wish he was fiddling with my volume knob or perusing through my driving playlist on my phone.

I really just wish he was here, with me.

But Christmas miracles only extend so far, and it looks like I'm going to have to face a pair of Grinches all on my own.

Evie's the one who opens the door when I arrive, smiling big and wide.

"Hey, kid," I say, pulling her in for a hug.

"Max," she murmurs, squeezing me around the ribs. It almost feels like getting a hug from Vick, despite the height difference. "You look awesome."

"It's because I have boring eyeshadow on," I say, waving a hand around my eyes.

Evie shakes her head. "No, you look...happy? Are you drunk?"

"No, idiot. I drove here." *I guess pretending can get me places. Huh.* I swat at her arm, but Evie dances away before it can fully land. She helps me out of my coat, and I toe off my boots, stepping into a puddle immediately as I set my foot down.

I'm trying not to take it as a horrible omen, and merely as a coincidence.

I follow Evie inside my childhood home, dragging along my giant bag of presents and my bottles of booze. I quickly make my rounds saying hello to my aunts and uncles, getting kissed and hugged within an inch of my life.

I don't know if it's my imagination, but the hugs I get are extra tight, and the kisses to the top of my head are extra long as if we all missed the close contact after spending a week away from everyone and everything.

I get swarmed by Vick and Amber, hugging me tightly. It's pretty glorious even when both Brody and Michael come in for a giant group hug, and my knees almost buckle under the combined weight.

"Well, shit, I'm happy to see you guys, too," I laugh, then start handing out presents, like I'm actually Santa Claus with fabulous makeup on. "Merry Christmas guys."

Vick's eyes light up when I hand her gift over. "I forgot yours. Michael and I were running late."

"Yeah, I bet you were," I smirk at her and enjoy watching my cousin squirm with embarrassment. I look over to Michael, who's blushing just as hard.

Well, shit. They're adorable. It's kind of not fair.

I ignore the jealous pang in my chest knocking around my rib cage and struggle to focus. I move into the kitchen like I'm walking on a battlefield filled with land mines. One wrong move and I'll set off the beast – my mother.

Izzy's in the kitchen, stirring the gravy for the turkey we're going to demolish soon. Mom's at the kitchen island, working on dressing the gigantic salad that'll disappear within minutes of being placed on the table.

The kitchen's too hot – there are too many people, and the oven's cranked high – but I still feel the chill when I head closer to her.

It's funny how after twenty-seven years, one wrong look from her, and my first response is to take a step back and bolt in the other direction.

My dad's pouring himself a rum and coke. He looks over to me when I sit his bottle of wine on the table, right next to the bottle of cognac for my mom.

"Merry Christmas, Dad."

He smiles at me, and the vice-like grip around my heart relaxes, just a little. "Merry Christmas, sweetheart. I thought you were supposed to have passed by earlier."

"I'm right on time," I say, glancing down at my sparkly watch. "Seriously, I'm right on time."

Dad shakes his head, finishes adding a couple of ice cubes to his glass. "That's not what your mother thought. She thought you were coming over to help."

I frown. "She has Izzy to help. I was busy, Dad. I had to finish up some work."

Dad looks down at his glass, effectively shutting down any conversation about my work and the hours I put in. "What work?"

This, again?

I bite the meat of my inner cheek, pull in a deep breath through my nose. "I had to schedule some more videos out and finish uploading one that'll be going live in a couple of hours. Do you want to know all the details?"

I know he doesn't, but sometimes it's like I have to list out every single little thing I do every day to get him to understand how much work I put in.

Dad shakes his head. He never wants to know about the details. He doesn't want to know what I do, and why I love what I do.

It's nothing new, really, but after the week I've had and the sore spot that Logan holds in my heart, well, I don't know how much more I can take.

"Go help your mother," Dad says.

"Why? She didn't ask me." Maybe I'm being obstinate, maybe I'm putting up a boundary too late. Or maybe I'm the asshole.

Dad's eyes flare wide. "That doesn't mean it isn't polite to offer to help your mother."

I raise my eyebrows. "Did you offer to help? Because you live here, and I don't. I'm a guest." Those are fighting words, and I find myself enjoying the Dad looks so pissed. He didn't expect me to answer the way I did.

My heart beats frantically, and there's blood pounding in my ears. My cheeks are warm, and I'm starting to sweat because it's so hot in here. But I'm standing up for myself, even if it's the wrong place and wrong time.

"Maxima," Dad hisses. There used to be a time when I would put my tail between my legs and do what I was told. Not today, not this Christmas.

"What? You know I'm right. Did you help her at all today, or did you watch some football?"

Maybe this is the Christmas where I stop speaking to my parents, maybe this is where the family rift tears us all apart.

I hate how I have to make the decision – ignore the way he talked to me and try to play nice for everyone. What if I don't want to play nice anymore?

I clench my jaw, give my dad a sharp smile. "Fine, I'll go see if she needs some help."

I move to stand by mom's side while she taste-tests the salad. She's frowning at the taste. Mom adds more salt, then starts mixing again. "Hi, Mom. Merry Christmas."

"Merry Christmas, Maxima," she says, talking down to the salad bowl instead of looking at me. Yup, I'm in trouble and I *just* got here.

Sweet.

My mood's starting to plummet, and it's getting hard to stay hopeful that Logan's going to show up at all. It's getting hard to believe that I'm going to make it through this entire evening without falling apart.

Mom lifts her head, raises an eyebrow. I look like her, I know that. But we couldn't be more different. "Don't you have someone you want to introduce me to?" she asks.

I lick my lips. "He's running late. He actually might not show up at all."

Mom purses his lips, and she turns away. "Would it have killed you to let me know that he wasn't coming? Now I have to rearrange the table settings *again*." She sighs, a sound closer to disgust than exhaustion.

"I'll do it. It's not that big of a deal, Mom. I'll take care of it."

I know she's frazzled. Mom's always frazzled whenever she does Christmas dinner. She cooks and cleans for a whole week leading up to the event. By the day of, she's so tired that she doesn't have enough energy to actually enjoy herself, the holiday, and her family.

"Well, you should have come earlier then, and helped prepare everything," Mom says. We all seem to be pushing each other today.

I pull in a deep, deep breath.

"You didn't tell me you wanted help, and you have Izzy here." I wave over to my younger sister, who flips me off. I slice my hand over my throat in retaliation, and Izzy grins. She turns back to the gravy, swearing at the saucepan.

"Mom, I can't read minds," I say, following her around from the utensil drawer back to the kitchen island and salad bowl. "You should have told me you wanted me to come over and help."

"Fine, fine. Go and set the table. I haven't put out the wine glasses yet. And bring this over, too," Mom says, tapping the salad bowl and walking away from me.

Vick's right there, nabbing onto the bowl. Amber's her backup, and she's already getting wine glasses down from the cupboard for me. I cart over what I can, two at a time.

"Jesus Christ," I groan in the relative safety of the quieter dining room. "Next thing you know, I'm going to get yelled at for wearing this shade of red lipstick." I wave a finger around my mouth.

It's cooler in the dining room, away from the heat of the oven. I take another deep breath to center myself.

Even if Logan *were* here, what could he do?

Maybe he'd look at me like he's one of the people that actually likes that I'm here.

"What's the problem now?" Vick asks, trying to figure out precisely where she's going to put the giant salad bowl. "Where's Logan?"

I shrug. "Looks like he's going to be a no-show. And apparently, I was supposed to read mom's mind and show up early to help with the preparations."

"But Izzy's here. You don't live here anymore," Amber points out.

I shrug again, looking down at the table settings. "I don't know. It doesn't matter. I'm happy to see you guys."

"She says as if we didn't have a sleepover a couple of nights ago," Vick grins. "Sorry about Logan."

The doorbell rings, and I freeze in the middle of placing the last two wine glasses down at their respective settings. My heart goes haywire in my chest, stopping and starting like a dying engine before all the blood rushes to my face.

"Oh, *shit*," Vick chokes.

I'm practically running for the door, bypassing Uncle Alastor, and nearly making him spin like a top. The hope builds out in my chest, blowing up like a balloon, making me feel like I can walk on air.

I quickly unlock the front door, barely clocking that I've stepped into another puddle on the carpet and now both of my feet are soaking wet. I throw the door open to find Logan standing there, panting, his breath pluming in the air.

"Hey, Max," he says with a quick smile that doesn't reach his eyes.

It doesn't matter. I'm so fucking *happy* to see him.

I grab onto his hand and tug him inside. I hug him so tight that I hear the breath rush out of him on an *'oof'*. "Shit, shit, shit. I'm so happy you're here. Really happy, Logan." I say against his coat, my voice muffled, refusing to let go.

Logan's arms move around me, and we're hugging each other in the middle of my childhood home entryway.

I lean back to blink at him. Logan doesn't look right. "What's wrong?" I whisper. "You didn't have to come if you were feeling bad."

Logan shakes his head, runs his thumb gently over my cheekbone as if I'm made of glass. If I wasn't already holding onto him I'd probably melt right through the floor.

"And miss out on seeing you? Never." He smiles again, but it looks forced, even to me. Logan's trying so hard for me. Tears start welling in my eyes, the back of my throat flaring hot with pain.

I pull back, taking and hanging up his coat. I hold onto the bottle of expensive gin he brought as a gift while he toes off his boots.

When he's done, he stands up to his full height, tilts his head. "Are you ready, Max?"

"Yeah, I'm ready. Are you?" I whisper. I reach out to hold his hands.

"I will be. I promise. I'm here now. You don't have to be afraid."

I mash my lips together, sniffing hard. The tears go back from wherever they came from. I clear my throat. I'm still afraid that I'll be called out in front of everyone at the dinner table. I'm still afraid that I'm going to be found wanting against my parents' lofty expectations.

But with Logan here? I'm not *so* afraid.

I squeeze his hand. He squeezes back.

I pull in one final, deep breath. "Come and meet my family." I tug Logan into the kitchen. My stomach's full with a swarm of bees instead of butterflies, buzzing angrily in my belly.

"Mom, Dad, everyone," I call out over the myriad of conversations being had in the kitchen. "This is Logan. Logan, this is my Dad, Isaac."

Logan extends his hand for a shake. "Hello, Mr. Prewitt. Merry Christmas. It's nice to meet you. Thank you for inviting me into your home."

Dad doesn't look at me as he shakes Logan's hand in a quick one-two pump before dropping his hand. It could have been worse. Dad could have tried to pulverize Logan with his grip.

"Hello, Logan. Welcome to my home. Merry Christmas."

Logan mumbles back another Merry Christmas, which is so adorable I wish I could hide him in a closet and smother him with kisses. Instead, I continue introducing him to everyone. I like that he particularly warms up to Vick without really knowing about her gamer background. They talk video games for a bit, while the rest of us chat.

I help Mom out when I can while Logan's occupied talking to everyone. We all shuffle into the dining room when the turkey's finally ready to be served.

A hush falls over my family as the bird is carted out into the dining room, my father showing it off like he's the one who did all the hard work. Dad sets the thirty-pounder in the middle of the table and starts carving it thinly, slice by slice.

The rest of us start passing around the sides: salad, mashed potatoes, stuffing, buttered dinner rolls, and roasted vegetables. I nearly drop the mashed potatoes into my lap, but Logan's there to save me, grabbing onto the other end before I could be blamed for ruining Christmas dinner.

Heart still in my mouth, I watch as my dad starts passing out the giant plate filled with turkey. Both the gravy and cranberry sauce are passed around and around until everyone's plate is full. Wine is poured, and soda cans are opened.

It's time to eat.

"Merry Christmas, everyone," Dad says, smiling wide. He takes his seat at the head of the table, Mom sitting to his right. "Dig in."

Everyone eats in stunned silence, the delicious food doing all of the talking for us. Logan murmurs to me whenever he wants something, and I make sure his wine and water glasses are always full as the meal progresses.

I'm antsy. As long as we're eating, people can't really talk. That would be a hell of a choking hazard. Doesn't stop them from trying, though.

I lick my lips, practically vibrating in my seat, waiting for the other shoe to drop, waiting for my parents to say something rude about me.

Amber sits to my right, sharing a dinner roll with me until we finally both decide to take a whole one each for ourselves. Vick sits across from me, eating slowly, smiling at us, twirling around her engagement ring absently, the sparkle flashing in the light.

My own wedding band is in my pocket, burning a hole through my dress just by existing. I hadn't noticed how I had quickly gotten used to the weight and feel of it on my ring finger. I'm acutely aware of what I'm missing.

"So, Logan," Dad says, and the mashed potatoes I'd been chewing on have gotten stuck on their way down. "Tell us a little bit about yourself. Max hasn't told us much about you. She hasn't told us anything at all." Dad looks at me as if he's waiting for one hell of a story.

If I could turn off the signal to my brain that makes me blush, then I would. Right now, though, that part of me isn't listening.

"Dad," I hiss. I gulp down some water to get the potatoes down and look over to Logan, a silent apology in my stare.

Logan clears his throat, coughs into his fist. "What would you like to know Mr. Prewitt?" he asks.

"Everything," Dad says, smiling like a shark that's scented blood.

Really? They're doing this to me now?

Of course, they are, of course. What else are they going to pick on?

My heart's beating hard and fast, and it's so freaking hot in here that I'm close to standing up and stripping all of my clothes.

"I'm afraid you have to be more specific, Mr. Prewitt."

"What do you do for work? Or do you play around on the computer all day like Maxima does?"

I roll my eyes. Playing on the computer all day. That's what I do. *Sure.*

"I work in video game development, actually. So, yes, I do play on the computer all day." Logan smiles politely, but I can see there's a razor's edge beneath it.

It shouldn't be hot, I should be turned on, but *I am*.

My cheeks burn even hotter. I can't be having this reaction at *the dinner table.*

Beat feeling like shit, though, no?

"Video game development? What does that even mean? I swear, would it kill any one of you to have a proper job like Amber?"

Logan licks his lips, his eyebrows moving down over his eyes in a scowl. It shouldn't be hot, too. I shouldn't find him hot when he's looking like this, but *I do.*

"A proper job, Mr. Prewitt? I work regular hours and receive a paycheck for those hours. I receive benefits from my job for those hours worked. I don't see why it doesn't constitute a real job."

Logan's tone is hilarious to me, the way his words are clipped and precise, sounding more like a robot. Dad's face is starting to get red. He looks over to Mom as if she's going to back him up.

Logan's being unfailingly polite, so I don't know what else my parents are going to do.

"Amber's a physiotherapist," Dad says, waving a hand to my cousin. "Vick plays video games all day long, and people pay to watch her. Max apparently uploads makeup videos and that makes her money. What happened to a regular office job?"

"Um, Dad? I don't think now's the time to talk about jobs and stuff." I shake my head, but Dad doesn't get the message.

"Why? Because you'll be out on the street if the people who watch your videos decide to go somewhere else?" he asks.

There's a hushed silence now and everyone's afraid to break it. I know some people here are relishing the fact that my dad's bringing all of this up. Family dynamics are special in that way.

"You know I have a contingency plan for that. I've told you a million times that I'm prepared for when it happens."

I mean, it's a fear of mine, sure, that people will lose interest in me, in my content. There's always going to be a limit to the people that will watch my videos, that will engage with my content. I can only grow so much until I can't grow anymore. Maybe the platform will one day die out as new platforms get introduced.

The only thing I can do is be prepared for when it happens.

"I have backup plans for that."

Dad shakes his head. "You have no employable skills, Max."

"Uncle Isaac, there are always going to be ways to make money," Vick says, coming to my rescue. "Besides, Max and I have already saved for our futures. Max is better at managing her money than I am, and she's basically set to retire in her thirties."

"Yeah, right. I'll believe it when I see it."

"Okay, Dad. I'll show you one day," I say, trying to defuse the entire conversation. "I've got a ton of spreadsheets that we can go over together." I'm still trying to get us back to Christmas talk. "And Mom, these mashed potatoes are really great."

Mom nods, spearing me with her dark eyes. "I had to whip them up this morning since you didn't show up early to make them this year."

Jesus Christ, somebody give me a break!

"Uh, Aunt Ella, I'm looking through the family chat here, and I don't see where you told Max to come early. Or Vick or me, either. Or hell, the uncles and my parents. Did your phone eat the text?" Amber asks, swiping down the screen of her phone, not paying attention to the aftermath of the volley she's just thrown down.

I fucking love my cousins. I really, *really* do.

Izzy and Evie are seated together, watching all of this unravel with wide eyes.

"Amber, don't talk to your aunt like that," Aunt Meg says, leaning forward to grab her wine glass.

"I'm just asking a question, Mom."

"You're being rude, Amber," Aunt Meg snaps, and throws back some of her wine.

Amber shakes her head. "Nah, I don't think so. So, Aunt Ella? I don't see it anywhere."

"I'm about three seconds away from throwing all of you out," Mom says.

I panic. I don't want to be blamed for ruining Christmas for *everyone*.

Izzy snickers, and then starts laughing like she's about to pee. "Mom, *Mom*. We've already eaten. What are you going to do?" she squeaks and holds onto her belly. "Oh my God. This is supposed to be a holiday about coming together, and holy *shit*, everyone's at each other's *throats,*" she sputters out.

It shouldn't be funny. I know it's not. But I can't help but laugh, too, seeing my sister so helpless. It doesn't take long for everyone else to start laughing, and then resume eating the last bits off their plate, as if nothing happened.

All the while, Logan holds my hand under the table.

Thankfully we get to the end of the main meal without any blood being shed. That still leaves dessert though.

Almost there, Max. Almost there.

When we're all done eating and I'm moving the plates over to the kitchen sink, Mom instructs me to do the dishes.

"Hey," Logan says, bumping me with his hips as I pull on yellow rubber gloves. "I'm here to help."

My cheeks still burn with what he's just seen, with what he's heard. They're not terrible people, my parents, my family. I know a lot of people out there have it much worse. But shit, not supporting anything I do, ever? Might as well be a bunch of strangers sharing the same space.

"I'll be okay," I tell him, mustering up a smile. "I'm really, *really* glad you're here. You've made everything better already."

Logan leans down to kiss my forehead. He reluctantly pulls back to smile at me. It's unfortunate how great his smile is, finally. Whatever's hurting him, I've said the right thing to chase away the pain.

"Me too, Max. Me, too."

TWENTY-ONE

Christmas dinner...

After the first round of dishes are put into the dishwasher and the remainder washed, the leftovers are put away for tomorrow, and coffee is being served.

The pies are being reheated in the oven, and the world smells like deep and rich espresso mixed in with the sugary accents of my mom's famous apple sour cream pie.

Amber and Vick have kept me company while dealing with the dirty dishes, and have helped to dry the clean pile and put them away.

"Girls, why don't you go and enjoy yourselves and let Max do the washing up?" Mom says, interrupting Amber and her funny story. Brody and Michael are hanging out with us, too. We're like an assembly line getting things cleaned, and food put away while everyone else is enjoying spending time together.

I'm being punished, I know I am, but my cousins, their boyfriends, and Logan seem determined not to let me suffer alone.

“Nah, it’s all right, Aunt Ella. We haven’t seen Max in a while, and we’re cool with helping her out. Where are Evie and Izzy?” Amber says with a straight face.

“Drinking wine outside on the balcony. Something about it being too hot in here.”

When Mom leaves, Vick lets out a low whistle. “All you have to do, Max, is survive through dessert and that’s it. Logan, welcome to the family, man. We’re sorry we’re not at our best,” Vick laughs. “Aunt Ella and Uncle Isaac are usually more passive-aggressive than this. I don’t know what’s gotten into them.”

Logan shrugs and doesn’t say anything.

I’m drowning in worry and guilt at having him here with me, in front of all of this.

“I’m sorry,” I say, bumping his hip with mine. “I’m sorry that I dragged you out here. *God*, I knew it was going to be bad, but not this bad.”

“It’s fine, Max. I’m here, yeah? Let’s get through dessert.”

I frown at him. “Are you okay? Because you don’t look okay.”

Logan’s lips quirk on a half-smile but it stops there. “I’d rather not talk about it right now. I’ll tell you after.”

“Is it about that text you got the other day?” I push.

Logan tenses, his jaw clenching tight that muscles ripple along his jawline. Unfortunately, I find that incredibly attractive, too.

“Come on, Logan. I’ve lived with you for a whole week, and we managed not to kill each other. I know you.”

Logan's eyes blaze with a mixture of emotions that I can't quite name. "Do you, Max? Really?"

I swallow hard, struck dumb by what I'm looking at. "I don't know all of you, I know that. And you don't know all of me. Isn't that the whole point though, of being together? Of learning more about each other? Shit, I thought you weren't going to show up."

"I said I would, Max." He looks almost *disappointed* in me for not believing in him.

I shrug, get back to washing the last dish, and give it a good rinse. "People say things all the time but never mean them."

"I don't Max. I'm here, aren't I?"

My heart starts beating fast and hard. "Yeah, but you look like you don't want to be here. And I get it, okay? I get it. This is a shit show, and my parents are being rude. They're just trying to take it out on me by going through you."

"I know they are. I'm not blind. I want to be here, okay? I do," Logan murmurs.

I squint at him. This is all so hard to believe. I'm so happy to see him, incredibly so, but none of this is adding up.

"You don't look like it, is all I'm saying." *Jesus Christ, why do you keep pushing it, and pushing it?*

"Max, you don't know what you're talking about."

"Okay, okay," I say, ignoring the panic that comes up at the thought of him leaving me alone with my family. *When did I become such a little shit?* "Why didn't you let me know you were coming?"

"I had a family emergency. Please, I can't talk about it right now." He roughly wipes the last plate dry.

I nod and snap my mouth closed, even if I have a hundred more questions.

"You look beautiful. Did I not tell you?" He leans back onto the counter, keeping me in his sights.

I tear the yellow rubber gloves off my hands and smile up at him, ignoring the fact that something is very wrong. I'm still learning when to give him space, and when to burrow in his arms and hold onto him and tell him everything is going to be okay.

Dessert is tense. I keep rolling my shoulders hoping to work the tension out of my body, but that doesn't seem to be working out so well for me.

Vick keeps sending me pained smiles from across the table, all while stuffing her face with apple pie.

The desserts are delicious and coupled with bitter coffee, the combination is heavenly. The conversation remains stilted. I keep getting looks shot my way like this is all my fault.

I ignore the hot tightness in my chest and the way my parents keep trying to catch my eye to engage with me. My stomach sinks when I realize that this is going to be the last Christmas where we're all together unless something changes.

Because I can't do this anymore.

Hell, I got a complete stranger to marry me so I wouldn't have to do this alone.

I glance over at Logan, sitting next to me, eating his pie slowly and methodically with great care. He's some of the things I'm not – patient and calm, relaxed and unafraid of what others think of him, kind and sweet, and loyal to the point where he showed up here today not knowing what he was getting into.

My heart shivers, and I have to pull in a deep breath while I look at him.

What's even better? He looks back at me, gives me a wink, and then smiles, eyes crinkling closed. It's the first real smile he's given me this entire evening.

My heart rate doesn't simmer down for the rest of the night as I slowly come to a conclusion that's always felt inevitable.

I'm *definitely* attached to Logan Porter, husband or not. I'm attached and yeah, maybe a little bit in love, falling, *fallen*.

Second cups of coffee are poured and we all sit, staring at each other. I stare at Vick. She stares back while pulling grade-school funny faces that make me laugh regardless of my age.

When I think I'm given a reprieve and all the cousins head down to the basement to watch our annual marathon of all the *Die Hard* movies, my mom asks to talk to me.

Great, just great.

Logan squeezes my hand, and I take what little bit of strength I can from the gesture.

This is going to suck, big time.

"Yeah?" I say while taking a seat at the kitchen table.

She's tired, I know she is. Her shoulders are slumped, and she's holding onto her mug of coffee like she's found the fountain of eternal youth and that's the last bit she's ever going to get.

"I'm disappointed in you, Max."

I snort. Mom's eyes narrow. I'm so sick and tired of being afraid of them, of jumping through hoops to get their approval. I'm *glad* I got married without them knowing. "What else is new?"

"Do not talk to me that way, Maxima. I'm your mother. We're not friends."

"Nope, we're not." I lay my hands on the scarred surface of the table, digging the pads of my fingers in the grain of the wood. "What did you want to talk about?"

"Why didn't you offer to come help today?"

"Why didn't you ask me for help?"

Mom clenches her jaw. "You should have offered."

"I'm not a mind reader, Mom. You should have asked if you were drowning in work to do. Besides, you have two other people here to help you out. I thought you would be fine." She doesn't like that I've pointed out the obvious.

"Who is this boy you brought over? Are you serious about him?"

So serious that I married him on a whim. How's that for being serious about him?

"You met him. His name's Logan."

Mom shakes her head, makes a disgusted noise. "I swear, every single time we talk, it's to get these non-answers."

"No, we don't talk because you don't listen to what I have to say."

"And what do you have to say that's so important? Please, tell me. I would *love* to know."

I cross my arms over my chest, right over the gaping hole in my heart. How can you love someone when they continue to hurt you? When does it stop?

Does it ever?

"I'm serious about him, yeah. Dead serious." *I love him, Mom. I love him.*

"For now?" Mom asks.

"For now. For two months. For five years. I don't know yet. That's supposed to be the fun part."

"You're not getting any younger," Mom says, waving at my body.

"So? What does that have to do with anything?"

Mom sighs. "You're working so much that you don't see that the world's passing you by. When are you going to get married? When are you going to have babies?"

I nearly drop the ball, but I save myself from...myself. "Whenever I feel like it and find someone worthy of my time and attention. Plus, babies don't seem like a good idea for me."

"What?" Mom's eyes are wide with shock. "Why not?"

"Because I don't think I'll be a good mother. And I don't want to resent a child I didn't want in the first place. That's my decision for now."

"Is that a jab at me?"

I shake my head, fight hard not to roll my eyes. "I'm just making the observation that not everyone should be a parent, that's all. I'm pretty sure I fall into that category. So there's no real reason to rush out into the world and find a man I would settle to have babies with. That seems...counterintuitive."

"You are taking a jab at me," she says, pointing her finger at me. I used to believe it was a magic weapon, but I know now that it isn't. She's hurt. "I made sacrifices, Max, to have you. I made so many sacrifices. I went without for years and years so I could raise a family."

I'm sad because she had to go through that, so very sad. "It's okay to be unhappy. It's not okay to take it out on me because I have the freedom you didn't have when you married Dad. None of this is my fault. None of it."

"What are you saying? I love your father."

"Okay," I say, not knowing what else *to* say. "Okay. You know, I'm pretty crazy about Logan," I tell her. "And I'm pretty sure he's crazy about me."

"He couldn't stop touching you throughout dinner and dessert. He always needed to be touching your back, or your chair, your wrist."

Shit, Mom looks envious. But that's a conversation to have another day.

"Is there anything else you wanted to talk about?" I ask gently.

"Why do you act like a stranger when you come into my house?" She asks, drinking down some of her coffee.

I snort. "Because you treat me like one. Do you know how bad it hurt when Izzy told me you guys were willing to pay the down payment so she can get a condo on her own? Do you have any idea? I could have used that kind of support when I moved out, Mom."

She shakes her head, waves a finger at me. "You wouldn't listen to us. You bulled your way through our protests and did what you wanted to anyway. There was no stopping you."

"I didn't want to be stopped, I wanted to be supported. I wanted to have a place to come back home to if I failed." Shit, my stupid eyes are starting to well with tears. Shit, shit, *shit*.

"We thought you'd come back home in six months, at the latest. It's been years, Maxima. Years."

I snort. "I showed you, huh?" I whisper.

The conversation's softer now, more delicate. I've said what I needed to say, all I can say right now.

"Yes, you showed me. Are you happy?"

"I'm happy most of the time, and then I'm stressed because of work, and then I'm happy again. It changes every single day."

"And this boy, Logan, makes you happy?" Mom asks carefully.

"He does, when I give him the chance to."

Mom laughs, just like I meant her to. "You were the hardest girl to raise, the most difficult. Always wanted to do everything by yourself, just to prove you could."

I laugh. "That hasn't changed, like at all."

Mom's eyes are glassy with unshed tears, and the look of her triggers my tear ducts. I sniff hard to chase them away.

"I hope you let Logan help you, even if you can do it by yourself."

"Is that what marriage is, do you think? Getting help, even when you don't need it?"

Mom nods. "Because then you'll be ready to accept it when you need it the most," she sighs, closes her eyes, and rubs at them. I get out of my seat and bend down to give her an awkward hug.

It's been years since we've shared one, and a lot of time has been lost between them. I'm still angry, and I'm pretty sure Mom is, too, but it's nothing that won't keep for another day.

"I'll help you wash up."

"No, no, leave it. I'll take care of it later. I can't stand to be in the kitchen another second," Mom says, glancing around. "I'll go sit with your aunts and uncles for a bit."

"Okay," I murmur, letting her go and stepping back. We awkwardly step around each other, and I head down to the basement, finding Logan already on the stairs coming back up.

"Hey," I say with a wave. "What's up?"

"I'm sorry, Max, but I have to go. I wanted to say goodbye to your parents."

My heart plummets down to my toes. I reach out for his hand, and he gives it to me, squeezing our fingers together. "Yeah, sure. Come on."

I watch numbly as Logan says goodbye to my aunts and uncles. I help him put on his coat after he gets his boots on. I move up to my toes and kiss his mouth gently before rocking back down to my heels.

"Thank you for coming. It means the absolute world to me."

He smiles, but it's so freaking sad, my heart aches at the sight of it.

Say those words you need to say, Max. Come on, say them.

"I have to go. I'm sorry that I couldn't stay longer."

"I know. You need to go, though. God, this whole evening must have been torture for you." Logan squeezes my hand and tugs me close.

"I don't care what anyone else thinks, Max, but you're the greatest thing that's ever happened to me. I need you to know that."

My eyes well with tears that eventually spill over. "Yeah? Do you mean it? Really?"

"I mean it with all of my heart. But I need to go, and I need to be alone for a few days. I'm sorry. Trust me to come back to you, okay?"

I gulp down all of my questions and nod. He came here and did what I asked of him, there's no reason why I can't do the same.

"Whatever it is, you don't have to go through it alone. I'm here, Logan, okay? Whenever you need me."

His eyes are shiny, his smile is brittle. "You promise?" He strokes his thumb over my naked left ring finger.

"I promise. Ring or not. I promise."

He kisses the back of my hand, and without glancing back, he's out the door, leaving me behind – again.

TWENTY-TWO

Boxing Day...

"Has he called you yet?" Vick asks.

I pace my living room, my phone pressed to my ear. I glance around my empty apartment, at the way it feels a little *less* without Logan in it.

"It's been like maybe twelve hours," I say. I'm not fooling her though. Hell, I'm not even fooling myself. I've counted down every single minute until this moment, waiting for Logan to get in touch with me.

Maybe today is not that day.

"As if you don't have the exact countdown to the second, Max. I know you. Have you figured out what you're going to do now?"

"Just ask me what you want to ask me."

"Fine, then. Are you going to stay married or not?"

"Whether I stay married or not doesn't change the fact that I want Logan in my life, for as long as we both decide."

Vick laughs. "Nice. It's good to finally hear you say it."

I frown down at my toes. "Say what?"

"That you've fallen head over heels in love with your husband. It's cute, through and through. I can't wait to tell Amber."

"Please, I know you two probably have a running bet."

Vick grunts. "There's no such thing going on. Maybe. Perhaps. All right, fine. I'm on a winning streak and I like taking money from her."

"Right," I say, grinning now. My apartment's warm and cozy, the heat blasting from the vents. My fridge is stock full of groceries and some leftovers from the night before. I even have a couple of plates of desserts that I can indulge in whenever my heart desires.

A week ago, I wasn't sure Logan and I were going to have enough food to eat. I wasn't sure if we were going to have to leave my apartment behind and seek shelter somewhere else.

I wasn't sure about my feelings towards him, but I am now.

Logan showed up when I needed him the most, and that's important to me. Very few people in my life have shown up when I've needed them to.

"How's the wedding planning going?" I ask.

Vick groans dramatically. "I don't want to talk about it. That's *all* anyone wants to talk to me about. It's like I've lost all of my personality and everyone expects me to turn into a bridezilla. I mean, I'd love to have a *Sky Castle*-themed wedding, but I don't think Michael will let me."

"Did you ask him?"

Vick clears her throat. "I was thinking about *how* to do the asking."

I laugh. "I'm sure you'll come up with something." A knock comes to my door, and I head towards it, wondering if my ice cream order has already come in. "Hang on a sec, Vick."

"I think that's my cue to leave actually. You'll get it soon enough. Bye, Max!" With that, my cousin ends our phone call, and I'm left frowning down at my doorknob. I check the peephole and gasp.

I pull open the door fast enough to twinge something in my wrist. "Logan. You're *here*," I breathe.

Logan looks an absolute wreck. His dark hair isn't styled with any kind of product, but wavy and frizzy. His clothes look disheveled as if he rushed to pull them on, and his coat isn't zipped. Hell, he's not even wearing a hat and gloves, and the skin over his knuckles looks red and raw.

"Logan? Are you okay?" I squeeze down on the doorknob, the cold seeping through my palm. Something's *wrong*.

He stares at me as though he's just realized where he's standing. "I...I didn't know where else to go. I had to get out of there." Logan's voice cracks and his eyes shine with unshed tears.

I carefully hold my hand out, palm up. He settles his hand into my grip and I gently tug him inside my apartment. It's like he's coming back home.

I move slowly and carefully, my heart beating hard and fast against my ribs. I don't know what's wrong, only that there *is* something wrong, and I don't know how to fix it.

I carefully remove his coat from his shoulders and hang it up. I crouch down to help him out of his boots. I hold onto his hand and bring him to the kitchen, and I make sure he's seated at the stool he always preferred when he was here last week.

It's only been a few days, and I've missed him so much. How is that possible?

"I only knew that I wanted to see you, no matter what," he says, voice rough and raspy.

"What happened?" I ask in a whisper.

"My mom...she passed away the other night." Logan runs a hand over his mouth, his gaze dropping from mine. Through our clasped hands, I can feel that he's trembling through my grip.

My heart twists and aches for him, even while I scramble to figure out what to do, how to make any of this better.

How can I do that when I don't know how to fix this? This can't be fixed, Max.

"I'm so sorry, Logan. I'm so sorry."

Logan nods, and sniffs hard. "I didn't want to tell you. She'd been sick for a long time, a *long* time. And last night, she finally looked like she wasn't hurting anymore. And I-" his voice cracks again and he ducks his head into his arms, a broken sob spilling from him. He cries so hard and violently that I marvel that his body is still together instead of falling apart, cracking wide open to deal with his grief.

I freeze for a few seconds, and then plaster myself to his back, aching with him, trying to keep him together.

"I'm sorry, I'm so sorry," I repeat over and over, rocking him gently from side to side. I let him go only to secure a tissue box and hand him a wad of them so he can clean his face and nose. My stomach twists into knots.

"And yet you came to my Christmas dinner even though... Fucking shit, Logan, why? Why would you do that?"

My heart explodes to three times its size, my rib cage too small to contain everything that I'm feeling, everything that I want to tell Logan.

I gently wipe the tears from his face. My thumb drags over the swell of his bottom lip. I gasp when he kisses me there, soft and quick.

I'll think about this moment in the future, I'm sure, the one moment that changed everything for me, and it'll be this one.

I love Logan Porter, my *husband*, and he's sitting here in front of me, utterly heartbroken.

"Because I said I would. Because she would have wanted me to keep my promises. Because she knew that there was someone in my life even if I didn't explain it all to her. That's why I asked you to marry me, Max. I was selfish. I wanted to let my mom know that I was going to be okay without her, that I had someone who loved me, who I loved back."

My mouth's dry, and my throat tightens, flaring hot with pain.

"I'm sorry I asked you like that. I'm sorry I wasn't being totally honest with you."

"Logan, you came to the dinner last night. There's nothing you can do now that'll make me think you're a shitty person. There's nothing you can do about it. Not one thing."

"I'm sorry, Max. I'm sorry about everything."

I pull in a deep breath, let it out slowly. "The whole time you were here, living with me. Did your feelings for me start to grow?"

"God, Max, how could you not know? I'm crazy about you. So crazy that I asked you to marry me, even if I had an end goal in mind."

"Well, so did I, so I think we should stop beating each other up for that, huh?" I shake my head, run my thumbs over his sharp cheekbones. "What can I do for you now? What do you need? Food? Sleep? Tell me and I'll make it happen. Let me take care of you now."

"I want to sleep, please."

"Okay. My room's right over there."

"No," he says with a shake of his head. "I want to sleep with you next to me. Please?"

"Okay." I mean, it's not like I'm going to say *no*. If my sleeping next to him brings him some comfort then it's the least I can do. It's my turn to take care of him now.

We head to my bedroom together. I let Logan climb under the sheets first. I turn on the TV hanging on my wall to play *Jurassic World* on Netflix for some background noise.

I'm hoping it's going to distract him and forget his pain for a little while.

"Do you want to tell me about her, or do you want to keep quiet? I've got a box of tissues on my nightstand right by your side there, and enough blankets so that you'll be warm in two seconds. Do you need anything else?"

Logan shakes his head. "Just you."

If this wasn't spectacularly terrible timing, I'd kiss Logan breathless. Right now, I'm trying to figure out ways to ease his pain.

"Okay," I mumble, snuggling up close to his side. "Hey, it feels just like when we were stuck in the storm, freezing our asses off together, huh?"

Logan grunts then blows his nose rather loudly.

I pet along his stomach, the thermal a little rough against the skin of my palm. We both watch the movie unfold and meet the new dinosaurs that weren't around in the original franchise.

"I'm sorry if you had plans for the rest of your day."

I lean up to look at him. "My only plans now involve you and playing a koala to your tree for the rest of the evening. You let me know when you get hungry, okay?"

Logan sighs. "You know what I said before, about wanting to let my mom know that I was getting married, that I found someone?"

"Yeah..."

Logan licks his swollen lips, ignores the tears that leak out of the corners of his eyes. He pulls in a shaky breath, sniffs. "It started one way, Max. But you know, right? That I love you?"

I lean back to look down at him. He gently places some hair behind my ear, careful with me even while he's so heartbroken I don't know how he can bear it.

"I know, Logan. Who else could stand my ass for a whole week straight of complaining than a man who'd fallen in love with me?" I joke, not knowing that at all.

I'm rewarded with a small smile from him, and I wipe more of his tears away. "Thank you for being there last night, for being by my side. It made everything so much better, you have no idea."

"Good. I'm glad. If you let me, Max, I'll be by your side as long as you want me."

"Does it work the same for you? Wanting me by your side, too?"

Logan laughs, surprised and wet. "Yeah, it does. I'm sorry I'm not at a hundred percent right now."

I wave off the concern. "You saw me nearly busting out of my skin. This is nothing. Come on, try to close your eyes, try to sleep."

"She'll still be gone whether I fall asleep or not."

"I know, but give your heart a break, just for a little while."

Logan sniffs again. "Would you come to the funeral with me? It's scheduled for next Monday."

"Yeah, of course, I will. You're basically stuck with me until I say otherwise."

Logan smiles again, even though he's still crying. "I wish I could stop. I wish I didn't have to think about how at ease she looked when she died. I think she was waiting for me before she finally let go."

My own eyes start to well with tears, and my throat is so thick and painful that I don't know if I can speak. I nod instead, wanting him to continue, to let it all out.

"Fuck, Max, she would have loved you."

"Yeah?" I whisper wetly, tilting my head. "Really?"

Logan nods. "Fuck, yeah. She'd have loved everything about you, from head to toe."

I raise an eyebrow. "Even if we had gotten married without telling anyone?"

"My mom wouldn't care about that. She eloped with my dad when her parents told her not to marry him."

"A rebel, huh? She must have been one hell of a cool lady."

"I thought so." Logan's face crumples as another wave of grief pulls him under. All I can do is hold him as tight as I can, and replace the sodden tissues for fresh ones.

After a while, he's able to fall asleep.

I text my cousins that I'm going to be AWOL for a few days while I take care of my...husband.

Shit, the word doesn't sound so scary now, not when Logan's in my bed.

I don't know how long we doze for, but when I wake up it's to find myself alone in bed, and the heavenly smell of leftovers being microwaved.

I head into the kitchen, finger combing my hair.

Logan's in my kitchen like he's always been there, like he never left.

"It's nice to have everything working for once," he says. His face is still red around his cheeks and eyes like he's been rubbing at the tender skin. "I was about to wake you up to eat, but you beat me to it."

"I wanted to make you food." I frown, take my seat at the island.

"It's microwaved leftovers, Max."

"Still, I should be the one doing it. Me. You're tired and sad and I wanted to take care of you. It's my turn to take care of you. Are you going to let me or what?"

"I've never been taken care of before."

I wrinkle my nose. "This is one of those cases, though, we talked about before. I'm going to give and you're going to take."

Logan stills He looks up at me, runs a hand through his hair. "I don't know how to do that."

"I'll teach you. I learned from the master himself, after all." I get a laugh out of that and I'm practically walking on air. "First, you have to let me do all the cooking and cleaning up. We both know you like to do the dishes but that's not going to happen."

"And after that?"

I shake my head, hands on my hips as I round the kitchen island. I tug Logan until he's seated where I want him. "I don't know. I'm just winging it and doing what feels right. You'll let me know, though, right, if you don't want something from me?"

Logan nods, wipes his eyes from the tears that have already fallen.

"So let me take care of you now."

"Why?"

I tilt my head, finally say the words that need to be said. "Because I love you. Are you going to let me do my job, or what?"

"Only if I get a kiss first. Please?"

I kiss him softly at first until Logan's the one that adds more heat to it, more emotion. I gasp against his mouth and let him take over.

It's my turn to give.

By the end of the night though, I'm still pretty sure that Logan's given me a lot more than I've given him.

I'm going to have to fix that.

TWENTY-THREE

The funeral was awful, as funerals generally are, or so I've been told. All I do is hang around the seating area and smile at Logan whenever he looks over at me.

I already paid my respects to his dad, who looks entirely shaken by grief that I doubt he could see me through the tears streaming down his face. It's clear that he loved his wife.

By the end of the burial, Logan's exhausted.

I offer to drive him home, but he wants to come over, so that's where I go.

My apartment's been quiet these past few days after Christmas. I've caught up on work. I also didn't completely disappear into my editing cave since Logan would be in touch throughout the day, making sure I had eaten or taken a walk outside to clear my head.

Mom and Dad are still giving me the silent treatment, but it doesn't hurt so much anymore. Izzy's always excited to talk about her impending mortgage countdown, but I don't have the energy to be so excited when Logan's hurting as much as he is.

Maybe in another week or so, I'll take her shopping for furniture.

Logan drops his duffel bag as soon as he steps inside my apartment. When I get to the kitchen, I'm hoisted up onto the kitchen counter and pressed back against the cupboards in a bruising kiss that steals my breath away.

"Please, I need you. Please, Max."

We barely make it to my bedroom without tearing each other's clothes off. At the end of the fiery storm, we're both panting, trying to catch our breath. My body's hot and satisfyingly sore. Logan leans downs to kiss me deeply, murmuring my name against my lips.

"I'm sorry if I was rough."

I snort.

Logan stares at me. "Does this mean what I think it means?"

I smile at him, teeth on display. "I don't know. What do you think it means?"

"I think it means we need to have a discussion."

I snort. "Maybe you're right." I run a finger across his collarbones. "How are you really?"

"It was hard, Max. Really hard."

I run my fingers over his eyebrow, down to his cheekbone. He nuzzles against my touch like a cat. My heart melts, especially when he dips down to kiss me slow and sweet.

"I'm sorry that it was hard for you today."

"She would have loved you, you know?"

This isn't new, but it helps him to talk about it and the least I could do is listen. He gives and I take; he takes and I give. That's the way it works.

"Obviously, I'm amazing," I laugh, leaning up to kiss his cheek. "Now, go to sleep. We have to start planning for New Year's Eve. There's a rooftop party I want to try to get into, and the tickets go on sale at five in the morning."

Logan tickles me until I squeal and then kisses me until I'm panting against his mouth.

Even though it was a pretty terrible day, it still ended well, with the both of us together.

·♥·♥·♥·♥·♥·

"Hey, sorry I'm late," I say, sitting down across from my sister at her favorite coffee shop. The air smells like roasted espresso beans and sugar cookies. If heaven were a place on Earth, this would be *it*.

Izzy shrugs. "Not a big deal. I just got here anyway." She glances away, more interested in what's hidden behind the glass case near the cash register.

We get up one at a time to get our orders of high-caloric coffee and a dessert because it's *still* the holidays and I want to indulge.

"So what's the matter with you? Why didn't you want to come over?"

Izzy snorts. "I thought you were going to be with your boyfriend, sucking face."

I nod slowly. "We do suck face a lot. I'm not even going to be sorry about it."

Izzy's mouth twists in a disgusted sneer. "I come bearing the family olive branch. Mom and Dad want you to come over for brunch over the weekend. You can bring Logan, too, if you want."

I nod. "I'll see if he's up to it."

Izzy frowns. "I thought it was pretty brave what you did, what you said to Mom. That's why I need to get out, Max. You get it?"

"Yeah, kid. I get it. Are you going to be okay paying for everything on your own?"

"I find it's pretty good motivation to stay on track because I don't have the option of going back home."

"Mom and Dad would love to have you back, you know that. Otherwise, they'll have to face the fact that they're empty nesters."

Izzy nods and crosses her arms over her chest. "That's not the real reason why I asked you here, actually."

"Turns out I have something to tell you, too. But you go first."

Izzy winces. "Fine, fine. I, uh, wanted to ask you if you wanted to go couch shopping with me. Because that's a thing I need now, a whole ass couch."

"Actually, no, you don't. Why don't I sub-let you my place? I won't charge you more rent than what I pay at cost, so it'll keep your expenses down. And you can have my place as yours if you wanted."

To my despair, tears start spilling over onto Izzy's cheeks.

"What? What? This is good news! Why are you crying?"

"Because! I thought you were going to be pissed at me because of what happened at Christmas!"

"Why would I be pissed at you? None of this is your fault."

"Max, I'm part of the problem, aren't I? I've been living at home forever, and I take all the handouts I can get."

"That just means you aren't as pathologically stubborn as I am, that's all. It's fine to ask for help, Izzy."

"Oh my God, who *are* you? My sister would never say those words to me. Not once, not ever."

I snort. "I don't know. Logan's said something like it to me a few times, and I've started to believe him. It's nice knowing he's in my corner, you know?"

"No, I don't know. I swear, all the guys in Montreal are the shits."

I shake my head. "I don't know. Maybe you'll meet the guy of your dreams sometime this year. I have a feeling."

"Yeah, right. I work at a bar, Max. What kind of future can I give to a relationship, huh?"

"Money isn't everything."

"Says the person who's richer than our entire generation."

I lick my lips. "Are you feeling better now?"

"You mean it, Max?" Her eyes are practically glowing with hope. "I can rent your place? Really? Where the hell are you going to live?"

"I want to find a place closer to Vick. There's a new development that's already built that I've been curious to check out. We'll see if they have any more condos left to buy."

A year ago, I wouldn't have thought I'd be married, and that I would be looking for another home with a mind to a future I can share with someone, let alone Logan.

"You're not just doing this because you feel sorry for me?"

I lick my lips. "I'm doing this because I want you to have a place to live that isn't back home where we grew up. I'm doing this because I can, and I want to help you."

Izzy grins. "I'm so lucky that you're my sister. Seriously. Evie's going to flip when I tell her. Holy shit, we can have sleepovers now with wine and sushi and brownies. I have to call her right now. Give me a sec."

I let my sister call my little cousin, smile when Izzy practically crows with happiness over the good news. I can't hear what Evie's saying, but I already know that kid is working her shift at the bookstore she adores.

When she's done yelling over the phone, Izzy turns her wide, wide smile to me. She pockets her phone and practically bounces in her seat. "I'm so fucking excited. I'm going to have my place, and it's going to be *glorious!*" she raises her arm and stabs her fist in the air.

"Merry belated Christmas, Iz."

Izzy about strangles me with her hug and screeches in happiness right in my ear.

·♥·♥·♥·♥·♥·

Valentine's Day...

"You're wearing your ring," Logan says, panting against my mouth.

"Less talking and more kissing," I say against his lips. I yank on the collar of his shirt and pull him on top of me, a welcome weight. "Now's not the time to talk about that," I groan.

"I can do both," Logan says, his smile pressed up against my mouth. It's unfortunate that I like that so very much.

I lean back, let my head fall onto the couch cushion. "Yes, I'm wearing my ring. So are you." I hold up his left hand as evidence. "What's the matter?"

"I didn't think you wanted to wear that ring anymore."

"Why not? It's a pretty ring. I chose it for myself."

Logan lifts my left hand and lays a kiss over my ring finger. "I know you did. I was there. You were very proud of choosing it, too."

I smile at him. He's really beautiful like this, soft for me, his mouth swollen from my kisses. It's a good look. A *really* good look.

"If a girl's only supposed to get married once, then she better choose her ring, right?"

Logan laughs, then nuzzles into the skin at my throat. Goosebumps erupt all over my skin, and I shiver in his hold. He licks along the column of my throat before laying down a ghost of a kiss, which only serves to make my horrible case of goosebumps *worse*.

It's been almost eight weeks since his mom died, and we've spent more time together than I thought we would. With the new year, I've set a new list of goals I want to achieve, and one of them was having a life outside of my channel and social media.

Logan's part of that plan.

"I didn't want to bring it up, but I guess I should," Logan says, leaning over onto his side. He moves me gently so that I'm settled on my hip, pressed up against his front. If I wanted, I could push him off the couch and watch him tumble to the floor, but he's been really sweet to me all night during our first Valentine's together.

Besides, there's still the bedroom games we're going to play later and I can't wait.

"Okay. Tell me."

Logan kisses my forehead, then down to my nose, then finally settles at my lips. We get sidetracked by more kisses, the deep and wet kind, the kind that steals my breath away.

"You were saying?" I pant, pulling back to catch my breath.

"Now that the holidays are over and you've given me time to grieve...what about that annulment, Max?" he asks, curious.

My heart slams against my ribs, hard and fast. I look down at my wedding ring, sparkly and perfect, nestled on my finger. It fits just right. "I think I could stay married for a little while. How about you?"

TWENTY-FOUR

Evie Prewitt sighs after a long day at work. Boxing Day was always a good day at the bookstore that had become home to her, and now she looks forward to climbing into bed, opening up her eReader, and reading one of her dragon shifter books.

Once in bed, she doesn't know why she does it – probably some perverse need to cry without actually feeling her feelings – she looks up her ex's, Ethan's, social media.

It doesn't take long to find out that she's been replaced, like a piece of worn clothing that's been discarded and left behind.

It shouldn't hurt as much as it does, Evie knows that, but she lies down, looking up at the ceiling ad wondering where it all went wrong.

She loves her job. Hell, she *lives* for her job. She gets to talk to people all day long about books, and honestly what could be better? Evie works hard and long hours, with lofty dreams of taking over the business within the next two years.

And her first set of trials and tribulations will commence when Mrs. Bristol, the bookstore's head manager, and owner, will be leaving for a long-overdue and extended vacation, leaving Evie behind to take the reins, all by herself.

It's exciting and terrifying in equal measure, and Evie loses sleep over it most nights. As if the store will go up in flames if she makes one wrong move, or the old building will suddenly collapse in on itself if she isn't looking directly at it, and there all day long.

Sometimes, in the darkness of her bedroom, with the fridge humming in the kitchen, and the faucet dripping in the bathroom that Evie finds more soothing than annoying, she wonders if this is *it.*

If this is all life is meant to be, all it can be.

She's been working at the bookstore for most of her adult life, and her dream of dreams is to finally have one of her own, holding onto it so tightly that her heart aches every time she walks into the store. She's pretended more than a time or two that it belonged to her, *really* belonged to her, the musty smell of paperbacks, the smell of wet cardboard that's been soaked through with snow in the transport from outside to inside.

Every little part of it is magical to her. The not-so-great part? The awful numbers on the overall financial health of the store.

It sits heavy on her chest, squeezing out every breath before she's ready to let it go.

Evie licks her lips, flops over onto her side, turning to her book for comfort.

She reads until her eyes slowly begin to close (through no fault of the book), and she falls asleep to an odd and very unlikely scenario.

Wouldn't it be nice that *she* could have a dragon shifter come and take her away from dreary Montreal and all of her problems, and expect her to save the world or something?

Wouldn't that be wonderful?

But stories are just stories, and Evie knows, right before she falls asleep that it'll never happen.

Besides, she hasn't dated a guy in forever, and really, there's never been any time for a relationship while her heart belongs to the bookstore.

Unless, of course, the man of her dreams shows up and tries to take it away from her. Then they're going to have problems.

But honestly, Evie's life is so predictable there's absolutely no way that could happen.

It might be fun, though, Evie thinks, before drifting off into sleep.

Fin

Want to stay in the know about upcoming books? You can subscribe to my newsletter here.

That's it for Max and Logan! Next up - Evie and Noah.

Read on for a sneak peek of the next Cuffing Season book, ***Cuffing New Year's Resolutions****, or you can pre-order it* ***here****.*

CUFFING NEW YEAR'S RESOLUTIONS

"Are you ready, Evalyn?"

I frantically shake my head, my brain stuttering and trying to recall the guy's name. I know that I know his name, it's just nowhere to be found in my memory. I'm drawing a complete blank, and all I can do is blink at him.

My feet have gone completely numb in these boots I'm wearing, and this jumpsuit is starting to feel kind of damp with how much I'm sweating.

And my heart? I don't even want to think about it.

I don't want to think about how hard it's beating right now, like a whole stampede of horses is trampling my chest. I don't want to think about the whooshing sound in my ears, the way my hair feels completely soaked underneath my helmet, and how my goggles are starting to fog up so now I really can't see.

Wonderful. Spectacular.

I'm going to die, I know I'm going to die. Why am I doing this to myself?

Because I made myself dumbass New Year's Resolutions, that's why. Like an idiot.

Because my last relationship ended in a bust, and Evan threw that terrible word at me that might not hurt other people, but it sure as shit hurt me, and it hurt me badly. The very word confirms what I've always known about myself—that I'm not that interesting of a person.

Evan called me boring.

Boring!

And it broke me a little if I'm being honest when I was trying so very hard to be what I thought he wanted me to be.

So what did my dumb ass decide to do?

Prove *him* wrong by taking my own stupid life in my own stupid hands and going skydiving—in the winter, of all times.

Who's boring now?

Still me! I don't want to do this!

I swear, if I end up jumping and the parachute doesn't open, I'm going to kill someone. And if that doesn't work out, I'm going to come back and haunt all the people who have slighted me over my lifetime. Twenty-seven years of life can drum up a whole slew of people that pissed me off or made me feel small.

They will feel my wrath.

If I die.

Which I don't want to do.

"Evalyn?"

"What?" I snap, fiddling with my goggles to get the gross fogginess out of them. I don't know how I'm moving as my body doesn't feel like my own, but like it's being controlled somewhere by master headquarters and people are scrambling to press buttons to override the fear paralysis that should be happening right now.

Except I am moving—sluggishly, yeah, but moving nevertheless.

My mouth's drier than a desert, teeth tingling as my breath whistles over them fast and hard as fear fogs my brain.

Funny thing is, we talked about this.

There's a whole orientation and signing of waivers, and all that before we even get on the plane. While I wanted to make a run for it the last second on the tarmac, I forced my stupid (boring) ass up those stairs and took a seat in the plane, rocking back and forth and wondering if *now* was the time to ask for a bathroom.

I'm an idiot.

A total idiot.

What am I trying to prove?

My heart gives a feeble kick against my sternum again, a paltry reminder that yes, I am alive, and I could not be once I jump out of this plane.

God, God, *God*, if I die, I'm going to come back as the best avenging ghost in the world. That's all there is to it.

"Are you okay?" the instructor, Noah, asks. Apparently, we're going to tandem jump.

He's going to strap me in with him, mount me like a stallion on top of a mare, and we're going to *fling* ourselves out into the sky and *hope* that the parachute opens, and I can make it down to safety without breaking my legs to stick the landing.

Sweat's my constant companion. Pretty sure there's a half cup floating between my boobs in my sports bra, and my hair feels veritably damp underneath the helmet, droplets of sweat pouring down the side of my temples—or at least, it feels that way.

"Do I look okay to you? Honestly," I groan, opening my jumpsuit just a little to get some air to my skin. "Does anybody look okay?" I swing my glance to the two other people who are jumping with me on this cold winter's afternoon.

I have a fleeting thought if the air will be so cold that it'll freeze the very mucus from my nose, but I didn't think of that when I booked this jump in the middle of the world's biggest pity party, getting drunk on wine coolers of all things, and eating too many pretzels to chase it down. I should have thought about a lot of things.

Evalyn Prewitt died because she didn't think things through.

No. No, no, no.

The interior of the boorishly loud plane has me yelling out my answers, my voice in an odd limbo between fighting for dominance over all the horrible noise coming from the plane, and the wind whistling through the open door that I will *not* look at until the time comes.

I double-check my jumpsuit, smoothing out wrinkles where I can because honestly, that's all I can do right now to not freak out.

Everyone else in the plane has nerves of steel, and I'm the only human being in here.

Apparently.

I sniff hard, ignoring the way my body's vibrating with the need to move but paralyzed to do so even while my hands pat down my body as if I'm checking for valuables when I have all of that safely stashed away in my car.

My cousin Izzy is going to get a kick out of this.

A kick.

I pull in a deep, deep breath through my nose, pulling it deep into my lungs and holding it there for a few split seconds before letting it out in a gush.

Noah looks less than impressed.

Which is the kind of look I want on a guy that's about to strap himself to me as we take a freefall out of this incessantly loud plane before I become a human pancake on the planet's surface.

I'll show you boring, Evan. Look! I'm about to pee myself, but I'm here! I'm going to do it!

Someone's going to have to push me out of here. I'm going to need a little help.

"Are you ready, Evalyn?"

I've told the guy to call me Evie a hundred times, and still, he uses my stuffy, annoying full name.

"No, no I'm not," I say on a pained growl, my teeth squeaking along with each other as I grind them. "But we're going to do this because I'm not a boring person," I growl to myself.

I should be embarrassed, voicing it out loud, the part of me that worries that I'm not enough for the kind of long-term relationship that always felt more like an adventure to me than anything else. And yet apparently, I am the person jumping out of a plane today on a *whim*.

What did the gladiators say before stepping into the arena?

We who are about to die salute you? Is that it?

"Let's do this," I say, jaw clenched tight, my entire body shaking in fear. "Let's do this."

"All right, we're almost there, another couple of minutes," Noah says, nodding at me, holding up a hand for me to wait.

I can't tell much else from his expression when all I can see is his mouth and chin, which I know will disappear under a neck warmer to deal with the icy air at this altitude.

Humans weren't meant to be at this altitude, oh my God. I'm going to die!

I probably won't die.

These guys, and jumpers/instructors, are the most popular in the city, and the most reputable.

Knowing my luck, though, I'm going to be that idiot person who gets stuck in a tree or something and dies horrifically.

The adrenaline's pumping through my veins so that time seems to move slowly, stretching across the seconds that feel like minutes as Noah steps up behind me once I permit him to do so and ties me to him, like a sad excuse of some sort of BDSM shit that I've only ever read about.

That's the problem, I think, with me.

I read, and read, and read—*but I never do.*

That's why I'm boring, I guess.

And this year was meant to change that.

I was going to transform into Evie 2.0.

While I've dyed my virgin hair to an icy blond that I love, and may eventually dip my toe into going pastel, and I'm wearing honey-colored contacts because I always thought those were the most beautiful warm eyes (not because one of romantic hero book husbands had those same eyes, of course not)—I don't *feel* any different.

Even when I'm standing in this plane, about to plunge to my death.

"Ready?" Noah practically yells into my ear, making sure we're secured together, close as two people can be (without all the clothes in between), Noah pressed up right against my back.

And how sad is it that this is the most I've been touched by a guy in the past couple of months? That it feels nice?

Am I allowed to like it? I don't know.

Noah walks us closer to the maw of the plane, where the great expanse of sky and land below has me dizzy for a split second, my heart beating *even* faster and harder in my chest as if reminding me that these are the last few beats I have left.

"Count us down, Evalyn," Noah says, and I resolutely shake my head. I am doing no such thing, *no such thing*.

I jerk my thumb back at him, trying to tell him without words that I want him to do it. Still, at this moment, I'm not brave enough to take that final step, it looks like.

Crushing disappointment makes my shoulders slump, and while my hands are placed on either side of the door, clutching on to the frame for dear life, I duck my head down and stare at this bird's eye view that gives me no reference at all to how high we are.

I'm just going to be jumping into space.

I give one last final nod, and Noah counts us down.

"Three, two, one..."

I take a step out into space, knowing that no one's going to catch my fall.

·♥·♥·♥·♥·♥·

"So how was it?" Noah asks after we've separated from each other, and I'm sitting on the open ground, in the middle of the snow, fighting to catch my breath. I did nothing but jump out into the air, and I feel like I've sprinted for too long.

I flop onto my back, staring at the gray sky, squinting up at it now that my goggles are off, and vow to myself to never regret the ground I walk on ever again.

"Good," I murmur, my voice hoarse from all the yelling I did. I didn't know I could yell so loud or long. "It was...good."

Noah glances down at me from his standing position, hands on his hips. We're currently waiting for the two other pairs of people to come down since I took the first crack at it. I stare up at him while my body fights the post-adrenaline shakes, and I have the awful urge to cry.

"You survived," he says, crouching down as I sit up so we're both at eye level. I sniff horrendously, trying to stave off the impending tears while I blink at him, a little too quickly. "You did it, Evalyn."

"Evie," I whisper, voice gone to shit. "Evie, remember?"

If I had time to think about it, I'd say that Noah is handsome, the kind of handsome that's overlooked. Not the movie star type that knocks you on your ass, but the kind of solid features that could feel like home.

Feel like home? What's the matter with you?

I shake my head, trying to dispel those kinds of thoughts, and watch as the two other pairs come down and eventually land in front of us, sticking the landing without anyone getting hurt.

We're driven back to the main headquarters, give back the jumpsuits, settle up what we need to, and head out to the parking lot to our respective cars.

Noah's leaving at the same time, too, since it's getting darker now the closer the time ticks over to three-thirty in the afternoon. He gives me a wave as I get into my car, legs still a little shaky as I just allow myself to breathe, to soak in the experience that I just had that felt like some sort of dream, or as if it happened to someone else.

I know that's partially because my brain is flooded with all kinds of neurochemicals right now, and the endorphin high should be hitting soon, but the crash is very real, and it all feels...hollow.

I cover my face with my hands as I curl forward, forehead meeting the steering wheel, and sob, letting it all out.

Everything feels too much and not enough, and my heart hurts and my nose is already starting to leak as tears fall down my cheeks. I press my forehead more firmly against the wheel, the tiny flare of pain grounding me.

What a way to start the year, huh? Trying to be a better version of yourself, and instead, you're moved to tears in Vick's car.

I jump when there's a knock at my window, and I hastily sniff hard and swipe at my cheeks, as if my tears are shameful. I glance over to see Noah standing there, frowning down at me. I give him a jerky wave, trying to shoo him to his car even though I'm sure he's freezing standing out in the cold like that.

He mimes for me to roll down my window, and I oblige him, opening it up a sliver once I turn the key in the ignition.

"Are you okay?" he asks again. "Are you safe to drive home?"

I nod hastily. My number one defining characteristic is being responsible (and boring, apparently). "I'll be fine. I'm just going to stay here for a little while longer."

"Do you have anything on you that you can eat?"

I grab the protein bars that I have stashed in the glove compartment, leaning back into my seat to show it to him. "See? I'm fine. Please go. I'll be all right."

"Take your time here until you feel safe to drive," he says, looking at me sternly.

Who the hell is this stranger, looking after my well-being? Why is he being so nice?

I wince, trying to shake off this web of conflicting emotions I seem to be stuck in. I clear my throat, cough into my fist, and rip open my protein bar, taking a vicious bite.

"I'll be fine. I'm sure you have somewhere to be."

Noah frowns at me, then nods slowly, taking me at my word.

He gives me another wave as he walks backward and then heads to his car across the parking lot where I imagine employees need to be. He waves again when he takes off, and I wave back, still feeling empty, but a little better now that I'm munching on the protein bar.

I sit awhile, letting my car get completely warm before washing down the bar with water from the bottle I always keep in my purse, and then start heading out of the lot and get onto the main road that'll eventually take me to the 10 and back into the city.

I cry intermittently on the drive home, getting mad at myself because I need my eyeballs to be free of tears to *see* the road.

I make it home just fine, my tiny one-bedroom apartment empty save for the lonely succulent sitting on the far windowsill in my kitchen – the only one that cares if I show up or not looks like.

I take a hot shower, easing my aching muscles from being tensed up for the last however many hours it was, wash my hair, and then put the whole mop of it in a hair mask, lamenting my decisions to go so extreme with my hair color. Maybe I'll go back to brown if I can find the time.

I pull on soft jammies and fuzzy socks because regular socks don't cut it anymore, and a giant hoodie that used to belong to Evan but that I kept because he left it more times at my place than I can count, and it's comfy and warm and reminds of a younger, better version of myself that I want to get back.

My phone lights up from where I've left it on the coffee table, my older sister, Vick, calling me.

"Hello?"

"Hey! You're alive! I'm so happy!" She screeches in my ear, and I have to put her on the speaker to deal with her at that decibel level. "So...how was it? Was it amazing?"

"It was...good."

"Good? Just good?" Vick asks, concern lacing her words.

"Yeah, I'm just...feeling a little out of it right now. I was so nervous and scared that I'm crashing down from it, and I just want to be a zombie in front of the TV. It's Sunday, and tomorrow's my first day on my own running the bookstore. It was a bad idea to do this today, but I needed to."

"Okay, okay. I get that you want to be alone. And because we both know you choose the same movies over and over, watch some of *Brooklyn Nine-Nine* so you can laugh it out. Plus, I know you're going to do great on your own at the store. I know so."

I nod dumbly and give no one but myself a tired smile. "Yeah, okay, that sounds like a good idea. I want to show Mrs. Bristol that I can do it on my own."

That's the last year on my five-year plan, anyway. That I can afford to take over the lease and run the store for the rest of my life, living the dream.

That's all I want. And if it makes me boring, then whatever.

I just skydived, so why aren't I exhilarated?

Where are all the happy chemicals for my brain? Where?

"Evie?" Vick calls when I'm quiet for a little bit. "Should I come over?"

I snort, but it sounds like a weak attempt at reassuring her, even to my ears. "No, I'll be okay. I'll see you tomorrow, right? We're going dress shopping."

"You hate dress shopping. But you don't have to wear a dress. I want you to be comfortable," Vick says, always giving me a way out when I shouldn't need one.

"No, no. I want to wear something unexpected for once," I say, my voice hard. "I want to pull off something different."

"Then that's what you'll get. I'm coming to get you around ten tomorrow morning. I'll bring coffee and donuts. Love you, you know?"

"Yeah, I know."

Vick snorts. "Gotta go, Michael's here. Message me if you change your mind about me coming over, okay?"

"Yeah, yeah," I say, give my last goodbye, and end the call.

I sit in my empty apartment, waiting to feel better.

I still feel like a boring person, bogged down in responsibilities. I've never taken a chance on anything in my life except for the one thing that mattered—the store.

And I'm going it alone tomorrow.

Somebody help me.

You can get *Cuffing New Year's Resolutions* **here**.

ABOUT THE AUTHOR

C.M. Kars lives in Montreal, Quebec, Canada where they speak French and say more than *voulez-vous coucher avec moi ce soir?* (I didn't just ask you that, I was just trying to make a point).

Cuffing and Tree Trimming is the third novel in The Cuffing Season series, and she hopes you like it a whole lot.

LEAVE A REVIEW:

You know what to do now, right? Tell a friend!

If you liked this book, please consider leaving a review. You can do so here.

If you're into indie (independent) makeup (or makeup in general) or beauty commentary on YouTube, I would recommend the following channels for information, but also a good time: Theresa is Dead, Audra at Home, Robert Welsh, Angelica Nyqvist, Kara C, Smokey Glow, and Amylovesmakeup.

I've frequently taken breaks during the drafting of this novel to watch these creators so I can have a laugh and sometimes talk shit about makeup. These people have no idea who I am, just thought I would shout them out here since they helped me keep my sanity while I was writing.

To keep up with me, you can find me on Facebook, and Bookbub, and you can sign up for my newsletter here.

CPSIA information can be obtained
at www.ICGtesting.com
Printed in the USA
LVHW042036021222
734242LV00013B/377

9 781990 603181